CHEST PAINS

CHEST PAINS

A Novel

Janet Nichols Lynch

Bridge Works Publishing
Bridgehampton, New York

Published by Bridge Works Publishing Company,
Bridgehampton, New York

Distributed in the United States by National Book Network, Lanham,
Maryland. For descriptions of this and other Bridge Works books, visit
our Web site at www.bridgeworksbooks.com.

First Edition

The characters and events in this book are fictitious. Any similarity to
actual persons, living or dead, is coincidental and not intended by the
author.

Library of Congress Cataloging-in-Publication Data

Lynch, Janet Nichols, 1952–
   Chest pains : a novel / Janet Nichols Lynch. — 1st ed.
      p. cm.
   ISBN 978-0-9816175-0-3 (alk. paper)
1. Music teachers — Fiction. 2. Ex-church members — Fiction. 3.
Life change events — Fiction I. Title.

   PS3562.Y4225C48 2009
   813'.54--dc22

                                        2008017478

10 9 8 7 6 5 4 3 2 1

The paper used in this publication meets the minimum requirements of
American National Standard for Information Sciences — Permanence
of Paper for Printed Library Materials, ANSI/NISO Z39.48 — 1992.

Manufactured in the United States of America

To my sister, Joyce

Acknowledgments

I am grateful to Steve Yarbrough and the Fresno State MFA Fiction Workshop for their comments on early chapters of this work. Thanks also to David Barofka for reading the first draft and offering insight; to Merrill Joan Gerber for her suggestions; to Franz Weinschenk, my host on KVPR *Valley Writers Read*, for his encouragement; to my editor, Barbara Phillips, for her help in shaping the manuscript. I appreciate Louise Gutierrez inviting me to observe her Susuki violin class, Jill Maxie for sharing her expertise in caring for heart patients, and my Visalia Runner friends for listening to me pitch stories at 4:30 in the morning. Ever supportive are my husband, Tim; our kids, Caitlin and Sean; my extended family, the Lynches, Fanshiers, Arthurs, and Fischers; and my lovely girlfriends Marsha, Jeffra, Caryl, Patricia, Penney, Lisa, Barbara, and Mary Jo. I am blessed by their love.

CHEST PAINS

Chapter One

Binder rings clicking, books slamming, cell phones singing announced fifteen minutes to go. Gordon Clay gave up on his Debussy lecture. No one was listening. Who the hell cared about Debussy? Grades — now that was interesting. He began returning a set of tests and his students perked right up.

"These were pretty good," he commented. This was a lie, of course. Half the class had failed, but he hoped that by trying to fool the slackers into thinking they were in the minority, he could shame them into studying for the next test. This didn't help, of course. A flurry of white drop slips stormed his table.

An exam plunged into the drop slips and a thundering textbook followed. A forefinger speared a check mark on the exam. "Show me where is in book."

"Excuse me?" Gordon's eyes trekked up the extended arm to peer into the brooding face of Bourhadur Chandrasekhara. A hard worker, and not just in his class. Bourhadur struggled with English, with making ends meet. The dark circles under his intense eyes were from laboring nights cleaning at the hospital.

"This guy — this Scriabin — where is in book?"

"Oh! I don't believe he's in there."

"I think this thing, too." Bourhadur folded his arms and raised his chin. "Not in book, cannot be on test."

"Anything we've discussed in class can be on a test." Gordon spoke calmly enough, even though a peculiar heat rose from his heart and radiated toward his shoulder. "Otherwise, why come to class? Why not just stay home and read the book?"

"Is not in book!" Bourhadur repeated loudly as if Gordon had not heard him the first time.

"Take it easy. An 88 percent is a good grade. One of the highest in the class."

"Is B. Always I be getting A's. I study science, I get A. I study maths, I get A. I study music — B. Is not fair test!"

"I'm sorry you feel that way." Gordon slid Bourhadur's test aside and resumed autographing drop slips. When he didn't respond, the student gave up and left. Gordon stared after him, rubbed his chest. It must be heartburn — the worst he'd ever felt. That greasy patty melt and fried onions he'd had at Mel's Drive-in. One drop slip remained, not for music appreciation like the rest, but for a whole slate of music major classes. He set down his pen and looked up to find his best student, his only bass student. "Joey. No."

"I told you this might happen, Mr. Clay. I got into the POST Academy."

"So you're going to play cop instead of bass?"

"Hey, you seen those rubber guns they give us, huh?" Joey Huerta was squat and round like the Michelin Tire man. He had the face of an angel, with tight black curls and an endearing gap between his front teeth.

"At least finish out the semester. You've got a good chance at the Will Herrington Scholarship for the fall."

"I gotta go full time at the Koffee Kup now." His grin widened. "Rosie's gonna have a baby, you know. "

"Oh! Oh!" Funny he hadn't heard. The grapevine grew thick and twisted in a small music department like the one at Goldhurst Community College. Rosie Pitbaum, the lowest, raspiest alto in concert choir, had an entire scene from Disney's *Beauty and the Beast,* dancing forks and all, tattooed across her back — the cost, the pain, the lifelong commitment! She and Joey were not yet a year out of high school, still living with their parents.

"My dad says I gotta be a man. Take responsibility. The hospital is gonna cost a lot. "

"You guys getting married?"

Joey shook his head. "We don't even got enough for an apartment. First we gotta get our baby born. "

Gordon nodded. "First things first. And what's wrong with the little feller having a musician for a dad?"

"Ah, it takes too long to get a degree. And then there's no guarantee I can make a decent living. I'll be a cop in fifteen months. Pay's pretty good and benefits."

"Yes, benefits." A generous settlement for the widow if he got whacked in the line of fire. *If* he got married. Gordon wished the boy luck. Joey grabbed the drop slip and ran, obviously relieved to get off without an argument. Gordon sat in the empty classroom, listening to Joey's retreating footfalls. A guy like Joey was quitting the department while someone like tone-deaf Sister Cecilia would probably make it through. The thing was when the Almighty was dipping into his sack of musical talent and doling it out, he'd completely slighted the sister, one of his biggest fans, but as for Joey . . .

"Joey!" Gordon dashed out the door.

The kid turned around, but kept moving, walking backward. By the time Gordon caught up to him he found he was gasping for air. "Don't . . . don't turn that drop slip in yet. Think what's important to you."

"I've got more than myself to think about now." Joey's face was set. He looked stern enough to be a cop, curls and all.

"Think what makes you happy."

"Like I don't see music makes even you happy, Mr. Clay."

Like a smack across the face, the remark struck Gordon speechless. Another pain struck him. He placed his hand on his heart.

Chapter Two

At the end of the day, he felt beat up. To save some steps, he edged around the perimeter of the music building. A pant leg nudged the white flowering jasmine, its cloying sweetness heralding summer, summer, *summer*. He had no plans; a rest from teaching was enough. This year more than ever, he couldn't wait for school to be over. Academics don't live in the real working world with a few weeks off each year, but lay off an entire season like the sick in need of convalescence.

Beneath a seamless arc of blue, Gordon could see the dusky peaks of the distant Sierra Nevada. The town of Goldhurst lay on the sloping foothills, northeast of Fresno. Across the street from the college, the carillon at Our Lady of the Apparition of Lourdes Catholic Church chimed four strokes. He passed the swimming pool and the smell of chlorine conjured up his college sweetheart, Carrie Malone, a cellist who swam laps for conditioning. Huddled together in his bed, his chest against her back, he had breathed the chlorine in her long brown hair like a heady perfume. The association had stuck in his head for nearly twenty years. Should he have married her? A moot question. He knew exactly what steps he had trudged to end up here, a place he didn't particularly want to be, and yet what could he have changed? His life wasn't a tragedy, he wasn't an addict on the streets, he had both legs, and yet . . .

He was a big man, over six feet. To anyone who asked — and no one did — he would say he wore a thiry-four waist, but he bought thirty-eights for the roomy comfort. He still had most of his auburn hair and wore it straggling over his collar in the fashion of his youth. He crossed the deserted quad. Most of the day students had left and the night students had not yet arrived. His mind kept running over Joey Huerta's drop like a tongue probing the spot left by a missing tooth. His only bass student gone. His only student who actually needed him.

Well, hell. Soon he'd be home, kicking off his shoes, popping open that first beer. Still it was a long walk in the sultry heat. The new president of the college had abolished staff parking to better accommodate the students. Gordon rarely got a space on campus and parked in the weeded lot separating Goldhurst Community College and Our Lady of the Apparition of Lourdes convent. By the time he reached his car, his shirt was sticking to his back. He got into the scorching metal box, cranked down the window, and turned the ignition. The engine whined, high-pitched and loud, as if it were about to explode.

"Mr. Clay, shut it off!" someone shouted from a distance.

Sister Cecilia was dashing toward him, her gray habit billowing around her ankles, her wooden rosary bouncing against her knees. She was loaded down with a bulging book satchel, clarinet case, and guitar. This was all he needed — the meddling sister. He dropped his face into his palm and burned his elbow on the steering wheel. "Christ!"

There she was, framed in the driver's side window, her open chalky face dusted with sienna freckles so faint they looked like someone had tried to scrub them off. Her modified veil revealed coppery bangs, chopped short and uneven like a child's.

"Whoa, Mr. Clay. Sounds like your carburetor is stuck."

"Nothing Triple A can't handle. You better get out of this heat, Sister. You look pretty loaded down there."

"Oh, I don't mind. I like carrying my instruments so everyone knows I'm a musician." She had said something similar about being a nun when one of her classmates had asked her why she wore a habit. There had to be something deficient about her and not just in music. Who would want to be a sister at the beginning of the twenty-first century when nearly every nun under the age of eighty had fled the convent?

"You remind me of the Singing Nun. You know, she had a big hit in the 1960s." He sang, "*Dominique, nique, nique, S'en al lait tout simplement.*"

"Oh, I've heard that song. A sister recorded it? Me, I'm no great shakes on the guitar. I just strum a few chords for the Youth Ministry Mass."

"Folk mass, we used to call it."

A light came on in her face, her skin the color of a sunrise. "Mr. Clay! I didn't know you were Catholic!"

"Was." Now he was in for it. He could see the way her body angled toward him, like a cat poised over a gopher hole. "I'd love to chat, Sister, but I've got to get back to my office to call Triple A."

"I'll see what the trouble is." She shed her possessions, the guitar twanging in protest.

"No thanks, Sister."

She moved to the front of the car and strained to lift the hood, emitting a guttural "Gah!"

"Hey, wait a minute!" He didn't know much about cars and probably she knew less. She was one of those do-gooders, always giving help to unsuspecting victims, even when they didn't want it.

He got out of the car, nearly stepping into her guitar as if into a shoe. She was bent over the engine, jiggling a lever. "Uh-huh, just what I thought. A little sluggish. Got any WD-40?"

"No. Please, just let it alone."

She raised her arms, pressed her fingertips together to form an oval over the top of her veil "Click! Lightbulb going on!" She dashed to her clarinet case, genuflected, and removed from it a small tube.

"Cork grease?"

"It's a lubricant, isn't it? It'll get you home, God willing."

God willing. How in the hell would his getting home go against God's will? He felt a constricting pressure behind his breastbone. He imagined his heart curling in its cavity like an old dog turning circles before plopping down.

Sister Cecilia was staring at him through an elongated vortex, her jaw slackened and her eyes dilated. "Oh, Mr. Clay, you don't look too good. You all right?" She darted out of sight.

The hood of the car rippled before floating back into focus. His breath caught as if he were trying to inhale and exhale at the same time. *I'm suffocating*, he thought. *I'm dying. So this is God's will*. Then the light faded. A dark covering descended over his face. It reeked of onion, rotting banana, and sour milk. Weakly, he batted at the paper lunch bag. The sister had a vise grip on the back of his head. First she would snuff him out, then she would go after his car with cork grease, all in the name of good works. With a rush of adrenaline, he twisted the sack and tore it away. Fresh air cooled his perspiring face. He inhaled sweet, life-affirming oxygen.

"Mary, Mother of God!" The sister stood on her tiptoes, flapping her hands like penguin wings. "Don't move! I'll call 911!"

"No!" He gasped. "I'm . . . fine."

"Mr. Clay, you were hyperventilating. Are you sure you didn't just have a heart attack or something?"

"Yes," he gasped, although he wasn't sure of anything but a desperate desire to escape her.

"What are your symptoms? I know a little bit. I volunteer at the heart patients' rehab at the hospital."

"I'm already feeling much better."

She made the sign of the cross and rolled her eyes heavenward. "Sweet Jesus, you gave me a scare."

Gordon nudged the guitar out of the way, sat in his car, his feet on the ground, his head on his knees. If he could just rest a moment, make the phone call to Triple A, wait an hour or so for the auto club guy to show up.

"Turn the ignition, Mr. Clay." The sister sounded muffled, coming from under the hood.

"I really don't think . . ."

Her head popped around the side of the car. She wore a little smile rumpled with uncertainty, like when she handed in her ear-training tests. "Just try it."

He sighed deeply, adjusted himself in his seat, and turned the key. The engine hummed normally. Cork grease! "You fixed it!" he yelled out the window.

"Not really. You need an overhaul." Sister Cecilia slammed the hood shut. She reached into the folds of her skirt and pulled out a handkerchief. A smudge of grease marked where the pocket was hidden. She wiped the grime off her cork grease, then replaced it in the clarinet case. "You know to turn the ignition off and pull over if the throttle gets stuck open, don't you?"

He nodded, although he hadn't thought about it.

She collected her possessions. "Better take it in tomorrow. And make a doctor's appointment. I know all the cardiologists in town. Donaldson is good, Spinelli even better. When was your last physical?"

Too personal. He changed the subject. "Uh, is Mother St. Paul still the mother superior of your convent?"

Her face froze. There was a pause, necessary perhaps, to force warmth into her tone. "Yes, she is — a fine musician! Well, you probably know."

"I know of her." The music department often inherited her piano students, young women who rarely missed a note, but played Chopin like typing business letters. "What does she think about your majoring in music?"

Her mouth tightened to a straight line. "She has reservations. She's afraid I'm starting out too late. But you know I'm willing to work hard. If I can get good grades, prove myself to her in other ways . . . Which reminds me: do you know . . . um . . . when the Will Herrington Scholarship winner will be announced?"

He thought he detected smugness in her tilted chin. There weren't many eligible freshman music majors for the prize, and no doubt she already knew Joey had dropped out of the running. "No, I don't."

She glanced down, fingered a rosary bead.

"Look, I'd better get going."

She raised her head. "You're sure you feel well enough to drive?"

"It's only a couple of miles."

"Well then, good-bye, Mr. Clay. Keep the faith."

What faith? In his rearview mirror, he watched her go. With her guitar hanging upside down across her back, her arms loaded with the clarinet and satchel, she resembled a hardy little pack mule. The self-assurance of the faithful always irked him. He had read that St. Catherine of Siena was visited by Christ and his mother only after fasting for weeks. Patron saint of the anorexic. Wouldn't any inquiring Catholic mind think she just might have been so hungry that she was hallucinating?

Chapter Three

Gordon let Bother, his indoor cat, out, and Target, his outdoor cat, in — the changing of the guard. Bother was a calico he had found as a feral kitten, chewing corn cobs in his garbage can, and Target was a gray tabby that had shown up at his back door and refused to leave. Standing at the counter, he drank a beer and gobbled peanuts. Target padded up to him, backed into his leg, and whipped him with her ringed tail, marking him with her gamy scent. He stroked her breast where the black stripes looked like a three-skeined necklace, his fingertips seeking the four clots under her skin. He had asked the vet if they were cysts or tumors, and he had said they were BBs, which had done all the harm they were going to do, probably the reason for her barely audible mew. She was damaged goods, but that was why he liked her.

He dropped a nut, picked it up from the floor, and began to chew it. It tasted fuzzy with lint and cat hair. He spit it in the trash. What the hell was wrong with him? He had been one of the most promising bass players at Eastman and now this — Bourhadur Chandrasekhara and Sister Cecilia, chest pains, and dining off the floor. For how many orchestras had he auditioned, for how many years? He sometimes got a callback, but that was it. He refused to admit even now that he had never been good enough.

He wiped his hand on his slacks, thinking he should get busy doing something. He could correct part-writing exercises, which always made him feel purposeful. Robert and Clara Schumann had studied counterpoint together one winter when Robert felt like he was about to lose his marbles again, and the intellectual discipline had staved off insanity, or at least postponed it. Unlike life, part-writing had rules everyone agreed on, and if you followed the rules, a simple chord progression came out sounding as pure and godly as a Bach chorale.

Gordon thought about the batch of papers in his briefcase, but just stood there at the sink, clutching the peanut jar. He hadn't touched the bass for months. He went into the spare bedroom where he stashed it out of sight. He thought of the tired old joke: *Hi, Gordon, I see you've got your girlfriend with you.* The bass, which was shaped like a woman, had to be embraced to play. He tried to shrug the teaching day from his slouching shoulders, sought to clear one corner of his mind to make music. All he could do was stare at his bass. She seemed to stare back, a bit resentfully. They weren't in a relationship anymore.

He was awakened by the rapid thudding of his heart, as desperate as the retreating footfalls of a fugitive. He propped up on an elbow, straining to hear sounds in the dark house. Nothing. All was well, no intruders. A nightmare then? It was more like anxiety, utter panic. Had he, in his sleep, suffered the sort of attack he had experienced with the sister that afternoon?

He was only forty-two years old. The ticker couldn't
be failing him yet. Thud, thud, thud. He hated the vulnerable sound and sensation of his heart, as if he had so
many beats doled out to him, and when they were all used
up — *poof* — he was a goner. If his heart stopped this instant, who would care? His parents were dead and so
were two of his brothers, Ambrose in the Gulf War and
Anthony in a hang gliding accident. Of his four living sib-
lings, probably only Ruthie would be affected much. How
long would his remains lie festering before someone came
looking for him? Would Art Bunch check on his absence
at the college? He hoped someone would find him before
the cats starved. Art once said a cat would eat the corpse
of its master, while a dog would lie down beside it to wait
for its own death. The sister was right; he should make
that doctor's appointment!

He glanced at the luminous blue digits of his clock
radio: 2:18. He'd never get back to sleep now. The tele-
phone screamed through the darkness, giving his heart
another jolt. Who the hell? He reached for the phone.

"Hello?"

A woman was sobbing. "Gordon?"

"Yes?"

"Oh, Gordon, thank God you're home. It's Carrie."

Carrie. His Carrie? He hadn't heard from her in years.
After all this time, she needed *him*? Two decades com-
pressed like the folds of an accordion; it seemed like yesterday that he had watched her in her overloaded, powder
blue VW bug drive out of his life.

"Carrie! My God! What's wrong?"

"Gordie is missing. He's not in his bed! I've looked
everywhere. Even went to the park."

"What park?" He realized then he didn't even know

what city Carrie lived in. Someone had told him that she had landed a position with the Denver Symphony, but that was years ago.

"It's the one his day care walks to — Sutter Park."

"And Gordie is your son?" Was it possible that she had named her child after him?

"Bastard! He's your son, too! Just because you're always off sailing that goddamn boat halfway around the world. Tell me — your mom won't pick up — do you know if she took him?"

His Carrie — the love of his life — instantly metamorphosed into a stranger. He gripped the receiver tightly to quell the trembling of his hand. "I wish I could help you. I know there's another Gordon Clay in Goldhurst. I've gotten calls for him before."

The woman released an anguished ejaculation, and the dial tone hummed in his ear. He lay back, the desperate woman's voice resounding in his mind. All alone in the world, a single mom, her little boy missing, perhaps kidnapped. How old was he? His naked body face down in a wooded ravine. Jesus, there were so many perverts out there.

Maybe it was okay. He'd read that in a lot of missing-children cases it's the estranged parent who snatches the kid — the other Gordon Clay terrorizing Carrie. When he thought of the stranger Carrie, he visualized the brown soulful eyes and smooth brow of his twenty-one-year-old Carrie, miraculously stuck in time.

Wearily he got out of bed, went into the bathroom to urinate. Bother, who was intrigued by any sort of running liquid, bounded in and jumped up on the side of the tub. Purring loudly, she pushed her orange and black head into his hand and gnawed on his fingers. Her sharp, spiky teeth hurt, but he endured it, at least for a short while, because she enjoyed it so much.

Gordon returned to bed and Bother settled into a furry comma on his stomach. Why, of all animals, were cats the only ones that purred? On the inhale her purr was soft and smooth, on the exhale rapid, louder, grainy. A little boy was lost in the world, his own, sweet Carrie gone forever. He tried matching the rhythm of his breathing to Bother's purr and finally drifted off.

Tchaikovsky's *1812 Overture* blared from his clock radio. He whacked the snooze button and groaned. He couldn't face another day. What he was doing had nothing to do with music. Fifteen years earlier he'd been hired to conduct the orchestra at Goldhurst Community College, but first the Goldhurst School Board cut the string program from the public schools, and a few years later the college orchestra disbanded, too. Now he taught theory and appreciation and an occasional string student — not Joey, not anymore.

His next thought got him out of bed. In the kitchen, he leafed through the phone book, and found the listings for "Clay." No Carrie Clay, Carolyn Clay, or C. Clay. There were the two Gordon Clays — he and the other guy. Once when he was downtown and had overshot a destination, he had driven down an alley to backtrack and had seen the words "Gordon Clay Imports" stenciled in yellow lettering on an aluminum garage door. He probably would not have noticed it if it weren't his own name. The place looked deserted and was obviously not open to the public. Now, he called the other Gordon Clay's number and heard, "The number you are calling is no longer in service, and there is no new number." He looked in the yellow pages under "retail" for a business phone and didn't find one. He slammed the phone book shut, thinking, *so much for the sleuthing business.*

Bother meowed to go out the back door and when he opened it, she bounded over Target, who was waiting on the outside mat with her gift of gizzards, the remains of her catch. Once inside, Target didn't even sniff the kibble but, having hunted all night, went straight to bed. Since she had moved in, he no longer found any rat turds in the oatmeal. When she first had arrived — probably dropped off — he had steeled himself against feeding her. Then he realized she was pregnant and had her spayed. When the vet tried to talk him into a series of costly shots, he insisted that the cat wasn't even his, but Target knew better. He had never even known he liked cats, but now he had two, both of them choosing him instead of the other way around. Maybe the reason he had never married was because no woman had ever arrived on his doorstep and insisted on staying.

As he drank his coffee, two missing children stared at him from a card that had accompanied some junk mail. The pictured children were Jeremy Conway, age eight, brown hair, blue eyes, missing about two years; and Stephanie Butler, age four, blonde hair, brown eyes, missing six years. The kids appeared to be years apart although their dates of birth were the same year. What good were these notices, anyway? He couldn't imagine walking up to a woman standing with a brown-haired, blue-eyed ten-year-old in the quick check line and saying, "This child looks like little Jeremy Conway, the missing child pictured on my junk mail. You must be his kidnapper."

He rummaged around the kitchen drawer and came up with the booklet of health care providers that his medical insurance had sent him. Only four cardiologists in Goldhurst were listed. He dialed Dr. Mario Spinelli — hadn't the sister said he was the best? When he asked for an appointment for a checkup, the receptionist gave him a date three months away, but when he described his symptoms she switched it to the following morning.

Next he called the auto shop three blocks from the college and arranged to leave his car there for a carburetor overhaul. When he was ready to go, he let Bother inside, then lifted Target off the bed, still in her tight ball. Her body stiffened, her claws fanned — she didn't trust human hands, no matter how gentle. She refused to use the litter box — whether she was too base or too refined, he wasn't sure — yet she would explode rather than crap in the house.

Chapter Four

Pulling out of the auto shop late that afternoon, Gordon decided to take a test drive through downtown Goldhurst toward Sutter Park. Little Gordie Clay had been on his mind all day, and he was hoping to find him there, alive and well. The Wells Fargo building and original courthouse had been restored to their appearance during the 1880s. The drugstore had a marble soda fountain and lettering on the front window, BELTS, TRUSSES, SUNDRY ITEMS. The stores were named Maude's Attic, Judy's Closet, and Aldo's Antiques. His first impression of Main Street fifteen years earlier was that it looked like Disneyland. Having failed as a bass player in the real world, he had decided to live in an imitation of life, in Never-Never Land.

Sutter Park was situated in an older, modest neighborhood of narrow houses. Elderly residents were selling out to young families in need of affordable housing. The park consisted of a couple acres of grass, with a duck pond encircled by an asphalt pathway. The playground contained a new blue and orange apparatus on which ten or so children were climbing. Gordon wasn't sure how he was going to find Gordie. Perhaps a playmate would call out his name. Perhaps a pretty young woman named Carrie, dressed in a business suit or a nurse's uniform, who did not look like his old girlfriend, would arrive to pick up the boy. Gordon would stride up to her and say, "Hey there, I'm the guy you accidentally called last night. I'm sure glad your son is okay." They would strike up a conversation, which would begin on the topic of his sensitive, caring nature and her trials as a single mom, and might continue over a cup of coffee or an informal dinner.

Insane. Why would he and this woman, who married a guy who happened to have the same name as his, have any interest in one another? *Gordon, it's Carrie.* That plaintive voice in the dark had washed waves of tender, nostalgic feelings over him all day. Was he going nuts, pining for a woman he hadn't seen in twenty years? Upon their graduation, Carrie had wanted to get married, but he wasn't ready to be tied down. Believing that ultimately they would end up together, that he could act like a jerk, and she'd forgive him, he went to L.A. to freelance. At Christmas, she reported that she'd found someone else. Getting dumped — the pain of it seared through his body as if it were happening that very moment. Regrets. Misery.

Looking over at the children's playground, he suffered a bout of stage fright, feeling self-conscious and out of place. He decided to work up his courage by taking a stroll around the duck pond. As soon as he began his circular promenade, he was greeted by an elderly couple passing him in the opposite direction. Four young women pushing strollers with toddlers trailing behind on small vehicles exchanged a few words with him. This cheered him more than it should. He didn't get out enough, that was his problem. Tomorrow the cardiologist would no doubt tell him he needed more exercise. He could get used to this, taking a few laps around the duck pond after school each afternoon.

Minutes later, he was sweating and panting, his feet throbbing. He noticed that the other walkers had on sneakers, while he was in hard-soled shoes. He hadn't done anything athletic since high school, when the baseball coach had made him choose between the team and the orchestra. Always he had chosen music, given his all to music, and where had it gotten him? Never-Never Land.

Well, if he was going to do what he came for, he'd better get on with it. He strolled over to the playground and sat on a bench near the climbing structure. On it, a group of kids was conducting a rocket ship expedition. He tilted his head, listening for names. Shawnté, Logan, Greer — none of the names he'd grown up with. The caregivers were two women embroiled in a heated dispute over which day was double coupons at the Shop 'N' Save. The one who dominated the conversation had bleached hair with dark roots and wore a long tunic with rhinestones over tight stretch pants.

A child, about three or four, sat on an immobile swing, calling "Swing me! Swing me!" in a flat, forlorn monotone, to no one in particular. He stretched his legs out and leaned back, tucked his legs in and leaned forward, yet remained stationary. He stared down at the ground, his brown face expressionless.

Would it be okay if Gordon gave the kid a little push? What was the harm? He walked behind the child, looked over at the oblivious caregivers, and gave a shove. The sensation of soft, solid, little boy against his own broad hand was startling. The kid threw his head back and looked at him upside down. An abrupt outbreak of a smile dipped into all the crevices of his face. His skin was the creamy brown of a cappuccino, what some would call black. Was he part African-American or Latino or Asian? His hair was not wiry, but silky, matted ringlets. His eyes were almond shaped, the pupils glistening like melted chocolate chips.

"Higher," commanded the boy, as if he were not used to getting what he wanted.

"Hold on tight." Gordon gave him a swooping push. "What's your name?"

The child pursed his lips together, making his chin bumpy.

"Not supposed to talk to strangers, eh? Well, that's smart."

"Moopuna," he blurted in a low tone, as if he were giving it over resentfully, pronouncing it in three, rhythmic syllables, a guttural punch to the "pu." What kind of name was that? Swahili, Polynesian, Filipino, Native American?

The heavyset blonde woman was abruptly at his side. "What's up?"

"Nothing much." Gordon's eyes shifted to look her in the face, but settled on the Tasmanian Devil tattooed above her clavicle. "Just giving Moopuna a push."

"You a friend of his?"

"He could use a friend." That came out wrong, as if he were in the habit of befriending lonely, little brown boys. "He just needed a push."

"What's in it for you?"

"Nothing," he said, speaking a half-truth.

"Higher," Moopuna pleaded in his low drone, but Gordon didn't dare touch him again.

"We have a lot of kids to look after here. No offense, buddy, but you better take a hike."

Buddy — he hated that. He looked over at the play structure, wondering which one could possibly be Gordie.

"You heard me," she said. "Get moving or I'll call the cops."

Gordon held his palms up. "There's no need for threats."

"It's no threat, buddy, it's fact."

"Swing me," droned Moopuna.

Potato Body stepped in front of Gordon, crowding him out of his station, and gave Moopuna a halfhearted shove. "Bye, now," she said, not even looking his way.

Chapter Five

The following morning, he was led into an examining room by an attractive, muscular woman, who looked less like a nurse and more like an aerobics instructor. She told him to remove his shirt and wait for the doctor. She seemed overly brisk, harried, almost angry. Perhaps she had too many patients to care for. She left him alone, perched on an examination table, the butcher-paper cover crackling beneath his haunches. Over the sound system blared a Strauss waltz, light, fluffy, cloying, as if the room were filling with cotton candy. It was too cold; his nipples tightened, the hair around them standing on end. With his legs dangling off the table, he felt like an uneasy child, placed in the care of someone who might do mean things to him.

Gordon rubbed his sore fingertips against his trousers. He had tried to practice the previous evening, but his calluses had gone soft. He had played a few scales and a Dotzauter etude. It felt like sawing wood. He kept checking the clock as he had as a kid practicing the piano. His mother would set the timer for thirty minutes and sometimes he'd tiptoe into the kitchen to push it ahead. Sometimes he would lie on the living room floor, feigning a stomachache so she would let him off. It was easy to get her to let him off most everything; she was burned out from mothering four kids before he was even born. Music meant nothing to him until he took up the bass. His junior high school owned one, nobody else wanted to take it on, so the bass became his destiny. Caught up in the rigors and routine of teaching, he'd almost forgotten that. Now he was going to practice every day, get his chops back, be a musician again.

He looked down at his hand that did not recall the feel of the bass so much as the small brown boy's sturdy back as he pushed him on the swing the previous day. Moopuna — he tried the name in his mouth. It was all up front, in the lips, like a kiss. He hadn't accomplished what he had come to Sutter Park for — finding Gordie Clay safe and perhaps meeting Carrie Clay. On the local news there had been no mention of a kidnapping in Goldhurst. Maybe no news was good news. Maybe Carrie had found the boy asleep in a closet or under the bed. Or maybe she was keeping the kidnapping a secret, going along with the demands of the kidnapper. But kidnappers didn't do it for money these days; they just molested and murdered for the fun of it. *Gordie — face down, naked in a wooded ravine.*

There was a cursory rap on the door, and in walked a big, burly guy with a full beard and dripping mustache, who looked like a pizzeria proprietor. "Dr. Spinelli," he announced. With a grunt, he slowly lowered himself into a chair. He peered into the screen of a laptop, grunted again, then asked, "What am I seeing you for?"

"Well, I experienced some chest pains and dizziness."

"Uh-huh." Spinelli poked the touch screen.

"I couldn't breathe and my arms went kind of tingly. I thought I was having some kind of attack, but then, after a while, it passed."

"Uh-huh."

"And I woke up at night, my heart pounding."

"Uh-huh." Spinelli seemed unconcerned by the account, bored, like he'd heard it all before and would just as soon not hear it again. "We'll run some blood and urine tests, do an EKG, put you in a Holter harness for twenty-four hours to record the activity of your heart."

Gordon imagined himself strapped into a torture device attached to a treadmill, on which he would be forced to trudge intermittently. "I'm going to have to hang around here twenty-four hours?"

Spinelli laughed, his paunch bouncing. "No, no, you put it on and go about your business. After a while, you'll forget you're wearing it."

Gordon remembered why he had put off getting a physical for over a decade: he hated doctors. He suspected that they knew more about *appearing* to know something than what they actually knew.

Spinelli braced himself on the counter and hoisted himself to his feet. "Nursie will be in to put you in the Holter harness and take your medical history. Oh, and don't tell her I called her Nursie. She's a doll, but she gets riled up easy. Feisty, but that's how I like 'em." He batted one eye in exaggerated winks. "Just be brave and stand up to her, show her who's boss, that's what I do." He patted Gordon on the shoulder and left the room.

Gordon rubbed the goose bumps on his chest. He waited some more. Now they were piping in the Bach/Gounod "Ave Maria" in palpitating strings. Funeral music — were they trying to tell him something?

A knock and the same athletic nurse swooped down on him. She looked at him with widely spaced, alarmingly lavender-colored eyes. Tinted lenses, had to be. "It's important that I know this," she said, reviewing the computer screen.

It was bad, really bad. That jokey, pompous-ass Spinelli wouldn't tell him squat, but this savvy woman was really going to lay it on him. A single word got lodged in his throat, then erupted in a croaky whisper. "What?"

"What did he say about me? Doctor Spinelli — did he call me 'Nursie'?"

"I . . . don't remember."

She sat down and leaned toward him. "Several of us nurses are trying to put together an harassment suit against him. He's a horrible man to work for. We're depending on our patients' cooperation."

Gordon fought an impulse to place his arms across his bare chest, not only for warmth, but to cover his nakedness. His gender had somehow become a bunch of child molesters and lechers. He looked covetously at his shirt, hung over an adjacent chair.

She hurled herself backward in an exasperated huff. "Well?"

"You seem to have some problem in your workplace. I don't believe I can solve that problem. In fact, silly me, I came here hoping you could solve my problem."

The lavender eyes were replaced momentarily with pink-rimmed alabaster lids, and then the lavender was back. "How do you expect us to serve our patients under such abusive conditions?"

"I don't know. Suppose you try getting things all squared away and I come back another day?"

She raised one eyebrow menacingly. It was already kind of menacing because she had plucked it in a higher arch than the other one, so that it seemed raring to go into active duty. "Do you do this frequently? Just flare up at the slightest provocation?"

"Flare up! Who's flaring up?"

"Mr. Clay, your voice is raised. Calm yourself, please. Let's start over. I'm Ms. Purcell, cardiology specialist. Tell me, on the job as a . . ." she peered down at the computer, ". . . college music instructor, do you frequently feel stress?"

"God, no. It's easy. I'm using about five percent of my knowledge, one percent of my brain power."

"So, you sometimes feel bored? Unchallenged?"

"I could not show up and no one would even notice."

"You feel . . .unnecessary?"

"On second thought, my students *prefer* I don't show up. They'd love it if class were canceled for the year!"

"Suffers from paranoia," she muttered, typing on the laptop.

"Hey, wait a minute, what are you putting down there?"

"Just what you're telling me. Do you smoke?"

"No."

"Drink alcohol?"

"Hey, have you heard about a kidnapping here in Goldhurst, of a little boy taken from his bed at night?"

She frowned. "I don't think so, no. About the alcohol. Beer? Wine?"

"A beer now and then, after work." Sometimes it was a whole six-pack, but he wasn't about to admit it to her. "Or two."

"I'll put several, okay? Patients tend to underestimate that. What about your diet? Do you eat lots of fruits and vegetables and whole grains?"

"Do potatoes count?"

"Not potato *chips* if that's what you're getting at. What about exercise?"

"I walk, and where I get stuck parking, it's quite a ways."

She looked to the ceiling, then back at him. "If you want a healthy heart, you'll have to work harder than that."

"Well, then, what do you do, for instance?"

"You don't want to know." She wanted to tell, she wanted to boast, he could see it in the bounce of her round, lavender eye.

"I asked, didn't I?"

"For one thing, I eat no red meat, no fat, no salt. I take step class three days a week, spin class three days a week, and lift weights three days a week."

"Are you sure? That's nine days."

"No, no, some days I double up on . . ." She caught herself then, glared back at him.

Gordon had to smile. He hooked his thumb toward the door. "And what about Dr. Big? What does he do?"

"Isn't it obvious? Operates a forklift." Her tone was so flat and accusatory he burst out laughing. She reached into a lower cabinet and withdrew an apparatus. "This is the Holter harness." She helped him adjust the straps over his shoulders and buckle it at the waist. She attached five electrodes onto his back and chest, adhering them with an icy goo. A hard plastic recorder, which resembled a Sony Walkman, was inserted in a holder on the belt. "Here, see this button? Press it when you feel any symptoms. Report back here tomorrow morning and we'll remove the harness and decode the data."

"I have to sleep in this thing?"

"You'll get used to it. We also want you to keep a

diary. We want to know when you eat, sleep, move your bowels, and about any stressful situation you might be in, like driving in traffic. If you press the button, make a note of the symptoms you experience and what you think caused them." She handed him an instruction sheet. "Here. Any questions?"

"Can I go now?"

"Just a minute. Let me have a look." She was reading over the notes on the computer. She was thorough; he had to grant her that. "About this incident when you experienced dizziness, heart palpitations, chest pains, shortness of breath, the doctor didn't note what was going on at the time. Was it a stressful situation?"

"Sort of, car trouble. It was hot, I was exhausted, and this . . . this nun . . ."

"Sister Cecilia?" Her ice-maiden countenance melted into a warm, open smile.

"How'd you know?"

"Sister Cecilia volunteers in our heart patients' rehab, and I know she's majoring in music at Goldhurst. She's got a real talent, hasn't she? So inspiring and uplifting! Her mere presence has a healing effect on our patients! I've heard her play her guitar and sing." She pressed her hand to her heart. "It comes from here. You're lucky to have such a gifted student. I'll bet she's at the top of the class."

It felt as if a boulder had been set on his chest, pressing down on him. Should he press the button, right now, in front of her?

"We'll see you tomorrow, Mr. Clay, and don't worry." Ms. Purcell's cool, long fingers encircled his wrist. "We're going to take extra good care of Sister Cecilia's music professor."

Chapter Six

The four members of the Goldhurst music faculty huddled in the chilly, cavernous band room reminded Gordon of the woolly mammoths of the Ice Age — a dying breed. Business was the major of choice now. It put the Mercedes and the BMW in the garage. Seated next to him was Art Bunch, his office mate and the jazz and reed man of the department. He was short and wiry with a reddish Vandyke beard. The only sign of aging was that his deep boyish dimples had elongated to creases. He and Gordon had been friends since their early freelancing days. Art had retreated from L.A. jazz clubs and recording studios, coke addiction, and his first tumultuous marriage, slinking into his teaching position at Goldhurst like some wounded animal three years before he helped Gordon gain his position there.

Gordon nodded toward Art's lemon yellow "Not ashamed" T-shirt. "What did you do this time?"

Art looked down to see what he was wearing. "Oh, this. My church had them made for the youth group. This one was an extra, just lying around, so I uh . . . you know."

"So you're not ashamed you stole from your church?"

"No, Gordo, not ashamed to be Christian."

This struck Gordon as ironic. With all the shouts of "Praise the Lord" these days, he thought the job of all the newfangled Christians was to make nonbelievers feel ashamed.

The head of the department, Lars Stelling, peered down at the agenda, holding it at arm's length. An energetic old guy in red Keds, he was a trumpet player who mostly taught piano class now. He'd been at Goldhurst since day one, some thirty years past.

"Our next item of business is selecting a freshman music major for the Will Herrington Memorial Scholarship."

Gordon sighed. With each breath, he felt the constriction of the Holter harness, the electrodes tugging his chest hairs.

"We have a short list to choose from," continued Lars, "Emmett Hammer, piano; Sister Cecilia, clarinet; and Joey Huerta, bass."

Gordon raised his head hopefully at the mention of Joey's name.

"Huerta crashed and burned," Art said.

Lars peered over his half-glasses at Gordon.

"It's true. Joey dropped all his music classes just this week."

"A pity," said Lars, crossing Joey's name off the list. "A talented young man."

"So that makes it easy," said Art, jiggling his right leg on the ball of his foot. "Let's give it to the sister and get the hell out of here." Art was always in a hurry. He let his classes out early, too, and even played music too fast.

"I have a worthy candidate: a Miss Victoria Truesdale," said Allegra Musgrave. Her long black hair was windswept and lacquered around her full face and she wore an Italian silk scarf that cost more than every stitch of clothing the men had on.

"Truesdale — I don't see her on the list of declared majors," said Lars.

"She's only the most talented soprano ever to pass through my voice class. Hmmm?" Allegra lowered her chin and peered into the eyes of the men, one by one, but none was moved to a response. "The most talented soprano" passed through Allegra's voice class nearly every semester.

"She has to be a *declared* major," said Lars patiently.

Allegra knew the rules, of course, but she often got her way because she cared about winning the most, grinding the men down with her persistent, coloratura harangue. A graduate of the Royal College of Musicians in London, she was a little too good for them all. Gordon hadn't expected her to stick around Goldhurst for long, but a few years earlier she surprised everyone by marrying a widowed pediatrician and llama rancher with four, nearly grown children. "I'll see to it then," she said. With each shake of her head, her handcrafted, wind chime earrings tinkled.

"We'd like to settle the matter *now*," said Lars. "I agree with Art. Although she's not exactly Stoltzman on the clarinet, Sister Cecilia is a diligent student, and shall we say, an *enthusiastic* musician."

"And ya know that creature, Hammer!" said Art. "Has a stud through his cheek, one through his tongue, and an iron band over his lower lip — a regular colander man."

"Hell, Art, none of that is against the requirements."

Lars bent over his notes. "Piano major. I've never seen him in my classes. Does he study privately?"

"He knows his way around a keyboard." Gordon

didn't know why he was supporting Emmett, who preferred rock over Chopin, except that he was, at least, not
tone deaf like Sister Cecilia.

"What if he gets his spinach hung up on his tongue
stud the day we present the scholarship?" Art's leg went
into double time, causing the table to rumble like thunder.
He was still a smoker, and, without a fag in his hands, his
whole nervous system jangled a ragged tune. Gordon
reached out and grabbed Art's kneecap, forcing his leg to
be still, but it didn't stop his rant. "These kids get scarier
every year. What are they going to do next? Jab out an
eye? Whack off a toe and hang it around their neck?"

"Arthur, please!" Allegra placed her flattened palm
against her ample bust, lowered her lids, and gasped. Gordon couldn't tell if she was grossed out or titillated. A few
dying embers remained between her and Art, even though
their love affair had been years earlier, when Art was still
married to his first wife and Allegra wore a size eight instead of an eighteen.

"Hey, Gordo, you got something against the sister?"
asked Art. "Like some twisted Catholic-boy thing?"

"Well, it is true the first day she walked into class I
thought, now is my chance to get even." He recalled his
first-grade teacher, Sister Clement, her face as wrinkled
as a walnut, her habit held together with straight pins,
her full skirt whispering his punishment. When she left
his desk, pink stripes the width of her ruler crossed his
palm. His private music had seeped from his mind; he had
forgotten where he was and had hummed.

"Sister Cecilia is a good, well-meaning person," offered Lars.

"I agree," said Gordon, "but this isn't Miss Conge-
niality. Twenty years ago she would have flunked out of

music and now you guys are saying we should honor her incompetence with a scholarship!"

"We have to encourage the few majors we have," said Lars, his white eyebrows rising above his wire-rim glasses. "Don't forget what happened to the drama department." He ran his forefinger across his throat.

"Damn it, let's just skip a year," said Gordon.

"You know how these trusts are set up," said Lars. "We're required to appropriate funds accordingly."

"But don't you agree that music majors, even award-winning majors, should be able to distinguish pitch?" Gordon suddenly felt lightheaded. The room shimmered. His face flushed, sweat forming on his brow despite the cold room.

Allegra leaned across the table, placed a bejeweled hand on his. "Are you all right, Gordon? Do you need a lie-down?" Anything could be solved with a cup of tea or a "lie-down," but her concern was genuine.

"I'm . . . I'm all right," he stammered. Where was that goddamn button on the harness? He'd press it now if he could only find it.

He entered his music appreciation class in a foul mood, a bad way to begin. He played an excerpt from George Crumb's *Ancient Voices of Children,* in which a mezzo-soprano trills her tongue, laughs, and sings into an amplified piano, while percussionists beat tuned tom-toms in a bolero rhythm, play a vibraphone, Tibetan prayer stones, and Japanese temple bells. The students winced, giggled, rolled their eyes, and clapped their hands over their ears. This was what he had come to expect, although he couldn't fathom why young minds were closed to startling, adventurous sounds. Nearing the end of class, he raised his voice over the din to ask if there were any questions.

"Do we have to know this?"

"Will there be listening examples on the test?"

He wished, just once, someone would ask something about music. After class, the students cleared out quickly, except Bourhadur Chandrasekhara, who approached him again.

Gordon opened the CD player and began putting away his CDs.

Bourhadur put his hand out. "I take CDs home. I make copies to listen for test."

The CDs were Gordon's personal property, and he rarely loaned them out.

"You can't just make copies of copyrighted recordings."

"Then I bring cassettes. You make copies for me."

"Look, Bourhadur, it's not feasible for each student to have recordings of everything I play in class. It's not necessary."

"You will not be lending me this CDs. You will not be giving me questions on test. You will not be cooperating me!"

Gordon felt his heart thumping, the harness clammy at his armpits. He spoke slowly to appear calm. "Just relax, Bourhadur, learn what you can in class, enjoy the music — that's what appreciation means."

"Don't need knowledge of music, need G.E. credit of A!"

Now was the time to press the button, but he could not reach for it, not in front of a student. "If you aren't interested in music, drop the class!" His voice — loud, edgy, heated — dropped off into a tense stillness. Some of his freshman theory students, who had already taken their seats, stopped talking and stared at him. Sister Cecilia, he noticed, stood behind Bourhadur, waiting her turn to speak with him.

"Teachers are to help the students, but you are the opposite method." Bourhadur's jaw was slack with rage. He was snorting deep drafts of air through quivering nostrils. "You are a damn guy."

The button, how to get at the button?

Sister Cecilia laid her hand on Bourhadur's forearm and talked so rapidly, Gordon at first thought she was having a mystical experience, speaking in tongues. Bourhadur answered her vehemently, flecks of spittle sprinkling her habit. They rallied back and forth, the sister calmly repeating the same phrase between his lengthy tirades that gradually subsided, until he bowed to her and shuffled out of the room.

Gordon stood dumbfounded, shaken. "What language was that?"

"Bengali."

"Bengali? You're fluent in Bengali?"

"Oh, no. I learned just enough to get by when I was a novice of the Missionaries of Charity."

"What were you saying to him?"

"Take a drink of water. It will cool you."

"That's it?"

The corners of her mouth turned up in an angelic smile. The pocket of her gray habit bore a faint grease stain, reminding him of her help with his car. "I thought hearing his own language would soothe him. He seemed so frustrated and upset."

"The Missionaries of Charity — you were in Mother Teresa's order?"

She nodded. "Serving the poorest of the poor. I got to meet her once. It was the greatest moment of my life."

"And you gave it all up to study music at Goldhurst?"

"I think it was having to wash my clothes in a bucket. I'll take a Maytag any day, but Mother Teresa is a saint. The Holy See works slowly and carefully. It may take one hundred fifty years for Rome to make it official, but Mother Teresa ascended into heaven the instant of her last breath."

"How would you know?"

"Because I once looked into her face and saw God." She walked toward her seat, but then turned back to him. "Oh! I forgot what I was going to ask you. Does the Singing Nun still make recordings?"

"Nope. She's dead. Suicide."

She gasped. "A sister committed suicide?"

"Oh, she'd left the convent by then. She and her, uh, female companion, who died with her, had a home for autistic children that was going bankrupt. The Belgian government was demanding back taxes on her recordings, even though she'd given all her earnings to the church years before."

She took the crucifix of her rosary between her forefingers and thumbs, contemplating it a moment. "How sad. To accomplish so much and then to despair at the end."

"Yeah. Burning in hell as we speak."

"God tests us all." She made the sign of the cross with the crucifix, then glided to her seat.

The button.

Chapter Seven

Gordon found himself back at Sutter Park, promenading around the duck pond, trading affable acknowledgments with the elderly couple and the assemblage of young mothers and toddlers. His second day there and already he was accepted as one of the regulars. This gave him courage to saunter over to the playground where Moopuna, a lone figure on an immobile swing, hunched forward, staring at the ground. Gordon settled on the bench, looking off into the distance, pretending to have no interest in the children at all. Soon he felt a very small presence standing before him. His eyes plunged into the solemn brown face.

"Higher."

"Well, hello, Moopuna. You remember me, huh?"

"Higher." He seemed old enough to speak in sentences, so why was he so taciturn? Maybe English wasn't his native tongue, but that was no excuse either; kids this little caught on fast. Gordon looked over at the caregivers, leaning against the climbing apparatus. The younger one was listening to a long-winded story from Potato Body. "I'd like to push you, Moopuna, but yesterday your caregiver told me I couldn't."

Moopuna looked over at the women. His face was as

blank as a drawn curtain, yet something was obviously going on backstage. "They don't give an ant's piss."

At least that's what Gordon thought he said. He'd never heard the expression and erupted with a loud guffaw.

Still yakking, Potato Body rummaged through her cavernous handbag. Gordon felt a light pressure on his hand as if an insect had alighted there. Moopuna's hand had encircled his forefinger. The child was touching him, which meant he was touching the child. Moopuna led him to the swing, but the caregivers didn't seem to notice; one was too busy punching numbers on her cell phone while the other watched with interest.

How long he swung Moopuna, Gordon wasn't sure. Five minutes, ten. His arm was getting tired. He was sweating under the Holter harness, and it was starting to chafe his rib cage. Dark blue flooded the periphery vision of his right eye, and he flinched with the realization of who had been contacted on the cell phone. She really had gone and done it — the bitch had called the cops on him.

"May I see your identification, sir?"

Gordon pulled out his wallet and opened it to his driver's license. His heart was pounding against the braces of the harness. He should press the button. "Is there something wrong, officer?"

"What is your business in the park, Mr. Clay?"

"Business? People don't usually come to a park on business." He thought of drug dealers, and it caused the heat to rise in his face. "Have I broken any laws?"

"No, but we routinely answer all calls about suspicious persons. Those women over there say that you've been loitering around this playground both yesterday and today."

The cop was a baby, overly scrubbed. "Hey, by any chance did you graduate from the POST Academy at Goldhurst?"

"Uh, yeah."

"I'm an instructor there, in the music department."

The officer considered this for a moment, but seemed unimpressed.

Moopuna dragged a toe in the sand, stopping himself. The kid cop bent at the waist and twisted his torso to peer into the boy's face. "Hey, man, I remember you. How ya doing?" He pointed to a bruise on his upper arm. "How did that happen?"

"I fell off the swing."

"He didn't!" Gordon exclaimed in alarm. He crossed his arms righteously, bumping the recorder of the Holter harness beneath his shirt. It made him feel weak, disabled, so that he dangled his arms at his sides again. Perhaps his shifting position made him appear nervous. Guilty.

"Got any more bruises like that?" asked the cop.

"No." Moopuna slid off the swing and bore down on the hem of his T-shirt, as if he were afraid the cop was going to undress him.

"Okay, man. Whatever you say." The cop straightened and addressed Gordon, "You better leave."

"But why? Don't I have the right to stand in a public park?"

"Sometimes it's just smart to back off from a situation — know what I mean?" The policeman withdrew an official-looking note pad and began writing on it in a tight scrawl, looking back and forth between it and Gordon's license. "I'm writing up my report. It just says I answered the call, that I spoke to you, and advised you to leave the scene."

"But I haven't done anything!"

"The courts are jammed with guys who haven't done nothing and guys who have. It's hard for a jury to tell the difference sometimes — know what I mean?"

Ugly *Goldhurst Sentinel* headlines reared up in his imagination. COLLEGE INSTRUCTOR ACCUSED OF CHILD MOLESTATION. GORDON CLAY ACCUSED OF STALKING WOMAN AND CHILD.

"You look kind of familiar," Gordon fibbed. "Did you by any chance ever take music appreciation?"

The cop sunk an incisor into his lower lip, suppressing a sheepish grin. "For a couple of weeks."

"Students think they're taking an easy class and it turns out not to be." Gordon looked over at the caregivers who were watching the scene with glee. "Let me ask you one other thing. Has anyone reported a missing child to the police?"

"Here in Goldhurst? Why?"

"Someone expressed concern to me about a missing boy."

"Most kids who are reported missing turn up perfectly fine, at a friend's or family member's place."

Gordon shrugged. "I suppose you're right." Moopuna had mounted the swing again and was trying to get it going on his own power. "Can you give him a few pushes? His caregivers don't seem all that interested."

"Sure." The policeman moved behind the swing, asking, "How'd you get that bruise again?"

Shuffling down the cement path, Gordon saw a runner approaching. She was a young woman in skimpy red shorts and a yellow running bra, an injudicious color combination, except on a hot dog. A part of his brain naturally assessed her body: a little narrow in the hips, not much waist, nice tits, probably, if they weren't mashed down in that Spandex thing.

"Mr. Clay!"

Uh-oh, a student. He was checking out the body of a student, something he had disciplined himself not to do. "How are you?" he asked vaguely, not yet placing the pale, familiar face, one which was perhaps framed in a different hairstyle some semesters ago.

She stopped before him, smiling. "You don't recognize me."

The voice, he did. "Sister?" Christ, he was ogling the T and A of a . . . how could a *nun* have so much skin? "You're um, running. Long ways from home, aren't you? Don't tell me you've come here on foot."

"Yeah. I'm training for a marathon."

A marathon-running nun? Music major, hospital volunteer. "How do you find time for everything?"

"Oh, I get a lot of work done on my runs. I study, meditate, pray the same as my sisters do in the chapel or their cells."

"Cells? You still call them cells?"

"Or rooms. Either." She extended her raised palms on each side, parallel to the sky, and cocked her head. "Can I ask you a question?"

"Sure." He thought it would be about music theory.

"Why'd you quit the church?"

"Well, I didn't exactly quit the church. I'm still a Catholic, culturally speaking."

"Huh?" She shaded his eyes to watch his face.

"I suppose I mean to say you can take the Catholic boy out of the church, but you can't take the church out of the Catholic boy. It's who I am, how I was raised."

"But you don't believe in it."

"The whole Catholic dogma thing? Along toward college it just didn't seem plausible."

"Oh! It's the opposite for me. I was raised as nothing, and then, a friend in high school took me to mass. From then on, I was hooked. The Lord is so good to me. He blessed me with music."

He couldn't resist playing devil's advocate. "Really? How so?"

"The first time I went to college I dropped out, not knowing what to major in. I left the country with the Missionaries of Charity to work in India, left that order, came back to the U. S., joined the Sisters of the Holy Restraint, and, since they're a teaching order, had to get a degree in something. I prayed and prayed for the Lord to guide me, and sure enough, first semester out, I took music fundamentals and everything clicked."

Just what had clicked, he couldn't fathom. Did she yet realize she had no musical ability whatsoever?

"Hey, did you make the appointment?"

"Oh, yes. Yesterday. The car's in tiptop shape."

"Not *that* appointment." She pressed her fingertips to her heart and rolled her eyes upward.

"Oh, yeah. I saw Dr. Spinelli." The conversation was getting too personal. "I don't think I ever thanked you for your help, both times, the car and Bourhadur."

"Oh, my pleasure. I was so happy the Lord sent me something to do for you. You've given me so much music. Poor Bourhadur, it's not easy for him, you know. Indians come to this country desperate to get ahead, to bring honor to their families back in India. And such struggles with the language, then in your class — western music is nothing like his own. It must be very confusing."

"Did you give Bourhadur a lecture, too?"

"Oh, absolutely! I'm afraid he didn't understand what you could offer him, Mr. Clay, but I think I set him straight. You should see a great change in his attitude."

He believed her. Miraculously, a weight had been lifted off him. He did not realize how much stress Bourhadur was causing him.

Sister Cecilia hesitated, swaying her body from side to side. "Uh, I was wondering, Mr. Clay, would you be willing to come check out our Youth Ministry Mass Sunday? I mean, I'd really like to know what you think of it."

So she was going to make a project of him, lure him back into the fold. "No, no, I don't think so."

"Oh, no? Well, then maybe some other time. Keep the faith," she hailed him, jogging backward. Her mouth fell open into an "O." "Keep the whatever," she corrected herself.

He headed toward his car, looking back toward the playground. He stopped, considering his next step, then turned back. Whether the sister had instilled within him a kind of courage or he was determined to demand some answers, he wasn't certain, but he stalked up to the two caregivers. "You called the cops on me?"

"You're back?" Potato Body began digging into her purse.

"Hold on. Let me introduce myself." He held out his hand, but the woman didn't take it. "I'm Gordon Clay."

Potato looked up from her rummaging. "Oh, so that's why you're hanging around. You're the deadbeat dad."

"Excuse me? Oh! Is that what she . . . er, Carrie . . . calls me? What else does she say about me?"

"Says you're always off on a sailboat somewheres — Fiji or Tahiti — one of those places."

"It just so happens that's how I make our living, the import business," he said indignantly. The words flying out of his mouth appalled him. He had meant to gain their trust by simply introducing himself. What could be gained by posing as the other Gordon Clay?

Potato Body narrowed her eyes at him, a nasty smirk on her face. "Is it true what they say about those islands? The gals go around with no tops?"

"Some of them. Where's Gordie?"

"Not here."

"Why not? I haven't seen him in months! Is he sick or something?"

"How should I know where he is?"

In a wooded ravine, face down, naked. Like some flaky TV psychic, he couldn't dispel the image.

"All I know is he wasn't there when we went to pick up his group after school yesterday and today. Tell your ex she's supposed to call if your kid's gonna be a no-show. She's a month behind in his payments, too. You wanna take care of that?"

"How much?"

"Sixty-two fifty."

Gordon reached for his wallet, pulled out all the bills in it — a twenty and four ones — and handed it to her. "Sorry, it's all I have on me."

"Better than nothing." Potato Body's tone, her whole demeanor softened. Money seemed to mean more to most people than it did to him. "I'll write you a receipt."

"No, thanks."

"Dealing with cash, it's hard to prove. You should always get a receipt."

"It's okay, really. All these people trust you with their kids. Why shouldn't I trust you with a few bucks?"

"All I'm saying is I could forget you gave it to me."

"Swing me," droned Moopuna.

"It's okay?" asked Gordon.

She held the twenty up to the light as if it might be counterfeit. "Knock yourself out."

Chapter Eight

Dr. Spinelli removed the tape from the recorder on the Holter harness. He pointed at sharp spikes, high and very close together. "Here. What happened here? A little before nine a.m.? Were you late? Stuck in traffic? Hey, I know: you couldn't find a parking space. My wife is taking a class over at the college and she says the instructor is always fifteen, twenty minutes late because there's no reserved parking for faculty — true?"

"Yep. It's the new president trying to increase enrollment by making it more convenient for students to attend."

"Doesn't make a damn bit of sense. What good is the students being there if the teachers aren't?"

Gordon merely shrugged. Typical college president thinking. Over the years he'd seen several presidents come and go. One had fired three POST instructors and the police academy lost accreditation until the next president reinstated them. Another president cut the college publicist position, the annual musical, and the entire drama department.

"I'm telling you, the day they take away my parking spot at this clinic is the day I walk."

Gordon thought of the harassment suit against Spinelli that the nurses were brewing. Parking was the least of his worries. "I remember now," he said. "It was just before my music appreciation class. I was at a faculty meeting."

"And?"

"Well, I opposed a decision the department made, and I couldn't do a thing about it."

"I see. Politics." Spinelli made a note of it. "What were your symptoms?"

"A little dizziness, I guess."

"And here." Spinelli pointed to another cluster of sharp apexes on the tape. "Soon after?"

In his mind's eye, Gordon saw Bourhadur's hand reaching for his CDs. "I was talking to a student. I guess he made me sort of mad."

"Didn't Nursie tell you about the little button thingie you were supposed to press?"

"Yes, but I didn't think it was that big a deal."

"And here. Whoa! Big ole blowup here, practically off the charts. What happened about four p.m.?"

The dark blue of the police officer's uniform flooded his brain like spilled ink, newspaper headlines looming over it: SUSPICIOUS CHARACTER. CHILD MOLESTER. STALKER. "Uh, I was at the park, taking a walk."

"A little walking caused this much stress? And then here, soon after? You really should've pressed the button here."

"Oh, that. I saw a woman runner."

"And?"

"Well, she wasn't wearing much."

The doctor laughed. "Oh-ho! A real looker, huh?" He cupped his hands out before his barrel chest. "Out to here, huh?"

"Well, uh, not exactly." Gordon felt two hot spots burning into his cheekbones.

Spinelli tapped the recorder tape. "Your response is perfectly normal. We won't even count this one." He scribbled a few more notes, then closed Gordon's file. "That's it for today."

"Wait a minute. What's your diagnosis? Is it bad?"

"Too soon to say. Blood pressure is borderline. Don't know about cholesterol. We'll have to wait for the lab work. Don't worry. I'll fix you up, whatever it takes, and Nursie will have some suggestions about changes in lifestyle. Boy, is she big on lifestyle. If I had to live a life as Spartan as that girl, I wouldn't wait around for a heart attack; I'd just shoot myself."

As Dr. Spinelli left the room, Nurse Purcell entered. He smiled and winked at her; she glared back at him with her lavender eyes. She took several pamphlets out of the rack on the wall and handed them to Gordon. "Here's some literature on heart health. There's shopping tips, recipes. You'll need to start an exercise program, too. Walking is easiest, and not just from your car to your classes, but a couple of miles each day."

"I told you: it *is* a couple of miles."

"I'll bet. And get some athletic shoes, with plenty of support. We don't want to see you in podiatry next week."

"Yes, ma'am." He saluted her, and she shot him a flinty look. "I mean, Nurse Purcell." He stretched one side of his mouth out and down, suppressing a smile.

"You think this is funny? Your blood pressure is high, too."

"The doctor said borderline."

"One hundred forty over ninety is high. Did he discuss the possibility of going on medication to control it?"

He had heard about those hypertension medications

that caused a dry, hacking cough, made your mouth taste
like metal, plus you had to get up to urinate half a dozen
times per night. "No, and I'm not interested."

"Then cut the salt and the stress."

"You really think these so-called lifestyle changes are
going to make a difference?"

"Absolutely."

"What if my heart is already too far gone?"

"What did Dr. Spinelli tell you?"

"Said I had to wait until the results of all my other
tests were in."

"Then you're going to have to wait."

"Look, you told me how bad stress is for me. Well,
this is the most stressful thing I've got going, this not
knowing."

She looked at him with those wide lavender eyes.
"This is completely off the record, but I can tell you something Dr. Spinelli never would." She tapped her temple
with a crooked forefinger.

It was his brain! Weak, constricted blood vessels were
causing the dizziness, the tingling in his arms and fingers.
His old man had dropped dead of an aneurysm, he'd go
that way, too. It was in the genes, like in the Mendelssohn
family; Felix and Fanny, their grandfather Moses, father,
and the little sister had all died of aneurysms. He gulped.
"You think I should see a neurologist?"

She actually laughed. She was very pretty when she
laughed; she should do more of it. "No, no. A psychiatrist. It seems you've got some issues to deal with —
stress, anger, profound unhappiness."

"But a psychiatrist . . . I really don't think . . ."

"I know!" She snapped her fingers. "You could talk
to Sister Cecilia!"

"The sister?" Gordon held his palms up. "Oh, no."

"Why not? She does wonders for our rehab patients, especially the despondent ones. A regular miracle worker. I'll mention it the next time I see her, if you like."

"I wouldn't like. I mean, please don't, her being a student and all. I wouldn't want this to get out."

"Suit yourself." She snapped the computer shut and stood. "We'll call you if we see anything of significance in your test results." She opened the door. He slid off the examination table and followed her out of the room

Glancing down the corridor, he observed Dr. Spinelli talking with another cardiologist. The two men in white medical coats were standing in profile, their toes about a yard apart, their bellies nearly touching. "How come those guys look like that when they know firsthand how much damage it can do to their hearts?"

Nurse Purcell threw up her arms and let them slap against her sides. "Oh, well, they think they can fix anything. They think they're God."

Chapter Nine

The next afternoon he did his shopping: running shoes, blood pressure monitor, bags and bags of groceries, more produce than he'd ever bought. Bother leaped up and wove her long, slinky body between the paper bags. She ducked her head into a bag and then, with one graceful leap, her whole multicolored body disappeared. He plucked her out of the bag and set her on the floor. She was a silly looking thing. Her head was too little for her body, and her ears were too big for her head. She had a patch of black around one eye, orange around the other, and a white stripe running in between. Her nose reminded him of Neapolitan ice cream. She rubbed against his legs, causing him to stumble. He selected a can of Kitty Tuna Casserole out of the cupboard and served it up, but that wasn't what she had in mind.

He got out the *Recipes for Your Heart's Delight* pamphlet and turned to "Meatless Chili." First things first. He removed from one of the bags a pound of ground beef. Bother jumped up onto the counter again. He poked a hole in the shrink-wrap, pinched off a bit of the meat and set it in her bowl on the floor. She leaped down, gave the meat a sniff, then went back to weaving between his legs.

"You don't know what you want," he told her, then realized he could be talking to himself.

He began to read the recipe. One medium onion, chopped. Three cloves of garlic, peeled and crushed. A cup of mushrooms, sliced. One and a half green peppers, seeded and chopped. Why one and a half? Why not one or two — what could it matter? He imagined the lone half pepper setting on a rack in the refrigerator, withering, then liquefying into a putrid, dripping goo. Three stalks of celery, minced. Skip it — didn't buy any. Three large tomatoes. He didn't have fresh; he'd use canned. One cup each of dried lima beans, garbanzo beans, pinto beans, and kidney beans, soaked overnight and drained. This blew his plans for making the chili for dinner, but he would read to the bitter end anyway. Oregano, chili powder, cumin — whatever the hell that was — basil, and dried parsley flakes. He checked his spice cabinet. Salt, pepper, and cinnamon — that would have to make up for all that other crap.

His eyes glazed over. All that chopping, slicing, crushing, seeding, soaking, draining, mincing — healthy cooking was beyond his powers. He popped open a beer, tilted back his head and slammed it down like those macho guys in the commercials. He raised the half-empty can in a solitary toast. "To my new lifestyle." Why strive for longevity with a rigid diet and exercise program only to increase and prolong his misery? He needed to straighten out his life. In the meantime, while he figured things out, he could use another beer and some more peanuts. Gripping the cool, solid glass of the peanut jar, he felt relief flooding his body.

He settled at the kitchen table with another beer and the nuts to correct second-year part-writing exercises. With his red pencil, he marked two lines linking the error of parallel fifths. He made another pair of slashes next to parallel octaves. The student had crossed the alto and tenor voices and written one chord with two wrong notes. Jesus, whose paper was this? He looked at the name. Rick Bay — that loser. When he had handed Rick his last assignment, he had glanced at the D, balled up the paper, and hurled it toward the wastebasket. Gordon crumpled up the paper and tossed it into the garbage. This time he beat him to it.

He took another paper off the stack. Parallel fifths again. Daily, for nearly two years, he'd been harping about parallel fifths. He slashed the error so vehemently his pencil poked a hole in the paper. Marking each correction, he held the paper firmly, yanking it to shreds with the point of his pencil. Subsequently, he marked each error with a small puddle of beer. He envisioned himself marching off to the nuthouse on the heels of Schumann, wearing a nineteenth-century foot-tall top hat. He swept his arm across the stack of papers and hurled them to the floor.

He settled into his recliner with another beer and a bag of sour cream and onion potato chips. Bother pounced on his lap and licked the potato chip in his hand. He threw it on the carpet for her. She jumped down, sniffed it, and walked away.

With the remote, he flicked on the TV and caught the local news. No mention of a kidnapping — by now he didn't expect it. The disappearance of the boy Gordon Clay would no doubt remain a mystery forever. He went into the spare room and flipped on the computer. Target padded up to him, backed into his leg, and whipped him with her black-and-gray ringed tail. He stroked the length of her belly, removing the loose fur, and she swiped at his hand, swiftly, concisely, drawing blood. Damaged goods, like himself.

He cruised the Internet, searching for orchestral openings. The orchestras on-line were interested in selling concert tickets, not soliciting bass players. Well, he had enough money socked away to have a student house- and cat-sit for the summer, move to L.A., and try the freelancing business again.

As soon as he got off-line, the phone rang. He started at the unfamiliar sound. The phone had not rung since Carrie Clay's late night call.

"Hello?"

"Twenty-four dollars, right? This is too bizarre, but Annette tells me that's what I owe you. I don't know why exactly, but . . . well, am I right?"

"Excuse me?"

"You *are* Gordon Clay — a Gordon Clay?"

"That's right, and you're . . . Carrie Clay?"

"I don't know why you helped me out, but Annette said a Gordon Clay paid her something and I don't feel like owing you anything, so could you please give me your address so I can reimburse you?"

Gordon's heart got to thumping. How could he explain himself? "I guess I was being a little self-serving, for my own peace of mind. I guess I thought if I paid her — Annette — I could get some information from her. What about Gordie? Have you found him?"

"I don't know what you're talking about."

"Remember, you woke me from a sound sleep at two a.m., crying, *sobbing*, about your missing son. It was natural that . . ."

"Oh my God. Wait a minute. You came to the park looking for Gordie? But how'd you know where . . .?"

"You mentioned Sutter Park on the phone. I tried calling the other Gordon Clay — your ex — to see if your son had been found, but his phone is disconnected."

"Which he neglected to tell me. I blanked out on his number. I looked in the phone book and dialed you."

"It's okay. I was hoping you'd call me back to tell me you'd found your boy."

"Why would I?"

This was no big deal. He would not make a big deal out of it. "Because you left me hanging! I've been worried sick. Any guy would be."

She laughed. "You think so? Well, then, you've got more faith in the male gender than I have. This is too bizarre."

"You did find him, I take it."

"Oh, um, yeah. It was my ex-mother-in-law. She came over to see him, decided to take him to spend the night at her house. I was in the shower at the time and she claimed she shouted to me and thought she heard me say okay. "

"At two a.m.?"

"No, no. This was eight thirty or nine. I got out of the bathroom, the TV was still on, but I didn't see Gordie. I thought he'd gone to bed. He does that, just slips away without a word when he gets tired. I had a test to study for. I didn't think to check on him until much later."

He wanted to ask what she was studying and if she was a student at Goldhurst. He shouldn't get too personal, though. "That's awful. Does grandma pull that shit often?"

"No. We're pretty civil. She's good to Gordie; she cares about him. I work full time and go to school. Gordon's no help — usually off on his boat."

"What does he import?"

"Wood carvings, coral jewelry. That's what he says anyway."

"What do you think he imports?"

"Hell, I don't know. Shrunken heads? He makes too damn much money for a few trinkets. One time he was gone a whole year. Forgets he even has a son."

"How old is your boy?"

"Six."

"Good age. I'd like to meet another Gordon Clay."

"You're suggesting — oh, no, that would be too bizarre."

"It might be fun."

"One Gordon Clay — two — is enough in one life-time. I appreciate your concern for my son, but . . ."

"What are you studying?"

"Interpreting for the courts. May I have your address, if you don't mind? I'll mail you a check."

"Skip it." Gordon set the phone in its holder. It was over — the Carrie/Gordon Clay thing. It had come to nothing, just like everything else in his life. Oh well, what did he expect? At least now he knew the kid was okay.

The phone rang again. It would be Carrie, agreeing to meet him. So maybe it wasn't over. "Yes?"

"Hey, Mr. Clay, did you realize that to call your number you make the sign of the cross?"

"What?"

"It's true. First you poke the first number off to the side, and then you really do make the sign of the cross."

"I don't call myself much."

"Oh! This is Sister Cecilia."

"I know." For a while the line hummed softly.

"I'm sorry to bother you at home. It's about the scholarship. Mother St. Paul and I were just, uh, discussing it. She wants to know if . . ."

"I can't say, Sister. Mr. Stelling will make the announcement soon."

"Oh, okay." She sounded disappointed, but then forced cheer into her voice. "It really is a blessing — your phone number, I mean. I know you don't think so, but God works in mysterious ways."

"Right, Sister. Good night."

He got another beer, and, without lifting the phone from its holder, punched out his phone number. Sure enough. He'd get it changed. Hopefully, if things went as planned this summer, he'd have it disconnected, put the house up for sale, move out of Goldhurst for good. There would be no hope of Carrie Clay calling him again. Sometimes losing hope was the kindest thing he could do for himself. To think he'd been mooning around over a woman and a boy he would never meet. She sounded nice, interesting. An interpreter. To hell with it. What did he care? He was going to stop thinking about Carrie Clay this minute.

He looked around the kitchen, surprised at the mess he'd made of the second-year papers. He tossed the entire pile out, thinking he'd have to make up some lame excuse about losing them, although he'd never lost a set of papers in his life.

He wiped the tabletop and settled down with the freshman ear-training quizzes. They were pretty good, until he got to Sister Cecilia's. She had notated an octave as a major seventh. Eighth notes and quarters were notated the same. She had scrawled a few figured bass symbols, then erased them with a smear, then wrote a big question mark. The dot was a circle, the way she dotted her *i*'s. She also encircled the *t* in her name with little dashes, suggesting the radiance of the cross. Everything about her irked him. She had a calling from God to go into music. Why then had he made her tone deaf? And why did the music department want to award her incompetence with a scholarship?

She wouldn't even be able to pass the ear-training final. She wouldn't be able to go onto sophomore theory, meaning she wouldn't be eligible for the scholarship. He slashed a fat, red F across the top of her paper.

Chapter Ten

It was the first day of the fall semester. Gordon stood in front of class after class of fresh, blank faces, repeating, repeating. "If you miss three classes . . . If you don't turn in . . ." The students sighed. He sighed. What else could he do? He was stuck. The experiment of the summer had been a failure in ways he'd never imagined. On L.A. freeways he had gripped the steering wheel in spasms of terror, his body tensed, his shoulders bunched. Once, changing lanes, he squeezed his eyes shut. He had auditioned for several orchestras, but the only gigs he could scrounge up were casuals in smoke-filled lounges and a six-week run of *The Sound of Music* in a dinner theater. Nuns — he couldn't escape them. The character Maria was like Sister Cecilia, only talented. In the stuffy, narrow, orchestra pit, he felt cornered, scraping his bow against one wall or slamming his elbow into the other. The conductor, a USC grad student, hurled insults at him. He was too old for that crap.

He'd been wrong about the money thing, too. Money meant little to him only because, teaching at Goldhurst, he had enough. The dinner theater job, which was nonunion, paid beans. He'd forgotten what that was like. Seedy bars, cockroach-infested studio apartments, and watery coffee in all-night diners. He had forgotten how, fifteen years earlier, he had shown L.A. his back, looking onward to tranquil Goldhurst, a respite from the real world. Now he was stuck here for good.

In his sophomore theory class, eight of the ten students bore familiar faces. There was also an elderly gentleman, who had written him quite a formal letter of introduction, stating he was the choir director at First New Hope, and would like to expand his "musical horizon." He continued on to explain that, forty years before, his music education had been interrupted when he heard a call from God; but ultimately, he decided he had a "hearing problem."

When Gordon called the name Philomena Gull, a mousy woman seated in the back row raised two fingers at half mast. She was wearing a shapeless brown jumper over a plain white blouse and a homemade crucifix consisting of a bunch of nails bound with leather thongs. Her washed-out face was framed by wispy orange hair cropped close to her small skull. Studying the woman's sober gray eyes, he was jolted by a shock of recognition, like spotting a family trait in the stern countenance of a distant relative in a sepia-tone photograph. In his consternation, he kept losing his train of thought during his routine explanation of the syllabus, muttering "Um," then breaking off into an embarrassing silence. He stammered through the cursory overview of his requirements, skipped the review quiz, and dismissed the class.

Philomena Gull tried to file past him, but he projected his voice toward her. "Uh, excuse me, I need to speak to you." She kept walking, not even turning her head. He called, "Sister, we need to talk."

She halted and dropped her head, giving him her alabaster nape beneath her chopped, jagged hairline. "I have another class right now."

"I only need a minute." He stalked out of the classroom, down the corridor, and into the office he shared with Art Bunch, knowing her obedience training would bid her to follow. Art was out; he could give her hell in private. He set down his books on his desk and nodded to a chair. She sat as he loomed over her. "You know you can't enroll in second year. The prerequisite is passing first year with a C or better."

She hung her head as if the grotesque crucifix dangling from her neck weighed it down. Addressing the pale hands in her lap, she mumbled, "I was hoping I could get the D changed to an incomplete, and then I could work on fulfilling first-year requirements while I continued with second year."

"It doesn't work that way . . ." He tried her name timidly, like testing an icy mountain stream with his big toe. "Uh, Philomena."

She emitted a muted sob, tears rolling down her freckled cheeks. "I hate that name."

He silently handed her a Kleenex. "In my roll book, it says you're registered under that name."

"I know." She honked into the Kleenex and swallowed hard. "I'll start from scratch. I'll go back to freshman theory."

"I'm sorry, Sister . . ."

"I'm not *that* any more."

That possibility had not occurred to him, even with the laywoman's clothing and the name change. And yet, there was something different about her. She seemed less of a person, no longer part of a greater whole. The wind

— no, the spirit — had been knocked out of her. Had she lost her faith? The thought was staggering. "It's against regulations to repeat a class you've already received a grade in, D or higher."

"But it's not fair. I could do everything but the ear-training, all the written work. I got an A on every part-writing assignment."

She had to be remembering wrong or exaggerating. "The ear is everything in music."

She nodded. "I think I can improve. I've prayed about it."

So she still had faith. Stripped of her identity as both a nun and a music major, she still had that. "Look, I'm not being difficult. I'm trying to save you a lot of heartbreak and disappointment. Obviously you love music, but there's two kinds of music lovers: those who play in the symphony and those who buy the symphony tickets. We need both kinds to make the music world go 'round. Why make yourself miserable over this?"

"Oh, Mr. Clay! Being a music major, studying music — this has been the happiest year of my life!"

"You've had a hard life then."

"I know I'm supposed to be in music. The Lord has told me so."

"Yeah? Then why didn't he give you the ear and a sense of rhythm?"

She shook her head in quick, short motions, clicked her tongue like he didn't get it. "You think the road to Calvary was easy?"

He had to grip the edge of his desk to steady himself. He could feel pressure pounding in his head, like diving deep under water. That morning, checking his blood pressure on his do-it-yourself monitor, he discovered that it was up to the borderline numbers of last spring. Oddly, despite the debacle of L.A., he had experienced no chest pains. No doubt his problem was situational and his situation was teaching.

Slowly he turned to his filing cabinet and pulled out his records for the previous semester. At a glance, he could see that she was right about getting all As on her written work. When had he begun putting grades behind students' names without making any connection between the two? It made him feel shabby, careless, prejudiced. He'd misjudged her, mistaking the faithful for the stupid.

He replaced the records in the file. "Well, it appears that you're right."

The corners of her mouth quivered, followed by a sniffle.

"This is what I might be able to do," he began tentatively. "Since you seem so determined, I might be able to separate your theory grade from your ear-training grade."

She looked up. The hope switching on beneath the nearly transparent skin of her face pained him. He was making a mistake, he knew it, but he followed through. "Some colleges do it that way. I'll have to check with Mr. Stelling, but I don't think he'll mind if I get a little creative. You know how few actual music majors we have."

She seemed to grow in the chair.

"You must understand that if we separate the grades, you've got two semesters of A in theory and two semesters of F in ear-training. In all honesty, I don't see how you're going to change that."

"I'll get caught up, I promise." She jumped up and began backing out the door as if she were afraid he'd change his mind. "Thank you for the second chance, Mr. Clay. God bless you!"

"Sit down. We're not done yet."

Meekly she sank back into the chair. "I'll get a tutor. I'll work extra hard."

"Didn't you have one last year? He or she didn't do you much good. That's why I'm proposing to be the one who gives you extra help."

"Oh, no, Mr. Clay, I'd be wasting your time. You've got more important things to do."

"Not true. My job is to teach."

She dropped her forehead between her outstretched forefinger and thumb. "I can't. I'd be too nervous. Nothing would sink in."

"That's part of the problem. When I'm giving dictation, instead of listening to the example, you're thinking, *I can't, I can't*, and you don't hear a note."

"True." She came out of hiding. She was staring down at the pile of brochures the nurse had given him. She looked at him, concern floating like a liquid film across her eyes. "What did Dr. Spinelli say about your condition?"

"Nothing much. A little high blood pressure — borderline, actually."

"It seems like more than that. Remember that day you had car trouble?" She clutched the ugly crucifix. "Lord, you gave me a scare. Mimi was quite concerned about you, too."

"Mimi?"

"Dr. Spinelli's nurse — Monica Purcell."

"And she talks about her patients?"

"Don't be offended, Mr. Clay." Her cool, pale fingers lighted on his hand, then flew off again. "We're friends. And she knows how highly I regard you, so naturally . . .

What she described to me — well, it sounds like you are undergoing a crisis of the spirit."

"A what?"

"I'm not kidding, Mr. Clay. It's making you physically ill and you've got to find some way to heal. Now, if you don't want to go to mass, perhaps you should check out the Ministry of the Living Faith Study Group."

"Not interested," he said, perhaps too firmly because her sienna countenance clouded to a rosy hue.

"What changes have you made in your lifestyle?"

Lifestyle — he hated the word. "I walk every once in a while." His pricey, snowy white, athletic shoes were still virgins, sitting in the trunk of his car in the shopping bag.

"Consistency is the important thing. You need to get started right away on a regular exercise program." She sat up primly now, looking askance at him. The tables had turned — she was no longer under his tutelage, but he under hers. "I'll make you a training schedule."

"Really, Sis — uh, Phil — uh, that won't be necessary."

She nodded toward the remains of his breakfast: a sausage biscuit wrapping and a grease-stained hash browns container. "You're not supposed to have any of this junk. You're going to have to eat differently, cook differently. I have this absolutely fabulous recipe for meatless chili."

With her confidence up, he reached over to the piano and played part of an ascending major scale. "Now, tell me, is this going up or down?"

"We're starting right now? I'm not ready!"

He repeated the scale passage. "Up or down?"

"Down?"

"Up." He played a descending scale. "And now?"

"Up again?"

"Not quite." He was making it too hard. "Let's try this. I'm going to play two pitches. You tell me if they are the same or different." He plucked down an A, then the same key.

"The same?"

He nodded. He played a B then a higher G sharp.

"Different?"

"Now we're getting somewhere." He checked his watch, her cue to rise.

"This means so much to me, you just don't know." Backing out the doorway, she bumped into Art Bunch, coming in from jazz band. "Oh! Excuse me, Mr. Bunch! Bye! The Lord be with you."

"And with your spirit!" he shouted after her, down the corridor. To Gordon he exclaimed, "Whoa! What's the sister's rush? Late for Matins?"

"That would be in the middle of the night. It's more like Terce about now." Gordon read Art's T-shirt aloud: " 'To do is to be,' — Plato; 'To be is to do,' — Socrates; 'Do be do be do,' — Sinatra. Hmm, does that mean you're a Sinatra fan?"

"It's a *joke*, man. Trouble with you, Gordo, you think too much. Me, I get out of bed, reach for a clean shirt — which are none too many since the little woman split — put it on, go to work. What's up with the sister, anyway?"

"She's left the convent."

"The sister ain't a sister no more, no shit? I thought she just switched one ugly dress for another."

"I liked the old ugly dress better."

"I liked the old *person* better."

"You noticed, too?"

"She was totally bummed at her clarinet lesson this

morning. Now I know why. Who would have thought she'd ever leave? She was so gung-ho. I called her Sister just like usual and she didn't say a word."

"I called her by her given name and she burst into tears."

"What is it?" Bunch never bothered with a roll book until grading time.

"Philomena."

"So that's why she burst into tears." Bunch checked his cell for messages, lit a cigarette, and inhaled deeply. Gordon didn't mind sharing an office with a smoker; he got a little contact high. The smell made him feel sweetly nostalgic for the 1970s, the good old days, when all musicians smoked and he was young enough to have hopes of a playing career.

Art blew smoke into a Ziploc bag, since smoking was prohibited in the building.

"I wonder why she left if it's making her so miserable."

"I think she's got the hots for you, Gordo." Art was always teasing him about women, about "not getting any."

Since Gordon had given up dating a few years earlier, he had surprised himself in his reaction to that Carrie Clay woman, a disembodied voice in the night pleading for her missing son. His desperate search, going off to Sutter Park twice, paying off that Tasmanian Devil caregiver to gain her trust. Had he actually envisioned himself with that woman and child — a sort of ready-made family? He had never confided in Art about the incident, and now he was glad he hadn't. He had had his sign-of-the-cross phone number changed to an unlisted one, so there was no chance of Carrie Clay calling him again.

He went on the offense, saying, "Your divorce is about final, right? She's all yours."

Art hacked a smoker's hack, waving the cigarette in front of his face to dispel Gordon's words. "Not my type."

"Maybe you can't afford to be all that picky anymore." Art had complained that his Club Med Mexican Cruise hadn't yielded a single one-night stand.

"I'll never say never. I made a myspace."

"Shame on you, Art. That's for kids."

"Ah, now. Some big kids are on there, too. And there's a couple of hot chicks in my church's Christians Without Partners Prayer Group I might be able to score. Besides, she wants you, Gordo. You ever noticed that cow-eyed look she gives you?"

He had noticed, but it wasn't what Art insinuated. It was how the rarely interested student looked toward an able teacher for the substance of knowledge. "That's only because I can give her what she truly wants: a passing grade in freshman theory."

"You went and flunked the sister, no shit?"

"No, she got a D. You know they can repeat a class if they get an F.

Art shook his head. "You're a mean man."

"Mean has nothing to do with it! This is about integrity."

"Ah, go on." He took another drag. "I see colander-face Hammer got the scholarship."

"Oh, Christ! Get married again, would ya, Art? You're a lot nicer when you're married."

"You think?"

"I think."

"Would if I could, Gordo. Marriage is the best deal

going for a little horny fart like me. You don't even have to call for home delivery. It's already *there*, man. Plus you get food *and* clean shirts, if you're lucky. Too bad for me, man. Fresh outta Mrs. Bunches."

Art withdrew a red Magic Marker from his desk drawer and drew a diagonal slash across the day's date on his wall calendar. "One down, a hundred seventy-four more to go."

A blur of movement at the door caught the corner of his eye. There stood the sister as quiet as the Holy Spirit. Gordon jumped up from his chair. "Oh! Sis . . . Phil . . . you're back!" How long had she been standing there? What had she overheard? "I thought you were going to class."

"It was short, the first day, you know. I just dropped by to, uh, ask you guys to dinner. See my new place and all."

"No, I don't think . . ." began Gordon.

"Awesome." Art clapped his hands together. "Just say when and we'll be there."

Chapter Eleven

He told himself he'd find a way to get out of it. Art had bailed midweek, claiming he was certain Gordon and Cecilia — no more Philomena, no more Sister — would want to be alone. "Be sure to pack a pocketful of rubbers. You know why she left the convent, so don't disappoint her, dude." He ignored Art's lewd comments, but as the week progressed his anxiety mounted. What if she really was interested in a relationship? Why didn't he just cancel out? Because he felt he owed her — *what*, he wasn't certain. Because it was one less Friday night he wouldn't have to spend home alone with the cats. He hadn't had a home-cooked meal in ages. It would probably taste like cardboard, but at least it would be good for him.

His mother had taught him to always bring a gift for the hostess. Wine, he was certain, was not appropriate this time, nor was candy or any other kind of dessert. His roses were practically gone, but he picked a bouquet, anyway. One white, one red, two salmon, three yellow.

The address she gave him was a run-down four-plex in the old Sutter Park neighborhood. Her apartment was in back, up creaking, outside stairs. She answered his knock with, "Oh, they're gorgeous!" and accepted his meager offering of mismatched roses bound in a soggy paper towel. Her face was bright with the heat of cooking, the flush of her cheeks clashing with her cropped, copper bangs. She appeared relaxed, wearing a long black skirt and a denim bib apron over her usual white blouse.

He stepped inside and his nostrils were filled with the mingling aroma of onions, garlic, and oregano. "Cozy little place you have here."

"Isn't it?" A pot boiled over, water sizzling in the flames of the burner. "Oh, just a moment." She set the roses on the table on her way to the stove.

The living room, kitchen, and eating area were all one room, shrouded in wallpaper of monster red geraniums. A path was worn into the greenish linoleum between the gas stove and the avocado refrigerator. There was an angel holy-water font at the door, a Holy Ghost sun-catcher in the window over the sink, and, looming over the sofa, the same portrait of the Sacred Heart — flesh ripped from his breast and his heart set afire — that had reigned over Gordon's childhood living room. Jesus's somber, accusing eyes had seemed to follow him around, so that he was afraid to be alone with the portrait, even to watch cartoons. How could anyone be consoled by the guy?

"Are all these units filled with . . . uh . . . nuns returning to the world?"

She walked toward him, smiling and wiping her hands on her apron. "You make it sound like we've been on spaceships. No, there's just my roommate and me from the convent." A roommate. Why did he assume she lived alone? "There's Buck, a homeless guy in front downstairs, would-be homeless. He's a handyman who's doing some work around the church when he's sober; there's a visiting priest from Colombia; and an elderly woman, Faye Marie, downstairs in back, who is just a regular tenant. Some wine?"

"Sure." He was surprised by the offer.

She poured herself some, too, then clinked his glass. "Cheers."

"Cheers." It was a full-bodied Merlot, very smooth. The price was still on the label — only a few bucks. "Very good."

"And good for you. A glass of red wine a day helps prevent heart disease. Like garlic. Garlic thins the blood."

"And wards off evil spirits."

"Oh, I believe it."

They laughed. Was it possible? He was having fun with the sister.

A knock on the door caused her hand to fly to her mouth mid-chuckle. "Oh, that must be Jack."

She opened the door to a young man in black Levis and a black windbreaker. His cheek was as smooth as a boy's and he had long curly lashes. He and she embraced warmly, like good friends. Were they having a dinner party? Was this her roommate's date? Then Jack unzipped his jacket, revealing a Roman collar.

"Jack, this is my teacher, Mr. Clay. Jack runs the Ministry of the Living Faith Study Group. You should check it out, Mr. Clay."

"Cool, absolutely, you should," Jack said, smiling and blinking fast.

"Will you join us in a glass of wine?"

"I'd love to, but I can't. No drinking on the job."

"Except at mass," blurted Gordon, attempting to join in.

"Technically that's the blood of Christ." Jack — not

Father Doyle or, at the very least, Father Jack — held up a circular, black leather case, and said, "If you'll excuse me, I've brought Tiffany her dinner."

Cecilia's concerned gaze followed the priest down the darkened hall, before she pulled her attention away and smiled at Gordon. "Well! Let's see. Dinner is about ready." She arranged two place settings on the table.

"The others — they're not joining us?"

"Oh, no. Jack's making his calls and Tiffany, well, she . . ." She stopped, watching the priest return to the living room.

"May I have a word with you,?" he asked her. "In private."

"Certainly. Excuse us, Mr. Clay." Together they slipped out the front door.

Gordon took another sip of wine. He sniffed the fragrant aroma wafting from the pots on the stove and his stomach growled. He helped himself to more of the wine and glanced toward the hallway. His hand slackened, the glass wobbling in his grasp. A woman stood in the dappled shadows as still as a statue. She wore the traditional black habit and veil of an old nun. Her eyes were set in dark hollows, a stiletto gleam aimed at him.

"I thought I heard a man's voice, other than Father's, I mean. Hello." Stepping into the light, she appeared younger, with a childish, heart-shaped face, accommodating massive, unblinking eyes.

"Uh, I'm Gordon. You must be Tiffany. Jack and Cecilia — they've just stepped out."

"To talk about me. They're always talking about me in hushed, fervent voices, as if I don't know. They're jealous of me." She walked past him and lifted the roses off the table.

"They're from my garden," said Gordon. "They're about finished for the year, but I thought . . ."

Tiffany grimaced. Her hand sprang open, revealing beads of blood swelling out of pin-sized wounds.

"The thorns! I'm sorry! I should have warned you." He took the roses from her hand. "Are you all right?"

"It is nothing. Compared to our Lord's suffering, it is nothing at all." The woman looked into his eyes, beyond his eyes, as if they were portholes through which she envisioned another world. He felt a chill ripple through his body. Creep show time.

Cecilia stepped back into the apartment. "Oh, you two have met."

"Sister, I need to speak with you," Tiffany said sternly.

Cecilia lolled her head toward him, giving a apologetic smile. "I'll be right back."

Eyes downcast, shoulders nearly grazing the wall, the two women filed down the hall with a noiseless glide they must have learned in nun school. The old structure was not well insulated and Tiffany's voice was raised. "You didn't say anything about your teacher being a man."

"Don't be ridiculous, Tif. It's perfectly fine. Jack is a man."

"Jack is a *priest*. This guy brought you *roses*. Does he understand . . ."

Cecilia began to speak quickly in a persuasive, hushed tone.

He thought the explanation was much too lengthy and totally unnecessary. Had they installed a nun in the apartment to keep Cecilia on the straight and narrow, to avoid the occasions of sin? Technically she was a free woman, out of the order; she could date if she wanted, not that he was a date. Then he remembered, according

to the church's teachings, vow or no vow, sex out of wed-
lock was a mortal sin. Murder and sex, sins of equal se-
riousness, both could get you eternal damnation. He
recalled the severe warnings of the old priest who had
taught his high school religion class, Modern Youth and
Chastity.

Tiffany was speaking now. "Well, you be sure you
aren't *too* nice to him."

Cecilia returned to the front room, still laughing.
"Sorry about that. Tiffany's too shy to ask you, but her
window is jammed shut. Could you try to open it, Mr.
Clay?"

He could imagine stepping into the nun's room and
her braining him with a rolling pin. "Are you sure? I
mean, isn't a nun's bedroom kind of personal?"

"I told you. Tiffany's not a nun. She left like me."

"She's dressed like one."

"That's what she's used to — her habit."

Timidly he stepped into the bedroom. If Tiffany was
aware of their presence, she didn't show it. She was kneeling at the side of her narrow bed, gazing up at a large crucifix, the lifelike Jesus in the last throes of his passion.
Blood streamed down his face from the crown of thorns,
the nails in his hands and feet, his pierced side. His knees
and right shoulder were skinned and bruised. Tiffany's
features crumpled, as if she were experiencing his intense
pain. Her expression shifted through fear, awe, and finally melted into an angelic serenity. He could not look
away from her beatific countenance, set aglow from beneath the skin.

Cecilia tapped his forearm. "Over here."

The arcane window was designed to slide upward, but
it was jammed shut at an angle. He dug his fingers under

the frame and strained to lift it. He happened to notice lying on the sill a metal rod; attached to it were four leather thongs knotted at the ends. He began to sweat; his heart pounded. He could use some fresh air himself. Mercifully, the window gave way.

Cecilia stepped into the cool breeze, plucking the opening of her blouse from her skin. "Oh, that's much better. My, it was stuffy in here."

Back in the kitchen, all appeared cheerful and inviting. He expected a meatless meal, but there on the mound of spaghetti she set before him were succulent turkey meatballs, each the size of a fist. He halved one with his fork and a mouthwatering steam wafted to his nostrils. The meal was rounded out with crusty sourdough and mixed greens with a tangy vinaigrette.

"How is everything?"

"Er . . . um!" She'd caught him with his mouth full. He swallowed hard. "Excellent, Sister. Oops! I just called you Sister."

"A lot of people do. I rather like it. In my heart I'm still Sister Cecilia. I left that sniveling wimp Philomena in the dust years ago. Do you know when a postulant becomes a novice she wears a bridal gown, sends out wedding invitations, gets a wedding cake? On that day Christ became my holy spouse."

"But he's such a sad sack, a killjoy. I can just imagine the apostles planning a party. 'Oh, come on, Pete, please don't invite Jesus. Then we can't have any fun. We'll all have to be good.'"

"Jesus was not a party pooper. He supplied the eats."

"Yeah, if you like stale bread and dried fish."

She held up the bottle of wine. "And booze. Remember the wedding at Cana, he came up with the best. Not to mention the terrific magic show he could pull off. Now, that's entertainment!"

"You don't have to answer this, but . . ."

"Please, ask anything you like. I've always imagined doing just this, just sitting and talking with you."

"I'm just wondering, Mr. Bunch, too, why you left the convent."

"I was kicked out, Tiffany and I both."

"Kicked out? Whatever for?"

"Well, let's see. Tiffany's not suited for community life, says Mother St. Paul." Her voice tensed when she pronounced the superior's name. "Doesn't get her work done. Prays too much. She prayed too much, I didn't pray enough — or so I was told. It's hard to get the praying thing just right for Paul."

"It's all up to her? That doesn't sound fair."

"We hadn't taken perpetual vows and, afterward, it takes an act of the pope. Paul got rid of us when she could."

"Is there someone you can plead your case to?"

"No, but it's all right. I was upset at first. You can imagine the shock, the disappointment. But I'm over it. The Sisters of the Holy Restraint wasn't the right order for me any more than it was for Tiffany. I've prayed about it so I understand that better now. You certainly can run and pray at the same time, something Paul doesn't understand. And Tiffany belongs in a more meditative order like the Carmelites. She's applied to several cloisters, even one in Bosnia."

"A cloister? That sounds mighty ascetic. How can a young American woman stand to be shut away like that?"

"Oh, it's not boring, not if you understand the communion with the Lord Jesus in prayer, and Tiffany understands that very well, too well, Paul thinks."

"She said something to me when you were outside with Father Jack. She said the two of you were jealous of her."

"I never thought about it, but I suppose we are."

He leaned forward. "Why?"

"Her communion with Jesus Christ. Personally, I can't sit still for all that meditation. I'm more suited for an order of service, like Mother Teresa's."

"So Mother St. Paul didn't like your marathon running?"

"It was more about my music. She ordered me to change my major and I refused. She was against music from the start, but she gave me a year to prove myself. I had big hopes of wowing her with that scholarship."

"Damn! Whoops, sorry."

"You can say 'damn' if you want. Here, I'll say it, too. Damn!" She gave the table a resounding whack with the heel of her fist, causing the plates to jump.

He thought back to the previous spring, the resentment he had felt toward her. Why had he been so hard on her? For the integrity of the music department? For her own good? He wasn't sure. "Now I feel bad. If only I'd known how much trouble I was causing you, I could have weighed the final differently so ear-training didn't count as much."

"No, no. I got the grade I deserved, right? Especially the way we're separating it now: an A in theory and an F in ear-training. I know I'll improve."

He changed the subject. "Uh, so, you're shopping around for another order?"

"Sort of. I'm not in any hurry to make another commitment, though. I've got to concentrate on my call from God."

"I thought a vocation *was* a call from God."

"I mean my call to music. I don't know what God's plans are for me, I just know he wants me to study music. Hey, maybe I'll be the next Singing Nun."

"You still participate in folk mass and other parish activities?"

"Oh, sure. There's no hard feelings. The church has been very generous to me. I get this nice place and the use of a car. In return I drive the sisters to their doctor appointments — some of them are quite elderly, you know — do their heavy housework, and look after Tiffany here."

"Is she ill?"

She hesitated. "It's so . . . she won't hurt herself."

"Oh, that kind of sick."

"No, no. Ascetics commonly practice self-mortification. Monks and nuns have been known to lie in the position of a cross on a cold cement floor, kneel in prayer all night. St. Francis wore sackcloth and when he acquired followers, he asked them to take up his habit. That's the origin of the word."

He reached for a second helping of pasta. "That wicked-looking thing on her window sill."

"Oh, that. It's not so bad. She doesn't leave marks, I've checked. You just lightly toss it over your shoulder as you pray. I'm more concerned about the fasting."

"She doesn't look like she's missed any meals."

"But she has. It's hard to know exactly how thin she is because she pads her clothes. She's subsisted on only one communion wafer per day and a bottle of water."

"Have you ever seen her eat?" He felt a pang of guilt; he was doing more than his share right now.

"Since moving here? No."

"Well, you're gone a lot. Here's what you do: count the number of slices of bread left, mark the level in the milk jug."

"Goodness, Mr. Clay! It's not about catching her."

"No? I'd want to. What if she's cheating?"

"This is between her and God. Whether she's sustaining life with the Body of Christ or sneaking a little food doesn't matter as long as she doesn't starve to death."

"Cecilia, if she's eating only one little circle of unleavened bread a day she will eventually starve."

"It's more than that. It's the Body of Christ. Saints have subsisted on it before."

"Let's agree to disagree then," he said, thinking about the roses. Had she deliberately driven the thorns into her fingers?

"You misunderstand Tiffany. She's really very sweet and dear. We were novices together. She had this way of watching people and then making funny observations about them. She always made me laugh. We were very close."

"*Were*? What happened?"

"Look who I'm losing out to!" Wisps of Cecilia's orange hair were backlit by the kitchen light. Her eyes were wide and her smile euphoric. "How can I compete with our Lord? I can only be happy for her, that she's found so much happiness with Him."

Tiffany McClary didn't look all that happy to him, but he didn't comment.

Cecilia cleared the plates and set out an attractive

arrangement of fruit. He would have preferred something rich and gooey like chocolate cake, but he was quite satisfied, munching grapes and sipping his third glass of wine.

"Too bad Mr. Bunch couldn't join us. He's so funny, always joking around."

"He's laughing on the outside, anyway." He felt compelled to tell her the whole, sad story: how Art and his crazy first wife, a drummer named Star, got too much into coke while working the L.A. jazz clubs; how their five-year-old daughter caught the run-of-the-mill chicken pox and died of a high fever; how they found Jesus, but Star remained depressed. They thought a change of scenery might help and moved to Goldhurst, but then Star got too much into horses and charge cards. Art started cheating, but Gordon didn't mention it was with Allegra Musgrave. After the divorce, Art fell in love again, this time with a dental hygienist named Suzy, but their marriage only lasted two years.

"Do you know why she left him?"

"Nope. Art doesn't either. He thought they were doing fine."

A piercing wail rose from Tiffany's room.

He nearly choked on an orange slice. The thorns, the whip. What was she doing in there? "Is she . . . okay?"

Cecilia waved her wine glass in Tiffany's direction. "She's praying. I knew his wife left him, but I'm surprised to hear he's a Christian."

"Oh, yeah. He's very active at New Beginnings Church. Performs in a Christian rock band, Loaves and Fishes."

"More wine?"

"Sure, if you're having some."

She stood, got another bottle from the kitchen and uncorked it. She had said a glass of wine a day was good, not a whole bottle. She filled their glasses. "Now, Mr. Clay, I want to hear your story and why you live as a monk."

"Excuse me?"

"Well, you're not married, no girlfriend. Everyone knows. Don't you know students always talk about their teachers?"

"What's there to tell? I never found the right girl."

"Well, sex is complicated, isn't it?"

"It doesn't have to be."

"Sure, if you can actually find someone to love and it's the beginning of the relationship and it's clear you both want it and each other, but how long does that last?" He was taken aback by her candor. He had somehow assumed she was virginal, and here she was clearly speaking from experience. "Making love, you can truly call it that about one percent of the whole span of an average sex life. Think how much a person has to concentrate on oneself to orgasm; it's truly a selfish, self-fulfilling act, and then there's all this pressure put on the relationship, whether the sex is good or bad, if one is going to someone else for it." She took a thoughtful sip. "Chastity is the equalizer, wipes out gender difference, liberates the spirit."

At his skeptical glance, she raised her one shoulder, let it drop. "Running takes the edge off. Chastity seems to be the easiest vow for me. Obedience is the one I failed at this time, and poverty — poverty was impossible."

He made a show of looking around the modest room. "You don't strike me as a material girl."

"Oh! This is opulent splendor! You should have seen

how I lived in India. If only I were granted some tiny pleasure: an electric fan, an afternoon to lie on my bed and read, a Hostess Twinkie! My sisters were wonderful, oh, such interesting young women from all over the world, and so giving. They were getting joy and subsistence from helping the sick and the poor, while I was angry, repulsed, disgusted."

Tiffany's moaning increased. "Oh, oh, Jesus. You love me too much. Oh, my Lord, yes! You love so . . . so . . . yes. Oh! Ow!"

Gordon's eyes darted and finally settled on Cecilia. She slightly raised her chin on her fingertips, a bemused smile on her face. "And you thought it was *boring*. St. Theresa Avila actually levitated in ecstasy, much against her will."

He'd heard plenty about St. Therese growing up. His mother had referred to her favorite saint as The Little Flower, but he'd heard stories about her that weren't quite so innocent — her visitations by an angel with a probing spear, her subsequent ecstasies which seemed more like orgasms, depicted in Bernini's statue *The Ecstasy of St. Teresa*. He hooked a thumb toward the hall. "You think she's flying around in there?"

"She might be." Cecilia burped quietly and gazed into her wine glass. "Such a pretty color. It's not too late for you."

"Oh, no. Not at all."

"I mean, you can still find someone."

He sputtered into his wine and gasped. "So, now you think you're Dear Abby or rather Dear Abbess?"

Chapter Twelve

"He's not gay," Cecilia said.

"I never said he was gay," said Gordon.

"A lot of people think it. They think all men are in the priesthood to molest little boys."

"Hey, being gay and being a pedophile are two different things."

"And Jack is neither." They were at the college's track. He was walking; she was doing something she called intervals, sprinting one lap, then jogging alongside of him the next, then going hard again. She was puffing air now, recovering from her last effort. She had on her skimpy mustard-catsup combo, apparently the only running clothes she owned. He wore long corduroy pants and a windbreaker, his hands burrowed into the pockets. He'd finally gotten around to lacing on his expensive running shoes, which felt as light and springy as mini-trampolines.

"Jack's kindhearted, sensitive, a very spiritual man. Once you get to know him, I think you'd really like him."

Gordon looked over at Cecilia, wondering if she might have a crush on the priest. He'd heard of that — priests and nuns falling in love and leaving the order to get married.

"You really should check out Jack's Ministry of the

Living Faith Study Group. The church has made a lot of changes over the last twenty years."

"Oh, no. No more Catholic hocus-pocus for me."

"Do you mean miracles?" She looked up, as if she were expecting one that moment. The big sky was stuffed with fat, fluffy cumulus clouds a mile high, with purplish underbellies and curvaceous golden crowns. It was a glorious sight; still, he hardly expected the Virgin Mary coming in for a landing.

She gripped his arm, startling him. "You must believe in miracles," she said fervently. Then she was off. She wasn't as fast this time around, but she bucked her head down, clenched her fists, and kept going.

"I'm expecting a miracle," she announced breathlessly on the next lap. "I'm praying to Mother Teresa for it. Killing two birds with one stone, so to speak." She left him to puzzle over that one while she sought out the drinking fountain.

When she returned, he said, "Explain."

She hesitated. "Gosh, I've never spoken this out loud, but here goes. I'm praying that I'll suddenly be able to hear well enough to pass ear-training. That will take a miracle."

"I was rather banking on the education process."

"Well, that, too. But I figure a saint's intercession couldn't hurt. It could be one of the miracles attributed to Mother Teresa and then she'll just need another one to be canonized."

"How do you prove which miracles are attributed to which dead person?"

"Well, it's not easy."

He laughed, imagining her traveling to Rome, clutching a briefcase filled with ear-training tests failed and those passed — at best they'd be C minuses — and pleading her case before a papal court of doddering old skeptics in crimson skullcaps.

Yet somehow she had coerced him into attending the Ministry of the Living Faith Study Group. What was the deal? Did she hold some magical power over him?

The group meet in the parish hall; about twenty people were seated at three long tables arranged in a U-shape. Jack started thrashing his lashes at Gordon when he saw him walk in the door, a nervous tick, evidently, or an expression of excitement.

The priest hugged him like a long lost friend. "Gordon! Cecilia told me you would be coming." Jack was wearing his usual attire — black Levis, black shirt, Roman collar. What was his story, Gordon wondered. Why this instead of the wife and kids?

Gordon took a seat at one of the tables, and Jack began distributing handouts. "These are your Faith Assessment sheets. Write the number that expresses how important each belief is in your life: four for very important, three for important, two for somewhat important, one for not important, and zero for something you might have questions about. Don't be timid. These assessments are for self-reflection."

Gordon read the first item on the list: God. Lots to question there. He put down a big, fat zero. Jesus Christ: one. Mary: one. The Church: one. He could kick himself for letting Cecilia talk him into this. Next was evil. Hmmm, now that one was a little more interesting. If a student like Bourhadur Chandrasekhara got really pissed off at him and gunned him down — that would definitely

be meaningful to his life. He gave evil a four. The Holy
Spirit. Its old name Holy Ghost was better, with those
little tongues of fire set over the heads of the apostles —
not flames, nor flashes, nor fingers, but *tongues* — those
were really cool. He'd give the Holy Spirit a two. The
Resurrection, the sacraments, heaven — they all got ones.
There. Done. Now for his gracious exit.

He felt something crawl over his forearm. A gnat? A
fly? A sheath of blue-black hair, thick and wavy, soft and
smelling fruity like . . . what? A melon liquor called
Midori that his Carrie had been fond of. A low, female
whisper, as raspy as Bother's purr, asked "What did you
get for 'evil?' "

Gordon tensed. A stranger was prying into his personal Faith Assessment. He thought to spread his broad
hand over his paper, like a priggish student warding off a
cheater, but he wasn't quick enough. A brown finger
tipped with a blood red spear scrolled down his answers.

The young woman peered up at him. She had almond
eyes, full lips, and flawless, dusky skin. She wore a tight-
fitting, velvet maroon jacket with white frills at the throat
and wrists, reminding him of Pocahontas in an Eliza-
bethan ruff. "You are not much of a believer, are you?"

He looked over at her paper: straight fours. "You
seem to be doing okay. A-plus for you."

"I've never seen you here before." Her lips parted,
showing large, very white teeth. "Did you come for
the fellowship?" Fellowship — another buzzword these
modern-day Catholics had copped from the Protestants.
What did it mean exactly? Getting together with people
who all believe the same to have one-sided arguments?

"A friend asked me to come."

"A girlfriend?"

"No, a nun."

"Here, at Our Lady? Which one?"

"Sister Cecilia."

"Oh." The youthful, tight skin of the beautiful face got tighter; at the corners of her full mouth was a barely perceptible twitch. "I heard she left the convent."

"Yeah, right. Where are you from?"

She shrugged. "From nowhere."

"Everyone is from somewhere."

"You think I am being evasive? Here is the story my father told me. There were one hundred sixty-six inhabitants on our island. The Americans told the chief that we must move because it would be engulfed by a big fireball — *kaboom*. So you see I really am from no place, like Princess Leah."

"Your people are from Bikini Island?"

"Not Bikini. Our island. Our people's. My family's. Do you think Bikini was the only island blown off the face of the earth before the Test Ban Treaty?" The longer she talked the faster she talked, clipping the ends of some words, dipping the pitch in others. He listened to the lilt and inflection of her speech rather than the content. She stopped short, slightly breathless. Jack was working his way toward them. "I think we are supposed to be talking about our Faith Assessments."

"Oh, Father won't mind if we take a moment for fellowship. I'm Gordon Clay." He pressed his palm against hers. It was warm and smooth, her grip firm.

"Mikilauni Kukula."

"Mikilauni Kukula from Island Nowhere, pleased to meet you. You have a very musical name."

"And you are a flatterer."

"Not at all. It is my business to know music. I'm a music instructor."

"At the college? Oh! I love classical music! "

"A symphony goer, huh?"

"Yeah. No, er, I mean, I just listen at home. I'm sort of afraid of actually going to the symphony."

She meant intimidated. He asked her what he asked his music appreciation students: "What's there to be afraid of?"

"You know, the rich snobs. High society."

"High society in Goldhurst? Really, where?" He looked under the table, clowning.

"I'm afraid I'd violate some unwritten code of manners, and they would find me out. I've heard it's tricky to know when to clap. It's like going to a different church, with everyone staring at you because you don't know when to sit, stand, or kneel."

"That's easy. At a symphony you sit the whole time."

"What about those standing ovation things?"

"I wouldn't recommend starting one. *That* would be scary. Wait until over half the audience is standing; that's the safest way."

"I guess it's not as hard as it seems. Still, I'd feel more comfortable if I went with someone who knows all the right things, for my first time, I mean."

It struck him then, like the light from heaven striking Paul when he was just Saul: this Polynesian princess of the almond eyes and flashing teeth was hitting on him! Maybe fellowship to her meant meeting men without going to bars. He looked around the room, noticing that most of the people were young men and women chatting and laughing together. Maybe fellowship was a euphemism for a Catholic singles club.

Well, this woman was too young for him, around thirty, if that. Then again, if would just be the symphony. He hadn't attended in years. It might be interesting to check it out, just like this meeting. "Well, uh, in that case the Goldhurst Community Symphony is performing on Saturday, but I imagine it's short notice."

"I'm not doing anything special. How do I buy a ticket?" He noted her careful use of first person singular.

"I can get tickets. I could meet you there or I could pick you up."

"Oh, I'd like it very much if you picked me up." Her hand lighted on his sleeve, again, ever so softly.

Chapter Thirteen

So he had a date. Self-reproach set in when he was driving home. A date sounded good, but it was more like a doughnut, those custard-filled, chocolate-iced ones that are so sweet they make the teeth ache. He had never been good at dates; they usually came to a bad end. She had even asked him to dinner. She worked in the office of a CPA, he had found that out. Not much in common, it appeared, but maybe that was what was so interesting about her. She was mysterious and gorgeous; he could listen to that exotic accent, that throaty voice all night.

By Friday afternoon he was more excited than he should have been. He should act his age, expect this date to be nothing short of a disaster. It seemed that this young woman was hoping for more fellowship than he could give. He recalled that she had seated herself next to him, draped her hair over his arm, bored her fingernail into his Faith Assessment before the subject of music had even come up. Something about him had attracted her. What was it? She was beautiful, too beautiful for him. Beautiful women had always been mean to him.

Saturday afternoon he went to the mall. He tried on shirts and trousers, all the while thinking of Thoreau's warning: "Beware of all enterprises that require new clothes." He ended up merely buying socks. His old ones were worn thin at the heels and needed replacing. New socks! He really knew how to drive women wild.

He was nervous, he had to admit. Driving to Mikilauni's house, he gripped the wheel so hard his hands cramped. He found her place in the Sutter Park neighborhood, not far from Cecilia's. Hers was a modest frame house, fifty or more years old, which she rented. Before he could ascend the front steps, the door opened. Mikilauni stepped out, shut the door with a decisive click behind her.

"I'm sorry, Gordon."

"What?"

She shook her head. "I can't go."

"Oh?" She certainly looked ready to go. Her mass of black, unruly hair was lacquered into a French twist. She wore a flaming red, mohair knit dress and big gold jewelry. Standing before him, with the knit material stretched across her breasts and soft, low-slung belly, she exuded such voluptuous sexuality that she could just as well have answered the door naked. It was hard to train his eyes on her face. She was heavily made up; her drooping lids, weighed down by shadow, liner, and mascara, intensified the exotic look of her sad, dark eyes. He possessed a fierce impulse to make everything right again, even though he had no clue what was wrong.

"Something's come up."

"You're not sick, I hope."

"Oh, no, no. I tried calling you, but you'd already left. I'm sorry you had to drive all the way over here for nothing."

Seeing her in the red dress wasn't nothing. He wished she'd just give him some idea what was going on. He saw the curtain move in a front room. Someone else was in the house, and the way she had stepped out of the house made it clear she didn't want to make introductions. Could it be she had recently broken up with someone, went out in a huff looking for fellowship, only to reconcile with the guy?

A face appeared in the window. It was little and brown, above a collar of blue flannel, rocket ship pajamas, the nose smashed flat and yellow against the glass. Funny, in all her chattering she hadn't mentioned that she had a kid.

Mikilauni reached behind her back, grabbed the door knob. "Do you think we could try again the next time the symphony is playing?"

"In two months?"

"Oh, that long? Well, I'll probably see you at the Ministry of Faith Study Group before then."

He shook his head. "I doubt if I'll be returning."

The face in the window rolled his cheek to press against the glass. Gordon knew how good that felt, warm skin against cold glass in a stuffy, overheated room.

As she opened the door behind her, he said, "Mikilauni, wait. In the window there . . ." He gestured by tilting his head in that direction. "Does he have anything to do with this?"

She leaned over the porch railing to have a look. By then, the kid had dropped his pajama bottoms and turned his other cheek against the glass.

"Ahhh!" she shrieked. "I'm going to warm that little backside good."

The boy disappeared, the curtains rippling in his wake.

"I didn't mean to get him into trouble. Last time I looked he hadn't gone bottoms up."

"I'll have to punish him. That was so naughty."

"Not so naughty. Actually, I think it was kind of cute."

She smiled ruefully. "You like kids?"

"Well, to tell you the truth, I haven't been around them much, but I think I like that one. What happened — the babysitter canceled?"

She nodded. "Old Mama said she'd be over, but then some of her beer-drinking cronies stopped by and she got all lit up and decided she didn't want to leave the party."

It was more explanation than he wanted. "Let me give you a little piece of advice, Mikilauni. Never explain. Your friends don't need it and your enemies don't care. I forget who said that, but it's an axiom I live by."

An uncomfortable silence ensued. She crossed her arms. "That's the one big trouble with you men. You always know best and will always be sure to tell a poor girl. A lot of men don't like to date women with kids, and I haven't had a date in months. All I do is work and take care of my son and the house and . . . well, I just wanted my chance at the symphony."

He had to admit her reasoning was justified. He had been guilty of avoiding involvement with women who had children. It was always so messy, the surly kids who usually resented you and the ex looming somewhere in the shadows.

They both stood there a moment longer.

He asked, "Are you going to invite me in?"

"What about the symphony? Don't you want to use your ticket?"

"The fun of the symphony was to escort you."

"You are a flatterer. Come in then and meet Moopuna."

"Moopuna?"

"That's right. In our language, it means grandchild. It is the custom of my father's people for the father to name the child. My dad . . . well, he was the closest thing to a father Moopuna ever had."

He walked up the steps. "Wait," she said. "There's something else . . ." She dropped her head, then raised it again; her heavy-lidded eyes seemed to grow darker. "I . . . I . . . have never been married."

"So?"

"You're Catholic and . . ."

"Not much of one. Come on." He touched her shoulder, steering her toward the house, toward Moopuna.

Inside, he looked around. Knitted afghans and crocheted doilies were strewn all over the furniture, giving it a closed-in look. He'd never dated a woman with needle crafts. Maybe it was something the missionaries had taught the islanders to do, and was passed on from generation to generation.

"Make yourself comfortable while I go haul the little bugger out. He's probably under the bed, hiding from a whipping."

Whipping? She called a spanking a whipping? "No! Please, don't punish him, not on my account."

She was gone. He wasn't sure she'd heard him over her high heels clicking on the hardwood floor. From down the hall came shrieks of protest, several sound smacks. Finally Mikilauni reappeared, half-carrying, half-dragging the whimpering boy, his face sullen and tear streaked.

Gordon squatted, his knees cracking loudly. "Hi, Moopuna, nice to see you again."

The boy hid behind his mother's leg and watched him with one eye.

"You know Moopuna?" Mikilauni asked in surprise.

"The park. I swung him. He was begging for a push and his babysitters couldn't be bothered, sometime last May. Remember me, Moopuna? I'm Gordon."

"Mr. Clay to you, young man. He's got to learn his manners. Kids nowadays don't have any respect for their elders. You'll stay for dinner, won't you, Gordon?"

"I thought we were going out."

"Not with Moopuna. It's nearly his bedtime."

They argued a bit, but Mikilauni seemed adamant about cooking him a meal, refusing his help, as if to prove something. She lambasted him with Beethoven's Fifth on a portable CD player, not exactly what he considered background music, but he didn't want to risk offending her by saying so.

She offered him a Coke when he was hoping for a beer. Apparently she didn't drink. She hacked her Sunday chicken to pieces, dredged it in flour, and dropped it into a pan of oil so deep he imagined his heart fluttering. She whipped up mashed potatoes from a box and opened a can of peas with a rotary opener screwed into a cabinet. As she cooked, she shouted over the music. Her biggest mistake was getting pregnant. She had been engaged to be married, she said, and, of course, birth control and abortion were out of the question.

She pointed the meat cleaver at him saying, "You see, the laws of the Church are sound. If I had obeyed them, I would not have this sad story to tell you." She bent over to put biscuits in the oven, tantalizing him with her round bottom stretching the red knit material.

When the symphony ended, he turned off the CD player, explaining he could hear Beethoven any time, but would rather hear her talk. She rambled on, like a person who lived alone, starving to be heard. His teaching life had the opposite effect on him — he was tired of the sound of his own voice and preferred listening. She referred to so many sisters, brothers, cousins, aunts, uncles, and friends that he couldn't possibly keep them straight, but instead let the lilt of names flow over him like music: Kali, Salote, Inoke, Peleki, Kahme, Manu, Filpe, and Old Mama — the nickname Moopuna had given her own mother.

He sat in her yellow kitchen, feeling too settled in, like a pot of crawling ivy. He was looking forward to the greasy chicken, but felt guilty. She was very clear about what she wanted in a man — not friendly sex and companionship, but a husband and a father for her child. The right thing for him to do was to not waste any more of her time. She needed to get back to fishing in the sea of fellowship at next Thursday's Ministry of the Living Faith Study Group.

One good thing had come of his chance meeting with Mikilauni: he was delighted to see Moopuna again. He watched the child playing silently with some toys in a corner of the room. "Moopuna," he called over to him, "what do you have there?"

Moopuna shuffled over, his curly head drooping to one side. Shyly, he placed a plastic letter magnet *M* in his hand.

"What is this letter?"

Moopuna stared, but did not reply.

"He doesn't know his letters yet," said Mikilauni. "He's only four. The day care people are trying to teach him some silly game, to make me think they earn the money I pay them. He's supposed to hand a person the letter that his name starts with, but you can see he's got it all wrong. He doesn't know Clay begins with C."

"*M* is for Mister." Moopuna blurted.

"Right!" Gordon handed him back the letter. "Here. You keep the *M* for Moopuna, and get me a *G* for Gordon."

Moopuna ran to his pile of letters and returned with an *S*.

Mikilauni laughed. "Oh, baby, you don't know anything!"

Gordon was very happy to explain, "This is an *S*. *S* is for Steve. *S* is for Sam. *S* is for —"

"Swing!"

"You do remember, uh? That I pushed you on the swing?"

Moopuna did not smile or nod, but something shifted and brightened beneath the creamy brown skin of his face, and he looked happier than Gordon had yet seen him. Moopuna reached out for the plastic letter. "I take back now. It not for to go to your house."

Gordon handed the boy the letter. "Oh, Mikilauni, he's so smart. You must be very proud of him."

"Oh, my whole family adores him because he's a boy. I don't know how I would have survived if God had given me a girl."

"You can't be serious."

"Oh, yes. It is our culture. No one was ever proud of me."

"Really? Not even your mother?"

"In her eyes I have failed because I have no husband. And to have the house and the job and the child means I'm admitting to failure, doing what a man would do if I had been successful. She would rather have me sitting around her house with my sisters, watching reality shows with her, collecting welfare, doing my nails and my hair, scheming to trap a man. I don't want the kind of man that kind of woman attracts. I'd rather be on my own, but I don't like being alone, either."

She placed the dishes of food on the kitchen table, then prepared a plate for Moopuna. She set it on his child-sized table next to the refrigerator, and pushed him up to it in his child-sized chair. "You sit quiet and eat up all of your dinner, even your peas."

He thought Mikilauni's attitude toward her son was odd, distant. He wished he could see what they were like together when no one else was around. Was Mikilauni putting on some act for his benefit to prove she had room in her life for a man? The other women with children he had dated had demonstrated that their children came first. He had admired their fierce mothering, yet it had not encouraged him to hang around. Then again, he hadn't much cared for those women's kids, but he liked Moopuna.

Mikilauni passed him the peas. Overcooking had turned them gray. He took a small spoonful to be polite. He looked over at Moopuna, banished to his own little table, fastidiously wrapping the end of his drumstick in his napkin before taking a bite.

"He's so cool," said Gordon.

She frowned. "I am worried about him. He needs a father to keep him in line. My dad was able to do it when he was alive, but he's gone now."

"He seems very well mannered to me."

She shook her head. "You wait. In my family the men are everything, the women nothing. My brothers Inoke and Peleki are spoiled and selfish. Soon Moopuna will see he can do anything he wants, and he will be out of control."

After the meal, Mikilauni stacked the dishes in the sink. "I have to put Moopuna to bed now. I won't be long, but he always expects a story."

"Can I listen to the story, too?"

She laughed as if he were joking. He sat on the sofa and thumbed through a *National Geographic*. He had to urinate. The bathroom was probably easy to find in this little house. He got up, walked down the darkened hall, and collided with Mikilauni, bumping chests and noses. He could not tell whose arms went around whom first. Their mouths joined. Her lips were full and eager for the kiss. Her breath came hard; she moaned. He cupped the weight of her breasts in both hands, the mohair soft on his skin.

She tensed and broke away.

"Sorry." He backed off. "I was on my way to the bathroom."

She reached behind her and flicked the switch. "There you go."

When he returned to the living room, he saw that she had taken out a Scrabble game — good, clean fun — and was settled on the floor with her legs curled under the coffee table, her high heels kicked off.

"Do you like Scrabble?"

"Scrabble's okay." He took his place on the floor opposite her, his knees creaking in protest. "I haven't played in decades."

"Not too many decades," she said, coyly. He had to be at least ten years older than she, but she was indicating that didn't matter.

He had done a little homework, studying an atlas. The archipelagos of the South Pacific are like the constellations of stars. He could imagine the Americans blowing her little island up, like one shooting star. It would not be missed, only by those who called it home. "After your people were forced off their island, where did they go?"

Her smile faded. "My people were deeply attached to their island, reluctant to leave the spirits of their dead."

"But what was the name of it?"

"You want to know the name of something that no longer exists?"

"I do."

The heavy lids dropped, rested. There was a long silence, then a sigh. "I forget. I will ask Old Mama."

"And then where did your people go?"

"Different places, islands in the Vava'u Group, some in the Tongatapu Group."

"So do you think of yourself as Tongan?"

"Not really."

"I thought Polynesia was all Mormon territory."

"Oh, the Catholics came, too. And the Methodists, the Presbyterians, the Seventh Day Adventists. You name it, they came. Nearly every island in the Pacific knows English, thanks to the missionaries."

"Do you still have relatives on the islands?"

"Oh, slews of them, aunts and uncles and cousins. Grandparents, too. Old Mama was calling over there so much, Kali and me had to yank the phone out of her wall and then, what does she do? She comes over and uses my phone, raises my bill up to the sky."

She fell silent, contemplating the letters on her racks. Then, she spelled *zoo* on the triple letter. Every once in a while her knee bumped him, which seemed to be an accident. Toward the end of the game, they began to fight like kids over the few remaining tiles. He kissed her again. She broke away and said, "Ever been married? In the Church, I mean?"

"Never been married anywhere." That usually discouraged sensible women, but this one was Catholic.

"Can I get you a Coke?"

While she was in the kitchen, he stood to stretch his legs. He had to find a gracious way out. Prolonging the evening much longer would only be frustrating, but it had been pleasant to kiss her. Maybe he'd steal another and then he'd be on his way. He settled on the sofa. She set the drinks on the coffee table and, with a wide grin, sank onto his lap. The weight of her body felt as if she were giving her whole self up to him, easily, freely.

He put his hand on her breast; she pushed it away. He put his hand on her thigh; she pushed it away. He thought how stupid the new rules of sex were now, how you could be accused of date rape if you didn't ask permission first. May I kiss you? May I touch your breast? May I enter you now? Besides being completely void of romance, what chance did a girl like this have, who wanted it, but thought it was immoral?

After three or four tries, he managed to get his hand up her dress and was pleasantly surprised. Instead of finding a hostile barrier of nylon pantyhose, he discovered stockings and garters and minute underpanties. He'd only begun to explore these delights when she tugged feebly at his arm.

"I like you, Gordon," she whispered. "I like you a lot. But this is how I got Moopuna."

"My hand won't get you pregnant."

Her eyes were closed, her face was tense with concentration. She began to move rhythmically against his touch, clutching at him and moaning. She needed him at that moment. He could not remember a time when he was needed more. He watched every bit of it.

It took her a long time to settle down afterward, gasping and clutching. "Don't think I usually . . . it's the release . . . oh, Mother of God, it's been so . . . I have not been with a man . . . so long." She was a talker, talking even when no words came.

At last her eyes flickered open and she tried to flash her toothy smile, the corners of her mouth quivering. "I have sinned."

He kissed her on her perspiring nose. "Nonsense."

She snuggled deeper into his embrace. "You are a generous man."

He felt guilty to take such a compliment. He wasn't being a martyr here, but he couldn't seem to convince her of that. She babbled on. "The moment I laid eyes on your scraggly little ponytail, I thought now here is a sweet, gentle man who will never treat me bad."

"Scraggly?"

"It is a little scraggly."

They kissed. She walked him to the door.

If he were the generous man she thought, he would be walking out for good, instead of getting her hopes up. He backed her against the wall and pressed as much of his body against her as he could. "When can I see you again? Next weekend?"

"Okay, sure. I don't suppose you go out on school nights."

"I go out on school nights. Name one."

"Wednesday."

"How's Tuesday? Or tomorrow? We can try the symphony again. It's a matinee, though."

"You can trade your tickets in?"

"Don't worry about that. I don't mind buying tickets twice. The Goldhurst Community Symphony can use the money."

Driving home, he smelled the scent of Mikilauni on his fingers. Ah, what a name! What a woman! He thought about their good-bye, how he had acted like a fool kid in love — in lust — as if he couldn't wait to see her again. It was no act; he really was a fool.

He sniffed his fingers again. Hell, high school sex, imagine that at his age. How long would it take him to get in? Was she really serious about waiting until marriage? Chances were the relationship would be over before he got his way, but even that didn't matter. He loved what had gone on that night. He felt content. He wouldn't wash his hand before taking himself to bed.

Chapter Fourteen

He awoke to the distant bells of Our Lady of the Apparition of Lourdes Catholic Church, thinking of her, unable to wait half a day to see her again. She had told him she attended the nine o'clock mass, the same one in which Cecilia's Youth Ministry of Music performed. He'd have to hustle to make it.

The first thing Gordon had noticed about Goldhurst was that there was a church on practically every street corner: the New Beginnings Church, the Faith Family Church, the First Church of the God of the Popular Man, the First Christ Believers Church, the Fortress of Truth Pentecostal Church, and the Salvation Lighthouse Church. There had been a Buddhist temple, built in the 1820s, but the Christians burned it to the ground.

Our Ladyof the Apparition of Lourdes was the only Catholic Church in Goldhurst, and it was jam-packed. Walking into the church, Gordon expected the arched, vaulted beams to creak and groan in protest. He dipped his fingertips in the holy water, wondering how a habit could survive with a twenty-year suspension of its practice. He stretched his neck in search of a dark-headed woman with a little boy squirming beside her. There were lots of women with black hair, some hanging like a curtain, some piled like a crown, some styled half-up and half-down, some ponytails and braids. What Mikilauni's mass look was, he had no idea.

He spotted a seat next to an elderly woman, but when he tried to squeeze in, she barely budged. She had set up camp with a water bottle, cardigan, cushion, satchel, rosary, missal, and her sandals, kicked off and stored under the pew. Seated at his right was a couple and their five little kids. He tensed, thinking how they would squirm and whine. A woman leading a black Labrador, decked out in red slippers and bandanna to match, passed their pew. A dog in church?

To his right was a little alcove that held a bloody crucifix. Why had this religion evolved on the basis of such a miserable death? A woman came around the corner of the alcove. It took him a moment to realize that she was Cecilia's roommate, Tiffany, in an ankle-length black coat, flaming red scarf, and Victorian black velvet hat pulled low on her forehead. She braced her palms against the wall and kissed one side of the crucifix and then the other. She knelt and kissed the feet, then stood and began to gyrate. A swing of her hip, a lip smack to Jesus's feet. She waved her arms, flapping like a swan. This was getting weird. Didn't anyone else see how weird this was? She bent and kissed, straightened and flapped. Kiss, kiss. Flap, flap.

Cecilia and her Youth Ministry of Music ensemble trooped before the altar. The musicians made a formidable noise: guitars strumming, electric bass thumping, piano pounding, synthesizer wailing out a tinny, fake flute timbre, and the mike screeching in protest. Cecilia weaved while the others bobbed, the light from within her shining through her small, pale face, her voice soaring above the others, slightly off-key. The music was not the folk rock he expected, but the cloying easy listening of a Disney cartoon soundtrack. When the song ended, the congregation applauded as if at a concert or a circus.

He turned the pages of his missalette, but apparently did not find his place fast enough, because the old lady reached over and found it for him. The Kyrie and the Gospel passed, and still no sign of Mikilauni and Moopuna. Father Jack began his homily on sex, how you shouldn't do it. Statistics showed that the divorce rate was higher among couples who lived together before marriage. Premarital sex led to disease and unwanted pregnancy and mortal sin. Father Jack seemed to be enjoying himself. Sex made Gordon hungry. He wondered in how many minds of the faithful were visions of ham and eggs.

A childish plea of "Let's go, Mama!" reverberated through the church, followed by a woman's soothing, "Hush, baby. Pretty soon."

Heads turned toward the source of the noise, several pews in front of him. It was no wonder he hadn't spotted them sooner. Mikilauni's blue-black hair was hidden under a hot pink hat the size of a waiter's tray. The soft, wispy hair of Moopuna's ringlets was barely visible above the back of the pew. There they were. His heart began to pound faster.

As the ancient words of the Nicene Creed sprang from his memory, his voice blended with the others to create a whole new timbre. He intoned the words with as much fervor as if he believed in them. Who were the other nonbelievers? He would have liked a show of hands. He imagined the heads of bald men, glistening like pennies in a public fountain, each represented a nonbeliever. What did they get out of this? Not saving grace, but perhaps a contact high. He worded a phrase differently than the rest

— they had changed the prayer without his knowing —
and the round, blue eyes of the little girl at his side rolled
up at him from beneath the wide brim of a white straw
hat, accusing him of being an impostor. His bold baritone
deflated to a mumble.

During the transubstantiation, he remembered how
his favorite task as an altar boy was giving the bells a
hearty shake when the priest raised the Host. The old
woman and the little girl startled him by taking his hands
during the recitation of the Our Father. What if he didn't
want to hold hands with strangers? The woman had
something encrusted beneath her long, yellow nails and
maybe the little girl didn't wash after using the bathroom.
If only he could be standing between Mikilauni and
Moopuna at this moment! The Our Father ended the
Protestant way with "For thine is the kingdom and the
power and the glory for ever. Amen," the people raising
their clasped hands in emphasis. When had the Catholics
gotten around to tacking that on?

At Communion, the faithful filed out to the center
aisle one pew at a time, an improvement on the traffic
jams of his youth. The old woman nudged his arm with
the business end of her prayerful hands. He sat down to
let her pass, feeling shame. He couldn't go to Communion because he wasn't in a state of grace, although it was
a lovely turn of phrase. A new development, laymen and
laywomen handing out Communion, shocked him.
Women still couldn't be priests, nor could they be trusted
with the collection baskets, but they could come in off the
streets and dole out the Body of Christ. The Host was
placed on the tongue — the traditional number one
method — or in the hands of the receiver — modern-day
number two.

Gordon took the opportunity to stand with the late-comers along the wall in order to bolt after Mikilauni and Moopuna when the mass ended. He watched the faithful stream by him: Nike ads, short skirts, bare midriffs. He kept Mikilauni's platter-shaped pink hat in sight, as if it were a docked ship he was desperate to board. He was glad to see her filing up for Communion, despite his hand up her dress the previous evening. He took sensuous delight in watching her exposed pink tongue accept the Host, to see the stark white wafer setting like a jewel on its pillow.

After Communion, while Father Jack quietly murmured his prayers, the keyboard player started up again, tinkling softly in the background, as if to say this guy isn't interesting enough. This upper register drivel was perhaps the most offensive thing of this offensive mass, this tinkling — this pissing on the Word of God. Couldn't a guy have any peace, a single moment of *silence*? Heat flared from his heart and fanned up through his shoulder. He rubbed his chest, thinking how badly he wanted out of this modern mass but first, he wanted to unplug it.

Mercifully, Father Jack said, "The mass has ended, go in peace."

Gleefully singing the recessional hymn with her group, Cecilia was up on her toes, looking his way, but he averted his eyes and ducked out the side door after Mikilauni and Moopuna. On the sidewalk, he took pleasure in watching them covertly. Among the fall golds and browns, wools and tweeds, Mikilauni, in her hot pink outfit, looked like a rose of summer. He quickened his step. Her short, flared skirt emphasized her round buttocks, the protrusion of which was further enhanced by black stilettos, that clacked on the concrete. On her hands were short, white gloves with ornamental pearl buttons at the wrists. Those minute buttons endeared her to him: that she would try that hard. Moopuna was wearing a suit, perhaps the only little-boy's suit in the congregation, powder blue and collarless. With one giant step, he caught up to them, coming alongside Moopuna in order to resist the urge to encircle Mikilauni's waist.

"Hi-yi," she said, the single syllable riding jauntily on two distinct pitches, her surprise sounding as sharp as if she had been caught doing something wrong. "I didn't know you went to Mass."

"Occasionally."

"It is what I thought."

Moopuna slipped his hand into his. It was warm and doughy and the color of coffee. People who didn't know them might have mistaken them for a family, a thought that he found both enticing and formidable. He was tempted to invite Mikilauni and Moopuna to breakfast, but resisted. After such a sustained ordeal in the community of the faithful, he was desperate for solitude.

"So. We'll see you this afternoon."

"Of course." The white smile flashed.

They stood there a moment, motionless, staring at each other before parting.

Driving out of the church parking lot, he had to slam on the brakes to prevent hitting an entire family who stepped out in front of him. Near the exit, a car going too fast almost sideswiped him. He felt piqued by the recklessness of those assured of their salvation. He took deep breaths to calm himself. He slipped a Gregorian chant into the CD player to clean out his ears.

Chapter Fifteen

The Goldhurst Opera House dated from the 1860s. The foundation had been jacked up and the walls reinforced, but then the restoration funds had run dry. The moldings were crumbling, the maroon velvet curtains were threadbare, and the springs in some of the seats had a way of spearing the audience. Still, if you had some imagination, you could conjure the splendor of its heyday.

Mikilauni twisted in her seat, a big, white smile on her dusky face. "I can't believe this place, Gordon. It is out of my dreams." She leaned into him to murmur, "You will tell me, won't you, if I'm doing something wrong?"

"You can't go wrong. Just don't talk during the music, that's all I care." He pointed out Lars Stelling's and Art Bunch's names in the program. "This guy is the head of our department and this guy is my office mate." Lars was loyal to the Goldhurst Community Symphony, calling it "darn fine," and Art was cynical about it, claiming he used it to keep up his "classical chops." Even Allegra Musgrave participated, taking the soprano solo in Handel's *Messiah* at Christmas.

"Why don't you play in it?" Mikilauni asked.

"I did the first couple of years I lived here, but . . ." Gordon raised one side of his mouth and shook his head.

There were a half-dozen good players in each string section, but moving toward the back, the players bent further and further out of tune.

That afternoon the orchestra was playing a user-friendly program: the *William Tell Overture, Scheherazade, Flight of the Bumble Bee,* featuring Lars as the trumpet soloist, and Tchaikovsky's *Pathetique* Symphony. During the *William Tell Overture,* the audience began to clap along with the beat. Mikilauni joined in, but stopped when she noticed he was not participating. The concertgoers conducted, talked, laughed, rattled candy wrappers, sneezed, and wheezed. The noise level of a typical Goldhurst audience usually so outraged Gordon that he almost always ended up tapping someone on the shoulder and asking, "Don't you have any interest in the music?" Now, sitting in the front balcony with the lovely Mikilauni at his side, he decided to relax and enjoy himself. He actually laughed when, at the end of the William Tell, a guy in the second balcony shouted, "Hi-ho, Silver!" Lars was an old bag of wind, but it took a formidable old bag of wind to pull off the trumpet solo in *Flight of the Bumble Bee.* He took a bow to enthusiastic applause.

During intermission, standing with Mikilauni in the lobby, Gordon greeted his students who approached him, notebooks lodged in the crooks of their arms.

"Good afternoon, Mr. Clay."

"Mr. Clay! Hey, man, glad you're here so you can explain this stuff to me."

After he had spoken several minutes to a young woman about the difference between texture and style, Mikilauni remarked, "Popular guy."

"They're my students. They all have to attend the symphony and write reports."

He placed her hand on his arm and escorted her to their seats.

He tried to tolerate the Tchaikovsky. His jaw tightened when the orchestra bogged down in the *Allegro,* and he winced when the audience clapped between movements. In the hushed *Adagio,* the old guy next to him began to snore, and during the *Finale,* a cell phone echoed the *William Tell Overture.* All the while, Mikilauni sat very straight, staring intently at the orchestra as if she expected a plot development.

When the program was over, she clapped enthusiastically, tears adding sparkle to the chandeliers in her eyes. "Oh, that was so gorgeous. Didn't you think so?" Her lower lip pushed out when she noticed his expression. "Oh, you didn't think so. What was wrong? Am I dumb or something?"

"No, no. You just don't have much concert-going experience. Some day we'll go up to San Francisco, and when you hear a real symphony, you'll know the difference."

"On the train?"

"Excuse me?"

"I'd like to go to San Francisco on the train. I heard they have a dining car and everything. "

"Sure, we'll go on the train." He was happy at that moment, his chest quiet. He was making plans with every intention of coming through with them, yet knowing such vague promises were often broken. He hoped she understood that, too.

After dinner, while they were walking from his car to her door, she remarked, "Oh, that Tchaikovsky song was so pretty." She sighed and leaned her head on his arm, her exotic eyes traversing the starry sky.

"Symphony, you mean."

"Symphony. It was so romantic. I think it must be the most beautiful music ever written."

He did not tell her that it wasn't romance but suicide that Tchaikovsky was contemplating, and that he preferred a male lover to a female one. He was not a Tchaikovsky fan, but he abruptly decided that it was foolish snobbery not to give the old Russian some credit. He would surprise her with the gift of a CD recording of the *Pathetique*. "Many of his melodies are beautiful indeed," he conceded.

She unlocked her front door. The house was dark and cold. When he had picked her up that afternoon he had missed seeing Moopuna, and she explained he had gone somewhere with Old Mama. He'd hoped to see him now and was disappointed to find the house empty.

She draped her coat and gloves over the armchair. "Can I make you some coffee?"

"It will keep me awake."

"I've got decaf."

"Fine."

She served the coffee on the coffee table, then sat quite a distance from him on the sofa, prim and proper. "So, do you like to dance?"

"Not really."

"I dance the hula."

"Oh?"

"It's not what you're thinking. Not a tourist attraction, but the real thing. My great aunt Lili taught me. In my culture, many things for women were taboo. If they ate pork or lobster it was death. Many times during the year it was taboo for them to speak. They had to invent

a vocabulary of body movement to express their feelings—the hula."

"Sounds more serious than I thought."

"Oh, it was for fun, too, like at the *Makahiki,* the holiday that is many weeks long. It was taboo to work then.
Just feasting, playing, surfing, lovemaking, and dancing."

"Sounds wonderful. Let me guess. They were all having too much fun, so the missionaries came and put a stop
to it."

"But that was a good thing. Our people's culture was
immoral."

"So the missionaries put clothes on them, made them
marry and stick to one sex partner."

"I'm not talking about sexual freedom. There was
cannibalism and human sacrifice and the worst to me —
infanticide. Women would have ten children and only
raise one or two."

"They would kill the others?"

"And no guilty consciences about it. No one told
them it was evil, a sin. If the parents had a fight, the
mother killed the favorite child of her husband, and in return the husband killed the wife's favorite. Most of the
children were gotten rid of as babies. The mothers stran-
gled them, stoned them, some were buried alive."

"You're sure about this?"

She raised a thin shoulder, let it drop. "They were a
very fun-loving people and kids can be a bother." She
laughed abruptly. "How we'd get on this?"

"The hula."

"Oh, yes! I want to show you." She put on a CD of
slide guitar music and disappeared down the hall.

He sat in the easy chair uneasily. This felt staged. She

returned wearing only a grass skirt, shell necklaces, and her hair. Her lithe arms rippled, her hips gyrated. As she moved, her hair and skirt parted, offering slivers of her body. She spread her bent knees and fiercely jutted her pelvis. If she was a tease, he'd never met one more enticing. She ended her performance with a pounce, her knees straddling his lap.

They kissed. Slowly he divided her blades of grass.

"Not here. Let's go to bed."

He gripped her shoulders, pushed her back to look into her face. "You're giving in? So soon?"

"You don't sound happy about it."

"I'm . . . I'm surprised. All the things you said last night about the church."

"It is all good in theory, but a girl gets lonely. I never wanted a man more than I want you now."

She got up, walked on silent feet, turned off the CD player. She swayed back to him and held out her hand. "Come."

He allowed her to pull him up. "I can't promise you . . ."

She stopped his words with a kiss. "Hush. I've never been a one-night stand, but I guess I don't mind being a two-night stand."

He smiled. She was funny, but sad, too. She talked too much. She led him down the hall. They undressed each other, got into bed.

He thought of all the names for what they were doing. It was not making love, not even for her. Having sex was good enough. He needed to turn off his thoughts, but he couldn't let his emotions take over yet, or it would be all over too soon.

"It is time," she whispered.

Time? Already? His hands and mouth weren't nearly done with all their explorations, but he would go with her tempo. He moved over her.

"Not that! I mean, it's time for the protection."

"Oh, that! Of course. Where do you keep them?"

"Where do I keep them? What do you think of me?"

"Oh, shit."

She sat up. "I thought every man carried one these days."

He hadn't, not since he was eighteen. He'd carried around the same condom from eighth to twelfth grade until, riding in his wallet on his hip, it wore out. Carrie had been his first; he was twenty and in love. After they broke up, when he went through his promiscuous stage, he was insensitive enough to think birth control was the woman's responsibility.

"Do you mind terribly?" she asked.

"No, of course not." He lay back in bed with a sigh that sounded more like a grunt.

"I mean, do you mind going out and buying some?"

He pulled himself out of bed. He dressed. He bent to kiss her good-bye.

"You will be back, won't you?"

"Are you kidding?"

"Just say so. I want you to promise that you'll come back."

"I promise."

Driving away, he felt tired. The idea of the all-night grocery and the nosey checker, Trudy Parker, put him out of the mood. If Mikilauni had choreographed the whole evening, why then had she neglected to procure the key prop? He thought of his own house, dark and peaceful. The cats were expecting their dinner. Sex, to him, meant he was *in* a relationship, and somehow after his relationships ended, the women never felt like remaining friends with him. He had the sinking feeling he wouldn't be attending Moopuna's First Communion.

He parked and entered the all-night grocery store. The place was too bright, too big, too empty.

"Hi there, Mr. Clay," Trudy greeted him. She'd been a music appreciation student years earlier. It was now unlikely for him to go out in public anywhere in Goldhurst and not run into at least one person who had taken a class from him.

"Hi, Trudy."

"Getting in for your groceries kind of late this weekend, huh?" Must've had a pretty busy weekend, huh? Whatcha been up to?"

"Nothing much."

He had planned to zip in and out with what he'd come for, but now he felt compelled to pad his order. He took a shopping cart and pushed it to the dairy case. He reached for milk, then realized if he spent the night with Mikilauni it might spoil. He reached for potato chips, then remembered he was trying to cut down on fat and salt. Christ, just toss some crap into the cart and get the hell out. As he was wheeling it toward the checkout, he realized he'd forgotten what he came for. He U-turned and headed for the Trojans.

He loaded his items on the conveyor belt, and Trudy began running them over the scanner. "No frozen TV dinners this week, huh, Mr. Clay?"

"Nope."

"No vegetables either." She clicked her tongue. "My guess is you need more roughage in your diet."

"So I've been told."

She picked up the box of condoms, turned it around to find the bar code, but mercifully she didn't comment. He paid her and she handed him the single bag. "Not much to go on for the whole week, Mr. Clay. Hopefully, your girlfriend feeds you better than you feed yourself."

When he drove back to Mikilauni's, she was waiting for him, not in the dark, as he had left her, but in full light, stretched out naked on the bed, propped up on an elbow to accentuate her exquisite breasts. The prolonged wait had increased their desire. He tore off his clothes and leaped into her bed. When they finally joined, her voice rose in a half-sob, half-laugh of joy.

Afterward she was chatty and cuddly, while he was sleepy and worried. Target's tummy would be growling with hunger. Bother had no street skills; she could get run over or torn up by a tom. He had to get ready to go to school in the morning. He had to get back to his own razor, his own toothbrush, his own life.

"Please don't be mad about this," she said, "but I can't let you spend the night."

"Oh?"

"My mother will be by early in the morning with Moopuna. It would be confusing for him to see you here. He might be hurt. I've got to look out for him."

He kissed her on her perspiring forehead. "You're a good little mama," he said, and sprang from her bed.

Chapter Sixteen

He arrived at the college Monday morning feeling as if he'd been on a long trip. When would he see her again? Next weekend seemed like an eternity. He imagined walking down the pathway at Sutter Park, holding Moopuna's hand, his other arm around Mikilauni's waist. He walked into his office and the whole blue sky, the great green of leaves and grass rippled and faded.

Art Bunch sat at his desk, wearing a "Breakfast is never served in hell" T-shirt. His leering grin caused the vertical crease on one side of his face to deepen. "Your girlfriend's been here looking for you."

Mikilauni? Here at the college? Gordon didn't like the idea. He set his satchel on his desk and slowly unpacked it.

"She wanted to reschedule her appointment with you."

"Appointment?"

"Something about the track"

"Oh, you mean the sister!"

"Not anymore, she ain't. She's a free woman. Done without for a long time." Art leaned forward on both elbows. "Or has she? I can tell by the look on your face you're getting some. Tell me, do you have her wear her habit in bed? Is that how you Catholic boys get off?"

Not even Art Bunch could ruin his good mood. Gordon opened his theory text and began to prepare the lesson.

Art was downloading ring tones from the Big Band Era, trying each of them out, while hitting his toe against the leg of his desk and popping gum in counter rhythms. Suddenly he was silent. "You make me sad, Gordo. You never share. Obviously, something's down with you and you won't give me a hint."

Gordon laughed loudly. "Okay, my friend, I'll share. I've met someone."

"Where?"

"At church."

"You don't go to church."

"I took her to the symphony, which wasn't bad."

"You don't go to the symphony. You sure you aren't talking about Cecilia? Dinner at her place, just the two of you, private tutoring sessions, just the two of you, and what is it the two of you do at the track?"

"Exercise."

"Jeez my knees, sounds like she already has you on a short leash."

"We're friends, Art. I remember when I couldn't stand her."

"You should take her to Allegra's Halloween bash. She could dress up like a nun. No, you dress up like a nun; she can dress up like a devil. Bad idea. I'm going as the devil."

"Oh? It's a come-as-you-are affair? Count me out."

"Don't be a party pooper, Gordo. I'm taking this lady Peggy from my church. She's a real sweetheart. Teaches preschool. Talks to me like I'm a four-year-old sometimes, but it's all good. You bring the sister. She's done wonders for your complexion." Heading out the door, Art actually pinched his cheek.

"I saw you at Mass," said Cecilia. "I'm dying to know. What'd you think of the music? Ah, don't tell me. I was horrible, wasn't I? I can tell by the look on your face."

They were at the track again, in their usual mode — he walking, she running intervals. "Don't take it personally. It wasn't you. It was all of it. Whatever happened to Gregorian chant, Machaut, Josquin, Palestrina? Now that's what I call Catholic music. I'd even settle for Bob Seeger's 'Turn, Turn, Turn' if it's a folk mass."

"Uh-oh. Sounds like you hated us."

"It wasn't just the music, the whole mass was so secular, so vulgar, so . . . Protestant."

She laughed. Her face was pink with the heat of her exertion, her sienna freckles across her nose and cheeks as faint as the first visible constellations on a summer evening. "I envy you, Mr. Clay. I wish I had grown up Catholic. What was it like?"

"Terrifying and magical, all at once. Most of the kids on my block were Protestants. They looked at me really weird when I told them I had to go to Mass, Confession, get ashes on Ash Wednesday. They didn't have any statues, saints, or the Virgin Mary. And how good could it be to bite off the head of a chocolate bunny on Easter, if you hadn't given up candy for Lent?"

She was off, pushing hard against the wind, knees and elbows flying. The air was gusty and cold. He turned the collar of his windbreaker up, thinking they were in for a storm that evening. He sensed a long, hard winter.

After her lap, Cecilia plucked her sweatshirt off the

bleachers. "I'm bushed. That was my sixth four-forty. I'm supposed to do eight, but that's it for me."

"Really? I feel fairly fresh." He lifted a foot and rotated his ankle. "I think I'll go a few more rounds."

"You've already walked two miles."

"Really? That must be my record." He smiled down at her to find her studying him with a quizzical expression.

"You're different. Something's happened, hasn't it? Something good."

"I had a date," he blurted.

"Oh, good for you! Tell me about her."

"She's . . . interesting. It's too soon to say much else. Why don't you trot alongside me for a few more laps so you can do a little interval practice of a different sort?"

She groaned. "I'm so bad at that kind."

"Come on, now." He sang a perfect fourth.

She sang up the scale, each step a bit flat. "Perfect fifth?" she asked, wincing.

"Singing up the scale really isn't the best method. Try this: associate the intervals with familiar tunes. What's this?" He hummed four notes.

" 'Here Comes the Bride?' "

"Uh-huh. A perfect fourth. Here's another one." He sang the opening bars of "Somewhere, There's a Place" from *West Side Story.* "That begins with a major seventh."

"Oh, I hear it. That's the same as 'Somewhere Over the Rainbow.' "

"No, that's an octave." He sang a major seventh, then an octave.

"I hear the difference. The major seventh is sharper."

It was actually flatter, but he understood what she meant: the seventh was strident, piercing, dissonant, whereas the octave was calm, restful, deemed perfect by the Catholic Church over a thousand years earlier. In the Middle Ages, the mighty Church had its fingers in every pie, music notation being invented by monks, perched high on stools in their drafty monasteries, dipping their quills into liquid gold. He thought of Cecilia's Ministry of Music and shuddered. How had the Church's glorious musical beginnings come to this?

Chapter Seventeen

He was out of control, he knew. Less than twenty-four hours, and already he was back in the sack with Miki-launi. Before dinner. When he got home from the track, she was on his answering machine. She met him at her door, undid his belt buckle as they kissed, and climbed into his arms. It was a bit awkward standing, bracing her against the wall, so he carried her down the hall to her bed. Where was Moopuna? Certainly not at home. The condom — they had forgotten it, he was certain. Hell, he didn't care; they'd make a baby. What was he thinking? Was he mad? He felt himself. The condom was in place; somehow she'd managed. She drew her sleek legs over his shoulders. He held her ass in his hands, his left thumb tracing peculiar, raised, circular patterns. She drew his hand away, placed it on her breast. "Here. Pinch."

Afterward she loved to talk. Salote, Kali, Inoke, Fipe — the litany of musical names lulled him into a blissful, relaxed state. Added to the mix were Ashley, Sarah, and Wendy, "the girls" at the Wiggins & Forrest Accounting Firm. She ended a sentence with a raised pitch on "okay?" and looked at him expectantly.

"Huh? Say again, honey. I must have dozed there for a second."

"Wendy's Halloween party, Saturday. We're going, all right?"

"No."

"What?" She sat up, leaving a cold spot next to him.

"The music department's having one, too. I just as soon —"

"Oh! That's even better. Let's go to that one." She snuggled down next to him again. "Now, what should we go as? It's costume, right?"

"I don't want to go. Halloween is for kids. Let's take Moopuna trick-or-treating, then jump into the sack. Where is Moopuna, anyway?"

"I see how it is." She shot out of bed, and he caught a glimpse of her backside, her right cheek, oddly scarred, as if a whole change purse of pennies was stuck to it. She whipped on a worn, purple bathrobe of knobby fabric. Some of the knobs had worn off, leaving pin-sized holes. She stomped into slippers that looked shorn from fluffy zebras. "I'm good enough for sex, but not to be included in your *set*."

"Set? I don't have a set."

"Everyone has a *set*." The last syllable erupted from her with a gust of breath, as she cinched her bathrobe sash.

"They're the people I work with. There're only three of them, and the cockroaches, but I don't know any of them except to say hi."

"Cockroaches?"

"Part-timers. They come out at night like cockroaches, and are paid about as much. This party is going to be a bust. I tried to warn Art."

"Who's Art?"

"I suppose I'd call him a friend if I had any friends.

You don't want to know him. I'm used to him; I know how to take him. And Lars is real old. Allegra isn't, but she's married to an old guy. Do you want to party with a couple of grandpas?"

She dipped her chin in the knobby purple material, her hair falling into her face. "Why won't you let me into your life?"

How had he forgotten this major point about relationships? Women invariably wanted something different from what he wanted. There were scenes and cold spots and ugly bathrobes. He had always entered the war zone bent on getting his way, and invariably he would lose the battle simply because the woman wanted her way more. Perhaps he'd learned something by now. He was bound to lose, so the sooner he gave in, the quicker the cold spot would go away.

"Okay, we'll go."

She lifted her face expectantly. "To which party?"

"I don't care. We can start early and go to both of them. Hell, we can go to every goddamn Halloween party in Goldhurst."

She twisted her shoulder forward. "You don't have to swear about it."

He was new at this giving-in stuff. He'd have to work on the being-gracious part. In seconds, he had her back in his arms. She nuzzled close, but her gaze was distant. "I know what you mean about friends."

Cautiously, he maneuvered down the dark, twisting road in the moonless night.

"Are you sure you haven't passed it?" asked Miki-launi.

"No, I'm *not* sure I haven't passed it." They had been

winding around in the sticks for what seemed like hours.

Mikilauni, wearing a sequined, Spandex mermaid costume, asked, "Couldn't you ask someone?"

"Do you see anyone to ask?" He grasped her hand as an apology for his strident tone. He had only been out to Henry and Allegra Musgrave's llama ranch only a few times and never in the dark. All the county avenues were numbered on the map, but few of them had signposts. Allegra had given him detailed directions, "When the road forks, bear right; in a few miles when you see a blue motor home bear left; at the first asphalt bridge with guard rails, set your trip odometer and bear left; after 4.3 miles, you will cross another asphalt bridge with steel guard rails; before the pavement ends; after the huge ABORTION KILLS WOMEN sign on the flatbed trailer, bear left again." Gordon was highly suspicious of directions that included the words bear, ending pavement, and movable landmarks.

Mikilauni stared through the windshield, her hand limp in his.

"I'm sorry. Getting lost in the pitch dark stresses me out." When she did not reply, he added, "You okay?"

She sighed deeply. "Sometimes I wish I could go home."

"It's gone, baby. Washed into the sea."

"It was beautiful. Perfect. Sandy beaches, coconut trees. My happy island."

And she was lost to him, gone there, a place that had ceased to exist long before she was born. He waited for her to come back to him. "Tell me something about this singing teacher. Allegra — right?"

"Yep. She's nice. Just thinks she's better than everyone else. A graduate of the Royal College of Musicians in London."

"What's she doing in Goldhurst?"

"Beats me. She married a widower a few years back with four teenagers. Surprised the hell out of me. I didn't know she had a maternal bone in her body."

"And the head guy is Lars, the guy who played the bumblebee song?"

Gordon chuckled. "Uh-huh. *Flight of the Bumblebee.*"

"Ow, I said it wrong, didn't I?" She pounded her thigh with her fist. "What if I say something dumb in front of them?"

"Ah, relax, honey. Have fun. Here's something interesting for you to watch for: Art and Allegra are in cahoots."

"You think they're having an affair?"

"Had one, but it's ancient history, long before she was married and when Art was trying to encourage wife number one to leave."

The headlights flooded a looming, plaster arch, glittering with embedded horseshoes.

"Are we here?"

"Nope. This is the you've-come-too-far landmark. I think I know where we are now."

He turned the car around. The Musgrave Llama Ranch sign was easier to spot in the opposite direction. Soon they were walking up the sloping pathway to the house. Gordon carried a Crock-Pot of his Healthy Heart Meatless Chili, spiced up with a little hamburger, and Mikilauni scraped along beside him in her stiletto heels, the narrow opening of her costume allowing her mere baby steps. They came upon a step too high for her to take and she stumbled, falling on her palms.

"Oh, honey, careful." He really didn't want to be

here. She held up one skinned palm for his inspection, and he kissed it. "Does it hurt?"

"Only my pride." She glanced toward the house. "I don't think anyone saw me. I'm going to have to go slow in this thing." The costume did seem insanely impractical and uncomfortable. It was at least one size too small, the blue-green sequined Spandex clutching her like a vise, the ponderous stuffed tail dragging behind her, the wired, strapless bodice digging into her armpits. She stretched a glitter-tipped finger toward the doorbell.

"Wait, my costume."

She reached into the breast pocket of his sports jacket, withdrew a pair of lensless glasses with eyebrows, nose, and mustache attachments, and placed them on his face. "It's not really what you'd call a costume."

"What? I'm Groucho Marx."

A Valkyrie — Brunnhilde, herself — answered the door. It was Allegra in her fantasy operatic role, her ample body robed in a purple satin gown with a silver, plastic breastplate, a helmet sporting two curved horns and fake yellow braids, with her feeble blonde spaniel Hunding yapping at her feet. "Gordon! Come in, come in!" She nearly shut the door on Mikilauni, before spotting her in the shadows. "Oh, gracious, hello dear, hello! Velcome to Valhalla."

"Allegra, Mikilauni."

Allegra's protuberant eyes took in the cleavage, the stilettos, the skin tone. "My what a beautiful *tail!* And where's your costume, Gordon?"

"I'm Groucho Marx."

"Honestly, Gordon. Here, I'll take that." Allegra reached for the Crock-Pot, then led them into what she called the great room where a square coffee table was laden with snacks, a black kettle of steaming beverage, and a row of ghoulish, flickering jack-o'-lanterns. Mirroring the jack-o'-lanterns were the party guests, perched on the curving sofa. The cockroaches wore no costumes, and Allegra's husband, Henry, was in his white lab coat and hospital name tag, his daily uniform. Lars and Adele Stelling were suited out in matching bumblebee outfits, a continuing theme from the symphony. Gordon had never seen Lars's old, scrawny legs in black tights and could have died a happy man without it.

Henry ladled into mugs what he called witch's brew, a hot, spiced cider spiked with rum. Mikilauni eagerly sipped hers, the first indication that she drank alcohol. He would have preferred a beer over the overly sweet cider, but none was offered.

He nodded at the cockroaches who all looked hungry and harried because they worked too many jobs with too little pay. Many of them were as accomplished as tenured faculty, but not as lucky. A cockroach rarely made full time because a cushy job like Gordon's was rarely vacated. When it was, a replacement was invariably hired from out of town. It was possible for a cockroach to get a tenure-track position at a college where he had never been known as a cockroach, and would then treat the cockroaches at that college with the same disdain with which he had been treated. It couldn't be helped: it was the law of the cockroach.

"No, no," Lars was telling a roach, "not so many music majors anymore. These days the kids are all business. You never hear them talking about what fires them up; it's all about money. Most of our students participate in music as an avocation." Proud bee that he was, he recited his favorite axiom of years gone by. " 'Music is an ideal, all-weather, lifetime hobby as well as a profitable profession.'" He asked Gordon, "Where's your costume?"

"I'm Groucho Marx."

"You are mistaken. The eyebrows are wrong. So are the nose, the mustache, and the glasses."

Allegra was heard from the foyer greeting newcomers, and then there arose a plaintive squeal, "Oh! Stop." Art Bunch, dressed in red tights, a red long john top, a matching black satin vest and bow tie, and a black felt beanie with red satin horns, leaped into the room, prodding Peggy, a chubby French maid, with his red plastic pitchfork. Their faces were flushed and their eyes looked bleary, as if their evening had started long ago. Art scanned the room, his eyes widening as they came to rest on Mikilauni's cleavage. He leaped over the corner of the coffee table, his wire-filled, arrow-tipped tail bobbing behind him, and squeezed in next to her. "I'm Art. You must be Ariel."

She scooted over to make room for him and his date. "No. I'm Mikilauni."

Art's head came to rest unsteadily on his pitchfork. "Stunning costume. You're new to the department?"

"No, I'm . . . I'm here with . . . ." She lolled her head against Gordon, the red hibiscus behind her ear grazing his cheek. He watched Art's baby face slacken, the caverns of his elongated dimples deepen.

"You're here with Groucho Marx?"

"At least someone thinks I'm Groucho Marx," Gordon said gleefully.

Art looked up at Allegra, who was standing behind the sofa. She cocked her head toward the kitchen.

"Need some help, Allegra?" he asked.

"I never turn down any offers."

"Would you excuse me, ladies?"

Peggy didn't reply, busy filling her plate with snacks. She didn't seem to notice how much attention Art had given Mikilauni and that he was now deserting her to go into the kitchen with Allegra. There was a lull in the conversation. Gordon checked his watch, wondering how soon they could leave. He longed to lick Mikilauni's skin, imprinted with the circular patterns from the tight, sequined Spandex.

Allegra returned with a bowl of popcorn. "Gordon, Arthur requires your assistance in the bathroom. Something about his devil costume wants attending to." A pool of white was showing beneath Allegra's wide brown pupils. Something was up, and he wanted no part of it.

"Maybe Peggy can help him."

"Oh, no, I don't know him that well." Peggy nudged his plastic pitchfork with her toe. "I don't think I want to."

Gordon walked through the kitchen, knocked tentatively at the bathroom door, and walked in. Art was sitting on the counter, his legs and wire tail swinging. "Who is she? A student? You lucky devil."

"I should have known." He turned to leave.

Art leaped between him and the door. "Is it serious?"

"It's our second date."

"Share, Gordo, share. Think you'll date her again?"

"Hard to say," he replied offhandedly, feeling like a traitor to Mikilauni.

" 'Cause she likes me, you can tell she really likes me. You wouldn't mind if I gave her a call?"

He couldn't bear the thought of Art's paws on Mikilauni, even if he never saw her again. "Yes, I would mind very much."

"You've gotten awfully greedy lately." Art made a circle with his left forefinger and thumb and moved his right
forefinger in and out. " — ing the sister and now this
Mikilauni comes along. She's out of your league, Gordo.
She's carnal. You can tell she's carnal. If I could only lay
my hands on that gorgeous piece of ass, I'd chain her to
the bed."

Gordon's hands closed and tightened. He tried to
relax them, but they balled up again. His heart was ham-
mering, and he had thought that Mikilauni was the best
medicine for his chest pains. "What about this Peggy? She
seems nice."

"She already hates my guts."

"What a surprise. She doesn't like being prodded with
a pitchfork?"

"Come on, Gordo, be a friend: hand over her number.
The sister is more your speed." His lips tightened to sup-
press a wry smirk. "I invited her to the party — as your
date. Me and Allegra thought it would be a good idea. "

"Jesus, no. Tell me it isn't true. What did you tell her
exactly?"

"Come to the party. That's all, big guy. I figured you
two could hook up here. Doesn't look like she's coming."

Gordon reached for the doorknob again, and Art
stepped aside. Returning to the party, they found that Allegra's great room had emptied considerably. The Stellings
had left and, without Lars to suck up to, the cockroaches
had also skittered away to the parties they actually
wanted to attend.

The doorbell chimed again, and Allegra answered it.
Into the room came Cecilia, wearing a brown monk's
robe, with her arms tucked under the stole. A stuffed
squirrel was sewn near the hem of her robe, a rubber rat

was attached to her sleeve, a rabbit was perched on her shoulder, and a Styrofoam sparrow decorated her headband. She greeted Art and Gordon. Allegra introduced her to Henry, Peggy, and Mikilauni.

"Oh, hel-lo!" exclaimed Cecilia to Mikilauni. "Nice to see you. How's Michael?"

"He's fine," Mikilauni retorted curtly.

"I'll bet he's grown!"

Mikilauni didn't reply. Instead, she helped herself to the pot of chili. Gordon had never seen her act this way, almost rude. Who was Michael? He'd have to be more attentive to her chatter about extended family. He greeted Cecilia with "Good evening, St. Francis. Great costume."

Peggy reached out to shake her hand. Cecilia unfolded her arms, revealing her palms, bound in gauze, soaked in a red goo. Peggy gasped and recoiled.

Cecilia looked puzzled a moment. "Oh! Excuse my stigmata! It's just tomato sauce." Hastily she handed Peggy a napkin. "So sorry! We saints are usually fun to have around. I'm the patron saint of animals."

"*Mister* Christopher is the patron of travelers," said Gordon. "He got demoted to Mister because no one could prove the saint actually lived. And I really liked my St. Christopher's medal."

"What's interesting to me," interjected Allegra, "is that Americans are all so confoundedly religious. Something like fifty-two percent of the population attends church, whereas in the U.K. it is merely three or four percent. Why do you suppose that is, huh?"

Henry's pager beeped.

"Not really, Henry," said Allegra. "Can't we have a single social evening?"

"It can't be helped, dear. You know Halloween is a

busy night for pediatricians." Henry stood. " 'Night all. Careful driving out of here."

Allegra followed Henry to the kitchen. They could be heard arguing in hushed tones. The back door was firmly shut. A car drove off. Allegra blew her nose loudly.

"I better go check on Allegra," said Art. He reeled slightly, his tail springing like something alive.

Mikilauni turned to Gordon. "I've always wondered — why do opera singers wear those Viking-type horns like Allegra has? Is it a certain character in an opera?"

"Good question," said Gordon, sounding like a teacher. "She's Brunnhilde, from Wagner's *Ring Cycle*."

"What's the story about?" asked Mikilauni.

"Oh! Brunnhilde is a wonderfully romantic girl, half-god, half-mortal, who has the job of carrying dead warriors off the battleground up to Valhalla. The plot is very complicated, based on Norse mythology."

"Mythology is heresy," said Peggy. "The true word of God is the Holy Bible."

"Oh, jeez," said Gordon. "Next thing you're going to tell us is the world was created in seven days."

"It was! Oh! I've had it!" Peggy stood, none too steadily, and staggered toward the front door. The door slammed. Tires skidded in the dirt.

"That was Art's ride home," said Gordon. "He always makes his date the designated driver."

"Didn't anyone ever tell Peggy the designated driver isn't supposed to drink?" asked Cecilia. "I hope she makes it back to town all right."

This Halloween party was wearing him down. He thought of his refrigerator and private stock of cold beer. He thought about Target out roaming. Halloween could be a rough night for cats "I'm going to get a drink of water. Be right back."

He found the kitchen empty. Allegra and Art must have slipped out the back door for a walk and a heart-to-heart. He heard a scraping sound behind the door of the walk-in pantry. Allegra's spaniel, no doubt, had gotten trapped inside. The door creaked when he swung it open. Allegra and Art were on the floor, his red tights pulled down to his bony ankles, his beanie with the horns twisted around, so that one horn was moving between Allegra's two Valkyrie horns. They looked up in a bewildered state, their eyes adjusting to the sudden slice of light. He shut the door with a reproachful click, walked over to the sink, and ran water from the tap. In the window, a stout, ponytailed man wearing prank glasses stared back at him. Feeling disgusted, he removed the glasses and jammed them into his breast pocket. He wished he were home, a beer in his hand, a vibrating cat in his lap.

Art came out of the pantry, adjusting his tights. "It's not what you think."

"I always knew you were a . . ."

"Never mind. I know what I am." Art nudged Gordon over and washed his hands and face, using dishwashing detergent, wafting Joy and sex.

"Is Allegra coming out of the closet?"

"Not while you're here, big guy."

"Is she okay?"

Art smirked. "Better than okay, I think."

Art sauntered into the living room, Gordon following. He saw the back of Mikilauni's head and winced. Seeing Art and Allegra together had somehow shamed him.

He was a brute, taking advantage of this sweet, trusting girl.

"The party's over, Mikilauni." He scowled at Art. "Grab your pitchfork, man. Let's go."

"I'm glad I can follow you guys out of here," said Cecilia. "It took me hours to find."

Gordon grasped Mikilauni's hands and pulled her to her feet. Art blew out the jack-o'-lanterns.

Not much was said on the drive back to town. He parked in front of Mikilauni's house and helped her struggle up the front steps, her tail dragging behind her like some dumb, dead animal.

"I think that went rather well," she said.

"You're kidding."

"I don't mean the party; I mean your set. I was a success, wasn't I?" She searched Gordon's face.

"You were great," he said. He kissed her hastily. "Goodnight."

"You're coming back, aren't you? After you drop Art off?"

"Uh, Mikilauni, no. I need some time alone right now."

She stepped back, hugging herself with crossed arms. "What are you saying?"

"I've been with too many people for too long. I'm not used to it. I need space. I'll call you tomorrow." He wasn't so sure he would, but he felt he owed her the hope of it.

Mikilauni dropped her head and entered the house. The door would not close behind her. She swung it wider. Her tail slithered sadly into the opening and disappeared.

In the car, Art began to explain himself, but Gordon

stretched out his palm. "Don't start, goddamn you. Don't even start." It was easy to take it all out on Art.

He dropped him off, then drove home. The cats were fine, waiting for him, one on each side of the door. He let Target in, blocking Bother's path with his foot. Safe inside, he scooped them up, and pressed them together beneath his chin. Target growled low in her throat, and Bother laid her ears back. He risked getting bit and scratched, but he held on tight. *His set.*

Chapter Eighteen

He awoke the next morning to a tapping sound on his bedroom window. The cats? No, they were both on the bed, Target, a black and orange ball on the pillow next to him, Bother, a gray lump pressed against his thigh. Mikilauni? He'd been wretched to her last night, deserting her in a panic. He crossed the room to the window, conscious of the knee-length flannel nightshirt he was wearing, printed with notes, rests, sharps, and flats that his sister Ruthie had given to him. He hated clothing with a musical motif and forgot he had it, until the previous night when he was looking for something warm. He flung aside the curtain and found Art Bunch, dressed properly in a yellow polo, tan corduroy jacket, and khakis, squinting beyond him at the rumpled bed.

Gordon stalked into the living room and flung open the door. "There's laws against prowling around in flower beds and peering into people's bedroom windows."

"Nice nightie. Where can I get one like it?" Art squeezed by him, and began circling the living room, looking like a man who had left his hat behind. "I didn't want to wake Sleeping Beauty."

"Mikilauni isn't here. You saw me drop her off first."

"I assumed you went back for her."

Target bolted for the open door, but she wasn't quick

enough. Art seized her between his legs. "Hey, Kitty-cat, nice boy." Target bared her rear claws, pushed off his forearm, and streaked toward freedom. Art lifted the sleeve of his jacket to inspect the damage. "She scratched me."

"Good judge of character." Gordon pressed the door against the November wind. In the distance, the bells at Our Lady of the Apparition of Lourdes beckoned the faithful to celebrate All Saints' Day.

Art was still snooping around. He had the gall to peer into the bedroom. Wouldn't that be a treat, finding Mikilauni asleep, her lovely, ebony hair draped over one bare breast? Gordon's fist balled involuntarily.

"Come on, get dressed, big guy. I'm taking you to the IHOP."

"I'm not hungry."

"Aw, come on, Gordo. You're always hungry."

"You can't stay married. So now you want to wreck Allegra's home life, too."

"Ah, now that wasn't planned. Allegra and I just came together. *Whammo!* It just happened. We haven't screwed in years. You don't understand passion, getting swept away." He waved his arms like waves crashing.

"I understand lust."

"I'll say. What other reason have you got to boink that sweet, young chocolate thang?"

It just happened. He punched Art in the nose. His arm cocked and straightened, making contact. *Whammo!*

"You punched me in the nose!" Art's accusing, beady eyes peered over his cupped palms.

Gordon dashed into the kitchen, spilled some ice cubes into a dish cloth, ran back to Art, and pressed the towel against his pink, swelling nose. There was quite a lot of blood. Gordon steered him backward. When the back of Art's legs pressed against the sofa, he fell into it. Gordon sank down beside him.

"Jeez, Art, I don't know what got into me. I guess, I was afraid you were right."

Art dropped the towel to his lap, attached his fingertips to the knob of his nose and wriggled it gingerly.

"It isn't just lust," Gordon reasoned, more for his own sake than Art's. "I wasn't straight with you last night. I wasn't even straight with myself. I'm serious about that woman!"

"Serious. In a week?"

"She's exotic, mysterious. She asks questions, listens to the answers. She's interested in everything."

"Sounds like a good student."

"I know she's too young for me, but — hey, she's got this great little kid who's smart and funny. Guess what his name is? Moopuna!"

"Those eyes, those lips, that costume. Oh, Gordo, God likes you better than me."

"He should. Wanna a beer?"

"Sure." Art followed him into the kitchen. "Henry is a hell of a guy. Allegra really loves him, but he won't do the dirty deed with her."

Gordon removed two bottles of beer from the fridge, opened them, and handed one to Art. "Won't or can't?"

"Won't, Allegra says. Just not interested. Little kisses on the cheek, hand patting, yeah. No whoopee. Allegra is a passionate woman. She practically tore my dick off."

"Too much info, Art."

"Sorry, Gordo."

"Henry's a good guy. You shouldn't be doing this to him."

"Oh, Henry's not gonna mind. He won't know."

"Sorry about the nose, Art."

"It's cool. I was afraid you were a better person than me."

"I *am* a better person than you."

They drank deeply.

Art stood. "Thanks for the beer. Gotta get to church."

"You're going to church with beer breath?"

"Can't help it, man. I got a gig." Out the door dashed Art, off to play sax in his Christian rock band, Loaves and Fishes. Gordon hurried to call Mikilauni, knowing he'd probably have to accompany her and Moopuna to Mass before digging into that breakfast.

"Monica told me you had a good checkup," said Cecilia, walking into his office for her tutorial the following Wednesday afternoon. Out of the convent two months now, she still wore the same white blouse and crucifix, but the brown jumper had been replaced by jeans which, she had told him, came from St. Vincent de Paul's Thrift Store. Her hair had grown out, and she wore it clasped at her nape with a tortoise-shell clip. She didn't look like a nun; she didn't move like one, either. He noted the subtle change in the toss of her shoulders, the tilt of her chin, how she extended her backside to reach for a chair.

"Yep. Blood pressure is down and so is the weight by seven pounds."

"No more anxiety attacks?"

"If I was still prone to them, that damn Halloween party should've given me one."

"Ah, come on. It was fun. I had fun. I thought the conversation was interesting." While her head was still bent toward her backpack, he reached behind him and removed his metronome from the shelf. He turned the dial to eighty beats per minute, set it in the middle of his desk, and switched it on.

Cecilia looked up, startled. "Oh, no! I can never stay with one of those. They mess me up."

"It just takes practice. Try clapping along with the beat."

She bobbed her head, watched the flashing red light, but still she couldn't clap when the metronome clicked.

"Slow down. You're ahead of it."

"I was trying to catch up to it."

"A common mistake. Try again."

Cecilia clapped and counted, "One, two, three, four, one, two—"

"Stop counting."

"Mr. Bunch says to always count."

"Sometimes it helps, but you're not listening."

He watched her struggle on, her face flushed with embarrassment. It was not a matter of listening, he realized, but feeling. She threw her arms up and let them slap against her thighs. "I'll just have to pray harder for a miracle from Mother Teresa."

"I want to try something. We'll have to go down to the band room."

It was nearing four o'clock, the corridors were empty. "I didn't know you knew Mikilauni Kukula," said Cecilia.

"Oh, well, I haven't for long."

"What's Michael like now?"

"I haven't met Michael."

"Really? She doesn't have custody anymore?"

"Wait a minute. You must mean Moopuna."

"Oh, she's using his Polynesian name now. He was enrolled in Our Lady's preschool by his baptismal name, Michael, but she withdrew him in the middle of last year."

"Withdrew him? Why?"

"You'll have to ask her."

"She didn't seem too happy to see you at the party."

"You noticed? I guess she sees me as an extension of Michael's teacher, Sister Margie. There was a problem between her and Mikilauni. Be nice to Michael. He needs someone to be nice to him."

He thought how quick Mikilauni was to scold Moopuna. He told Cecilia about meeting Moopuna several months before Mikilauni, in Sutter Park. She questioned him further, and he ended up telling her the whole story, how Carrie Clay had accidentally called him, looking for her son.

"What a fascinating story!" Cecilia stopped walking and stared down the hall, deep in thought. "Maybe she was an angel, guiding you toward Michael."

"I don't believe in angels."

"Which doesn't mean they don't exist. Think about it, Mr. Clay. A disembodied voice summoning you in the dead of the night." Half of her mouth was turned upward, her lips pressed together to prevent the form of a complete smile.

In the band room, he adjusted the metronome back two notches to seventy-two, plugged it into an amplifier, then twisted the volume knob full blast. With the ticks reverberated around the cavernous room, it was like standing in the chamber of a human heart. "Sit there." He gestured toward the large, black, amplifier.

"Right on top of it?"

"Right on top of it. Close your eyes." He paused. "Feel it?"

She nodded. "Shall I clap?"

"No, just sit. Let the beat seep into your body, become a part of you. When it's there, move to it."

"Move how?"

"Don't think how. Feel how."

At first she was still. Only the hopeful flutter of her pale lashes indicated that something was happening beneath her translucent skin. Her shoulders pulsed up and down. Her head began to nod. She slapped her hands on her thighs. She opened her eyes. "I've got it, haven't I? I *feel* the beat."

"I can tell. That's good. It's very good."

She was conducting in duple meter as she spoke, making short, sweeping curves with her fingertips. "It's already there. I just have to join it. I think I've been trying to make up my own. Can I try a rhythm now?"

"All right. Quarter, two eighths, two quarters."

She rushed the first eighth and was late for the third and fourth beats.

"Never mind. Go back to the beat. The important thing is that you're feeling the beat."

That evening, he stayed late at school, thinking he had only a little more work to do on his Wagner *Ring Cycle* lecture. He heard footsteps and voices in the hallway when the Community Chorus was dismissed, then silence. Nearing ten p.m. he thought he was alone in the building, when he felt a distinct presence on the opposite side of his desk. He started, looked up. There stood Allegra Musgrave in her black London Fog trench coat, knee-high black boots, and black driving gloves. Her collar was turned up and her hair tucked into a black scarf. She looked either like a mourning widow or a secret agent. "I suppose now you think I'm an awful person."

Oh, for Christ's sake! First Art came crawling to him and now Allegra. Was he a priest running a confessional? "Why would I think that?"

"Arthur told me you were horribly shaken. He said you hit him."

"There was more to it. He insulted Mikilauni."

She sank into the chair. "Arthur and I—it's been years since we, *years*— and then at my party we just— came together with a desire so . . ."

"Allegra, why are you telling me this?"

"You must understand the passions of the human heart, Gordon. I thought for a while maybe you didn't, but you must, or you wouldn't be with that young girl."

"It's getting late and it's nasty out. Henry will be expecting you."

Allegra drove a silver Corvette with a radar detector on the dash. She drove fast, and when she was late she drove faster. He hated the thought of her bearing and twisting on those slick, black county roads this time of night. He pushed back his chair to stand, but she laid her hand on his, her black kid glove soft to the touch.

"I do feel the need of a heart-to-heart, Gordon."

"The first time you two got together, Art wrecked his marriage — I guess he was looking for an excuse to divorce Star — but this time it's you and Henry, and wrecking that would be a damn shame."

Relief softened her face into an ironic smile. "There, you see? You really did want to give me a scolding. I came here to talk to the only person who knows Henry and me and Arthur well. You never have quite approved of me, have you, Gordon?"

"I never said . . . I never felt . . . Well, I've always thought you acted a little too important to teach here, like you should be singing at the Met instead."

"Oh, good heavens! I haven't that sort of talent."

"Are you sure? See, I think a professional career is a matter of luck."

"Maybe for you, Gordon. I can't be a judge of your talent because I've never heard you seriously play. You really don't play, now do you, Gordon?"

"In the Goldhurst Community Symphony?" He sniffed.

She tipped her chin, showing the white beneath her pupils. "Now who's being too good for whom? I heard you tried your luck in L.A. last summer. How did that go?"

"I'm back here, aren't I? I think I'm finally ready to make my peace with that."

She smiled. "It's that charming girl, isn't it? Mikilauni. Such a musical name. She makes you happy."

"Allegra, is Henry your soul mate?"

"Heavens, no."

"Neither is Mikilauni for me. Did you ever have a soul mate?"

"His name was Rudolfo. He left me for another singer . . . another tenor." She shrugged.

"I had someone in college. I let her get away. Mikilauni's not exactly . . ."

"Give it a chance, dear. I like her. I like how you look when you're with her."

"Do you still love Henry?"

She cocked her head, smiling ruefully. "What's not to love about Henry?"

"Then how does Art fit in?"

She fluttered her lashes. "Art fits perfectly. He's my body mate. It's fantastic how we get along in that department."

"When you came in here, I was afraid you were going to ask me if you should leave Henry for Art."

She pressed her hands to her cheeks. "Heavens! Such a dreadful thought! Arthur makes a dreadful husband, don't you think?"

He walked her out to her car, shielding her with his umbrella, her ample bosom grazing his arm. She opened her car door and settled in.

"Allegra, would it help if Henry saw a . . ." For some reason he couldn't say the word sex in the same sentence as the word Henry. ". . . therapist?"

"Whatever for? Henry is the most well-adjusted person I know."

"Just a thought. Goodnight. Drive carefully, now."

He watched her speed away. Allegra wasn't at all straightened out, as far as he could tell. She was used to getting what she wanted, and she wanted both men and his blessing, too. He wasn't so sure he could give it, but why the hell not? Who was he to judge?

Chapter Nineteen

Gordon removed the dinosaur sheets from the plastic wrapping, shook them out, and smoothed the fitted one over the daybed mattress. He had thought of this room as various things: the guest room, although he rarely had house guests; the spare room; the computer room; and the music room, since he stored his bass here. Now he hoped it would be Moopuna's room, his home away from home. Having dated Mikilauni four weeks, he was taking a major step. This would be the first weekend she and Moopuna would spend at his house. Out of the shopping bags he extracted kid videos and picture books. He had bought a child-sized table and was now equipping it with drawing paper, scented markers, and stickers. There was so much cool kid stuff on the market that Christmas was going to be a blast, the best he'd had since he was a kid.

He settled down at the kitchen table with recipes for shark. Cecilia had showed him how easy it was to sauté shrimp, steam mussels and crab, and grill fresh fish fillets so that they flaked succulently with the touch of a fork. It was all delicious. Previously, his only fish-eating experience had been his mom's cooking. Everyone in his family had grimaced at the thought of fish on Friday: dry canned salmon loaf, creamed tuna on toast, and frozen halibut, baked until it turned to brick.

Bother leaped onto his lap and lunged for the package of shark, wrapped in butcher paper. He held her back by petting her soft white bib, then nudged her to the floor with his elbow. Both cats rubbed against his legs and purred loudly.

He still didn't understand what he felt for Mikilauni. He could recall how it felt to be in love with Carrie, and he didn't feel that way about Mikilauni at all. Was he in love? He thought back to those bleak days of last spring, when all he seemed to have the energy to do was listen to his heart thud away the beats that were allotted to it; now he was happy most of the time. How many people had told him he looked like a different person, a new man? Not only did he enjoy his time with Mikilauni and Moopuna, but his friendship with Cecilia, and his teaching, cooking, and walking.

Target leaped onto the table, and he batted the gray tabby to the floor. He hadn't paid much attention to the cats since he had met Mikilauni, but they didn't seem to notice. That was what was so great about cats — no real commitment. He stared at the cookbook he held, not really seeing it. What if Mikilauni or Moopuna were allergic to cats? The cats would have to go. He heard that the pound gave cats twenty-four hours to find a home before they were euthanized. Bother might find a home, with her docile personality and vivid calico colors, but Target was a loser. He imagined loading them in the pet taxi, driving them to the pound, taking each of them out on the counter, tracing the black coils on Target's back, running his finger down the white stripe on Bother's nose between the black around one eye and the orange around the other. He wouldn't check back to see if they had found homes. The deadly needle would penetrate the unsuspecting, trusting cats — or not. He would never know. He unwrapped the fish, sawed two corners off one of the steaks, and set them on the floor. Bother sniffed hers and sauntered away, one forepaw placed in front of the other, but Target devoured them both, tossing back the fish like a greedy dog. He stroked her head, thinking if Mikilauni or Moopuna had cat allergies, there was medication for them.

Moopuna sat on his heels in the center of his new room, watching Target approach him. The gray tabby brushed her mouth against Moopuna's knee, twisted around, raised her backside, and thrashed his leg with her tail.

"He's whipping me."

"She. It means she likes you," said Gordon.

"Can I pet her?"

Gordon looked anxiously at Mikilauni. "He's not allergic? Either of you?"

"Oh, no. He loves animals."

"Just hold your hand out," said Gordon.

Moopuna extended his hand and Target ducked under it, pushing her head against his palm. Moopuna giggled. "She likes me."

"Why did you name her Target?" asked Mikilauni.

He showed her where to feel for the BBs lodged in her chest.

"How sad," said Mikilauni, "people are so cruel."

They went out to the kitchen, leaving Moopuna to play.

"You've really gone to too much trouble, buying all that stuff for Moopuna."

"Naw, it was fun. I want him to feel at home here." He poured them strawberry daiquiris from the blender, handed her one, and lifted his own glass in a toast. "To the first of many weekends you'll be spending here." They clinked glasses and drank. This reminded Gordon how gratifying it was to share a drink with a lover, and of Mikilauni's pretension of not drinking during their first meal together. But she had had her reasons, he supposed, and there was no point in spoiling the fun now.

Mikilauni was quiet, gazing out the window. "I don't think you coming to Mama's for Thanksgiving is such a good idea," she blurted.

This was something they had quarreled about the previous weekend. He hadn't wanted to go and she had implored him into saying he would. Now that she seemed to be reneging, he was surprised to find that he was looking forward to the day. "Why not?"

"You will not like the Kukula clan. All of us at once is too much."

"All families are scary all at once."

She smiled ruefully. "My family is like no other family you have ever met."

"That's a good thing. I delight in diversity."

"Delight in diversity? Did you get that from a book? I know you do not like loud crowds and chaos."

"Maybe it's time I got more tolerant." He went on to say that he drove up to Oregon only once in several years because he found his sister Ruthie's big Thanksgiving get-togethers hard to take. In large gatherings, good conversation was nearly impossible. Topics had to be kept general and superficial so no one would be offended and, with all the screaming kids and raucous football fans, there were numerous interruptions. Even so, he was always glad when he made the effort to attend.

Mikilauni insisted, "You will not like them. You cannot believe anything Kali says because she hates me and Salote says nothing because she is slow. Old Mama speaks only pidgin you will not understand and my brothers . . ."

"Whoa, whoa, whoa!" He held up his palm. "Honey, what's gotten into you? Is it the daiquiris? Only last week you were saying . . ."

"Inoke and Peleki are fat." She crossed her arms and sat back in her chair in her disgust.

He laughed and patted his belly. "I'm fat."

"Fatter."

It was not the response he was expecting, and it hurt. He had wished her to say how great he looked because he had firmed up a bit lately, but she was too determined to babble on about her family.

"In our culture a large physical presence demands respect. It is a form of prestige."

"So?"

"It's embarrassing. Inoke cannot fit in a theater seat. And a roller coaster — forget it. He will never ride one. Even if he could fit in, he would knock it off the tracks." She threw her arm up and out in emphasis.

He laughed at the image. Her face went still and somber, heavy lowered lids, drooping mouth, what he had come to think of as her Easter Island, stone-goddess look. He encircled her wrist and squeezed. "Honey, I will like your family, I promise."

From the spare room came a low twang, a great thunk, and a shriek. There was scampering in the hall, and Target, her ears flattened and her back slung low, streaked through the kitchen.

Mikilauni cringed, raising her hand to her cheek. "Oh Lord, what did my kid do this time?"

Gordon knew. He loped down the hall with the harrowing image of Moopuna crushed under his massive bass. Instead he found the bass flat on its back and the boy huddled in the corner, his arms crossed over his head.

Mikilauni darted under Gordon's armpit. "Did he break it? This thing must cost a fortune."

Gordon turned the instrument over, checking for damage. The bridge had slipped, and he began to adjust it. "It's fine. No harm done."

Mikilauni clutched Moopuna's upper arm, dragged him to his feet, and gave him a firm shake. "Don't touch Gordon's things. Do you see? Some of these things are for you and some are for him. Leave his alone."

"Hey, Moopuna, do you know what this is?" Gordon stood the instrument up, leaned it against his chest and reached for his bow. "It's called a bass. It's like a big violin. Here, I'll show you." He tightened the bow and played "Twinkle, Twinkle, Little Star."

Moopuna stared crestfallen for a moment, then shifted his weight from one foot to the other in time to the music, his eyes growing soft.

"Did you like that?"

Moopuna nodded.

"I'll play some more later. Right now, I have to fix dinner." Gordon leaned the bass in the corner again and he and Mikilauni returned to the kitchen. She sat at the table sipping her drink while he heated olive oil and crushed garlic in the skillet, then added the shark steaks.

A quiet strum reverberated down the hall.

"That kid! He's at it again." Mikilauni stormed through the kitchen, her arms pumping.

"Hey, hold on. It's all right." Gordon was reluctant to leave the fish. A minute too long and it would be ruined. He could hear the crack of flesh against flesh. Would striking a child the first time he touched an instrument destroy his interest in music for life? He hurried to the rescue.

He stepped between Mikilauni and Moopuna. She tried to swat around his large frame and inadvertently hit his thigh. She gazed up at him with a fierce, wild look in her almond eyes. Her lips were parted, and she was slightly winded.

He knelt down to Moopuna. "Hey, man. You'll have to pick on something your own size. How about the violin? I'll bet you'd need a quarter size. Would you like that, Moopuna? An instrument of your very own?"

He nodded, stealing glimpses at Mikilauni.

"He wouldn't be able to learn it. He's too little."

"He's four. Some Susuki teachers take two-year-olds."

"How do you hold a violin? Like this or like this?" Mikilauni demonstrated air violin, first to her left side, then to her right."

"Like this." He leaned to the left. "Why do you ask?"

"Make the song come out," said Moopuna.

Why was Gordon so pleased? His career in music had been nothing but disappointment. Why then did his heart race at the mere hope that he could nurture Moopuna in string playing? He reached for the bow and drew it across the strings.

"Let me." Moopuna grabbed the bow in his fist and tried to yank it out of Gordon's grasp.

Mikilauni's hand struck like a snake. Moopuna scowled at her, then spat on her shoe. Gordon caught her arm, mid-swing.

"Come into the kitchen, Mikilauni. Moopuna, draw me a picture, will you?" He steered Moopuna to his little table and sat him down, carried the bass down the hall to his bedroom, then met Mikilauni in the kitchen. He flipped the charred shark steak, and turned to her, his heart palpitating with rage. "We need to talk."

"I'm sorry, Gordon, I really am. He'll stay out of your things. I will see to it."

"I don't care about my bass. Well, I do care, but I care more about Moopuna. You need to stop hitting him."

Mikilauni's black eyes snapped at him. "I got knocked around plenty as a kid."

"And I got the belt plenty of times, too. It hurt me the most inside, my self-worth."

"He's got to learn right from wrong. You see how disobedient he is, how disrespectful? You don't know how it is to raise a kid. You don't know what it's like to be a parent."

"I would like to."

She raised her head. The moisture in her eyes magnified their vulnerable hope. "What's this? You are saying you want me to have your baby?"

"No! I'm saying I want, I might want . . . if things work out . . . I'd like to adopt Moopuna."

She tilted her head, looked askance at him. "All men want their own kids. They can barely tolerate another man's son."

"All men are not me. I love Moopuna." A vertical crease formed in her brow, and he immediately understood why. He had not yet told her he loved *her*. He rushed on. "It's too soon to talk about marriage, but if things work out . . ."

"I see how it is. The dinosaur sheets and the violin lessons. It's not going to happen, Gordon. I'm not moving in here to play house with you, not without marriage." She crossed her arms and jutted forward her jaw. "I've got my own house. I don't need to shack up with a man to keep him."

"I wasn't suggesting it! I mean if things work out, I would want to marry you." This was not what he had meant to say, but now that it was out, he rushed on to his main point. "In the meantime, I think we should agree on how to discipline Moopuna."

She looked away, considering this, and then she said, "All right. We'll try your way. I'm telling you it won't work, but I suppose you'll have to find that out for yourself."

"No more hitting?"

"You're the boss." She clasped her hands around his neck. He wasn't too pleased with her answer, but he kissed her anyway. It was a relief to see her white smile again. He had made it through *the talk*.

She pressed her whole body into his. He opened one eye and looked behind her. Moopuna was in the doorway of the kitchen, staring at them, his mouth slightly open. Gordon broke away from her, calling over her shoulder. "Oh, Moopuna! Dinnertime! You like fish, don't you?"

"Can you make a tray for him, Gordon, so he can eat at his little table?"

"I've got a place fixed up for him right here." He pulled out a kitchen chair revealing a red plastic booster seat. He hoisted Moopuna by his armpits and settled him in. "There you go." He pulled out the chair to the right of Moopuna, and steered Mikilauni into it. "And here you go. Isn't this fun? Tonight I get to serve you." Gordon cut Moopuna's portion into tiny bite-sized pieces, then set the plates on the table.

Mikilauni cut a corner off her steak. She took a bite

and chewed. "Mmm. Very good. Very tender. What kind of fish is it — halibut?"

"No, shark," said Gordon proudly.

"Shark?" Mikilauni repeated incredulously. She leaned over and spit her mouthful on her plate. She leaped up, reached across the table, and with her finger, scooped the fish out of Moopuna's mouth. She took his portion and Gordon's and scraped it all on her plate.

"Are you two allergic?" he asked.

"It's taboo! My people worship the shark."

"What? I thought you were . . ."

"Catholic? Have you no respect for my ancestors? My people evolved from the shark." She jumped up and dashed out the back door, carrying the plate of fish.

Through the kitchen window, Gordon and Moopuna watched her down on her knees, digging a hole in the rose garden with her hands, apparently giving her people's creation god a Christian burial.

"Is Mama planting the fish?"

"I guess."

Moopuna shook his head slowly, his eyes like brown, wet buttons. "It will not grow. Fishes grow in the sea."

Late that night, the phone cried out. As always, it got his heart thumping. He thought of Carrie Clay. He reached an arm out of the bed, patted around the night stand. On the second ring, Mikilauni moaned in her sleep and rolled over. He picked up the phone.

"Gordon, I'm sorry to bother you so late. I need your help. Can you come over?"

It took all those words for him to comprehend who she was. She had never before called him Gordon. "Of course. What is it?"

"It's Tiffany. Something's happened. I can't leave her. Could you stop at the store?" She rattled off a list of supplies.

"My God! Hadn't you better call 911?"

Mikilauni sat up in bed. "Who is it? What is wrong?"

"I don't think it's necessary," said Cecilia. "I can handle this with your help."

"I'll be there as soon as I can." He hung up and swung his legs over the bed. Mikilauni caught his wrist. "What's going on?"

"I've got to go help a friend. It's an emergency. She's having some crisis with her roommate."

"She? Who is she?"

"Cecilia."

"Why is she calling you? Let the convent take care of her troubles."

"She's not in the convent any more."

"This is what worries me."

"Mikilauni." She knew how much time he spent with Cecilia, in tutorials and on the track. Every time he mentioned her name, Mikilauni pursed her lips. Lately he'd stopped mentioning Cecilia.

"Why didn't you tell her I was here with you? What kind of a man leaves one woman in his bed to go to another?" She rose to her feet and reached for her clothes.

"Don't go, honey. Please stay. Cecilia doesn't have anyone else to turn to if she's calling me."

"What happened?"

"I'm not sure. Some accident with her roommate, it seems. I'll tell you when I find out myself." He took the panties from her hand that she was trying to step into and pushed her gently into bed. "Here, now. Cover up. Brr!

It's cold." He tucked her in tightly. "You're going to have to keep the bed warm for the two of us."

When he tried to straighten up, she clutched his shoulders. "I don't like this. I think she's pulling something."

"Cecilia?" He laughed. "Cecilia doesn't pull things." He dressed quickly and kissed her good-bye. "Don't worry. I'll be back soon."

He was pulling on his overcoat, heading out the back door, when Mikilauni called through the house a final time. "Tell her you won't do this again. Tell her you're my man."

Chapter Twenty

Blood was splattered across the front of Cecilia's night-gown, caked on her hands, and encrusted in her cuticles and the fine lines of her knuckles. He stepped inside and she hastily shut the door behind him, then accepted the plastic grocery bag he offered. "Thank you, oh thank you for coming. Come on back, but let me warn you — it's grisly."

She led him down the dark, shadowy hall, and he stopped at the threshold of Tiffany's room, staring blankly. She was in bed, wearing the same type of convent-issue white flannel nightgown as Cecilia, but the cloth over her abdomen was soaked in blood. Cecilia had cut strips from a sheet and bound tourniquets around her wrists and ankles. Tiffany's right shoulder, which appeared at the neckline of her gown, was swollen and bruised; crimson trickled from her knees and her feet were caked in rust. Flailing against her pain, she seemed to be in a sort of hypnotic state, conscious, but unaware of Gordon, Cecilia, and her surroundings.

"There's too much blood," he said. "She needs medical care."

"And we're giving it to her," Cecilia replied calmly. From the grocery bag, she withdrew sponges, gauze, and adhesive tape. "Get the pot of water off the stove. It should be cool enough to use." When he did not respond, she added, "Please, Gordon. She'll be all right. She's in God's hands."

Lots of people in God's hands were not all right, but he didn't argue with her. Together they sponged away the blood, toweled Tiffany off, and wrapped and taped the gashes on her hands and feet. As they worked, he noticed the air was heavily scented, a familiar smell, which reminded him of church. Frankincense, stale sweat, decaying roses? No, those manifested a ponderous feeling, and this was light, tranquil, despite the violence that had occurred here. Tiffany lolled her head back and closed her eyes; her breathing was shallow, but steady. They changed the soiled bed linen, gently rolling her from side to side. Cecilia asked him to leave the room so she could bandage the wound at Tiffany's midriff and change her nightgown.

He reached down and ran his hand through the bloodied Kleenexes in the wastebasket by the bed. He dropped to his stomach and searched under the bed. He rummaged through the drawer of the nightstand, even looked between the mattress and springs.

"What are you looking for?" Cecilia asked.

"You know." In the bathroom, he looked in the trash, the toilet, the clothes hamper, the tub. He went into the kitchen and checked in the garbage behind the curtain under the sink, then started going through the drawers.

He became aware of Cecilia, standing quietly beside him, now changed into jeans and a T-shirt. "She's sleeping peacefully."

"How do you know she isn't unconscious due to blood loss?"

"I know."

He remembered then that she had administered to the

sick in India and did volunteer work at the hospital. She must have had some medical training. "Do you know what she used as a weapon?"

"Weapon?"

"What she cut herself with. It looked like she scraped the skin off her knees and shoulder with a razor, maybe. She must have hit her shoulder with something heavy like a hammer, maybe a rolling pin. The palms and feet, those wounds looked like they were done with an ice pick. Oh, right, the wounds of Christ. Do you have an ice pick in here?" His hands were shaking as he stirred up the contents of a drawer, clanking together spatulas, potato mashers, and serving spoons. "Ah, here, it is." He held up the ice pick, but its worn, paint-chipped wooden handle was bone dry. "No, this hasn't been used lately."

"You still don't get it, do you?"

"Get what? That she's a lunatic? It could have been scissors or a knife. The police will want to know. And we are reporting this, Cecilia. If you aren't, I am. You aren't doing her any favors keeping it quiet. Anyone who self-mutilates this drastically needs psychiatric care." He scooped up utensils and let them crash onto the counter. He was beginning to sweat. A thought was creeping up the back of his head like a hood, and he felt if he made enough noise and kept busy with his frantic search, he could keep it from completely forming.

He stopped. He turned, leaning heavily against the counter, panting slightly. Cecilia's face was more pale than ever, but calm, radiant. Now he was beyond the dawning. Now he was just slow to acceptance. "*It's real?*"

She made the sign of the cross. "Truly, she is blessed."

He stepped toward Tiffany's room as if witnessing her one more time would make it more believable. He knew it would not. He froze, faced Cecilia again. "How'd it start?"

"The sensation of it has been coming on for some time, I think. She's been bedridden for weeks; the fasting has made her weak. For days she's been rubbing her palms, complaining of itching. I thought she just had dry skin from dehydration. Then today, Friday . . ."

"Friday, of course! It usually happens on a Friday."

"I didn't actually see the wounds open. It was around 10 p.m.; I was already asleep. She called out to me for help, frightened at first, hysterical. When I rushed into her room, there was already quite a lot of blood. I knew the moment I saw it what it was. That unearthly fragrance in her room — did you smell it?"

He nodded, hugging himself. "She had more than the five wounds. Her knees and shoulder . . ."

Cecilia nodded. "That's fairly common, too. Their afflictions tend to reflect the crucifix or image they contemplate."

He could picture the bloody crucifix she had kissed and gyrated before in the church. It was much like the one hanging over her bed. "What an amazing thing the human brain is!"

"God is the amazing one, the one who created the human brain, the one who chose Tiffany!"

He shrugged and added offhandedly. "Or it could be the devil."

"Oh, Sweet Jesus! I've thought of that too!" Her face tensed, her body swayed. He reached out to her, not because he thought she would faint, but because she needed support. Her arms came around him, and they held each other a few moments, almost dancing without moving their feet. "Oh, Gordon, I was so frightened at first, but then I prayed to the Lord Jesus and he sent me strength and peace." Firmly, she pushed away from him. "Then I was able to attend to her. I'm afraid I overdid it. I must go to confession tomorrow, today, I mean. My faith has not been pure. It was wrong of me to tie the tourniquets on her wrists and ankles."

"You were only trying to save her life!"

"God's laws of nature do not apply to miracles. It was up to him to decide how much blood would flow out of her. Do you think I can stop the hand of God? In interfering with his work, I have sinned." She looked down at the worn green linoleum, and then back up at him. "Something else is on my conscience. Remember my Halloween costume? Oh, I meant it as a tribute to St. Francis, of course, but maybe he saw it as ridicule. It may have been blasphemous."

"Cecilia, stop. You're beating yourself up for nothing. I imagine St. Francis is glad anyone remembers him at all." It was a ludicrous thing to say, as if he believed someone dead for over seven hundred years had any consciousness at all.

"There's more. Tiffany saw my costume. Could that have had something to do with this?"

"The power of suggestion? But not because of your costume—it's all those hours she's been meditating on the crucifix." He held out his hands before himself and studied them. "I can't imagine. It really feels as if the nails are being driven in?"

She nodded. "It's excruciatingly painful. Already she's suffered such agony."

"What's next?"

"I don't know. Sometimes it only happens once.

Sometimes it lasts for years or an entire lifetime. We'll have to see."

"Are you sure you're going to be able to handle this?"

"Yes, yes." She pushed her hair off her brow, exhausted. "Thank you for coming. I didn't know who else to call, who else could keep a secret. You understand how important it is that no one finds out, don't you? Droves of people would be prowling around here, trying to get a look at her. We'd never have any peace. It would hurt her chances for placement in another convent. The Church frowns on miracles. This sort of thing is bad publicity."

"Suppose it gets to be too much for you?"

"There's Jack. He'll have to be in on it, too. He comes over every day to give her Communion. He'll understand about secrecy. "

He wondered why she hadn't called the priest instead of himself.

She looked into the distance, trying to think it through. "I hope he can handle it. I like Jack, he's a dear friend, a good priest, but he's kind of a wimp, you know?"

"It will be a learning experience for him: his first stigmatic."

She smiled wearily. "You make it sound like there's going to be a second and a third."

She walked him to the door and they said goodnight. Outside the heavens were jammed with stars; four planets were lined up beneath the moon in a kind of arc, Venus and Mars glowing brightest. The universe seemed too huge, too ancient to make much difference to it that some guy on this puny planet had been crucified a mere 2,000 years ago. Gazing up, Gordon was filled with awe and wonder and gratitude. He would never understand its mystery; he figured he wasn't meant to. He was only glad he had got his chance, his life, his pinpoint of existence, here, now, with the people he loved. He did love Mikilauni, he decided, and Moopuna and Cecilia. With such a great outpouring of feeling, he might even love Art Bunch.

The stairs creaked beneath his step. A voice in the darkness hissed, "Shame on you."

It was an expression his mother had used on him; he hadn't heard it in decades. There, in the lower apartment, an old woman's face appeared from around the curtain. The window was open, and only the screen was between them. Gordon remembered her name — Faye Marie. "You think you can sneak away in the night, but God is watching. God knows what you do with that harlot up in that apartment."

He did not reply, but he had to grin to himself. Hopefully, her old eyes were not keen enough to see his expression in the dark.

At home, he found Mikilauni's car gone. He rushed into the house and phoned her, but there was no answer. Probably if he drove to her house, she would not open the door, either. Well, it was best to give her time to cool down. He had already decided half-truths would merely ensnare him; it was better to give her no explanation at all.

He undressed and, shivering in the dark, he put on his musical flannel nightgown. He slid under the covers, but could not sleep. When he closed his eyes, he saw blood. What was so terrifying about blood? It was supposed to stay on the *inside*. He dozed. He dreamed of bloody crucifixes, whippings, decapitations, Art in his devil costume,

the devil himself. The Christ Child appeared at his bed-
side and told him to believe that Tiffany was a saint. He
was arguing, reasoning with the child. His active brain
woke him. The Christ Child was still staring at him, the
whites of his sad eyes glimmering in the dark. Gordon
screamed.

The child screamed. He recoiled and began to cry.

Gordon sat on the edge of the bed. "Ah, Jeez, Moopuna, you scared me."

"Not-uh. You scared me."

"I guess we scared each other. I'm sorry."

Moopuna smiled, catching a tear on his tongue.
"You're wearing a dress."

"I think for us guys they call them nightshirts."

"I've never seen an uncle in a dress."

"I am not an uncle! I'm your . . . friend." He ventured
on. "Sort of a papa."

Moopuna shook his head. "No, you're not. Papas
beat kids."

"Not all papas. I didn't know you were still here. I
thought you'd gone home with your mama." What was
Mikilauni thinking, leaving him alone? What would have
happened if he had awakened and found no adults in the
house? Where *was* Mikilauni? He doubted now that she
had gone home. Had she run to her mother or sisters or
a friend, sobbing and spilling out horrible accusations
about him?

Moopuna looked around him, checking to see that his
mother was truly not in the bed. It seemed to give him
the go-ahead. He crawled into Gordon's lap and put his
arms around his neck.

"That's a boy. Come on, I'll take you back to your
bed."

"I'm afraid of my bed."

"You are? How come?"

"I'm afraid the dinosaurs will bite me."

"I thought you loved dinosaurs."

"Not in the dark."

"I see. Well, how about you sleep here and I sleep in the dinosaur bed?" This was a big sacrifice, since his bed was much more comfortable than the daybed. Moopuna rolled out of his lap and wriggled under the covers. He batted Gordon's upper arm, trying to get him to lie down. "Let's both sleep here."

Gordon stretched out on his side, certain he was breaking some code of ethics, having a child in bed with him. He could get arrested for child molestation or psychologically warp Moopuna for life. He took a deep breath. Moopuna clutched his bicep and cuddled into the small of his back. The child's presence was a comfort, a blessing. Gordon took a deep breath and let his body go limp. He'd rest for a moment while Moopuna fell asleep, then carry him back to his bed.

He opened his eyes to daylight.

Chapter Twenty-one

Old Mama's place was only a few streets away from Mikilauni's, but it might as well have been halfway around the world. Her neighborhood was little more than a slum, and her house was one of the most rundown. She lived with her four grown children, sons Inoke and Peleki and daughters Kali and Salote. No wonder, thought Gordon, that Mikilauni took pride in having escaped with Moopuna.

In front of the house, the small patch of scruffy lawn was now a parking lot with four pickup trucks of various colors, heights, and conditions, and one small dump truck, which, Mikilauni explained, was used for Inoke's and Peleki's tree-trimming service. Beer bottles, apparently, were a source of valued decor because they was pressed into the ground to border the flower beds that contained various vegetables — tomatoes, squash, and some Gordon couldn't identify.

Inside the house, one wall was nearly covered floor to ceiling with a pyramid of beer bottles. Several lawn chairs and a sagging brown couch were shoved aside to accommodate mammoth plywood boards set on sawhorses. Gathered around the makeshift table was Mikilauni's immediate family and another dozen family members and friends. Gordon was wedged between

Mikilauni and Inoke — a giant of a man, seated on two chairs, one for each butt cheek. He and Peleki had cooked a whole pig in the backyard in an underground rock oven called an *umu,* and then hacked it to pieces and set it on a huge platter, positioning the head in front of the ruined animal.

"They could have left the head outside," Gordon muttered to Mikilauni, but Inoke heard him.

"That is to fool you, *palangi,*" he said. "Dis really dog," and everyone in earshot laughed.

Gordon took a helping of the pork and a little bit of most everything else. He recognized mashed sweet potatoes, mashed squash, mashed taro, but it was hard to tell what the mash of sweet-tasting meat was.

"What is this?" he asked Mikilauni.

"Fruit bat," said Inoke.

Should Gordon believe him? There were thousands of bats in Goldhurst; some evenings he could count as many as thirty stacked in a heap and clinging upside down in a dark corner of his porch, but he didn't know what kind they were, and he had never heard of anyone eating bats of any kind.

"You like fruit bat, *palangi*?" Inoke asked him. "Dis cooked in de *umu,* but better barbecued."

"Tastes like chicken," said Peleki. The younger brother was about two-thirds of Inoke's size, but well over two hundred fifty pounds.

"It's my Aunt Mauli's mincemeat," said Mikilauni.

"What kind of meat?" Gordon asked.

"Beef," said Mikilauni.

"Dog," said Inoke. "Dog good eating. Very sweet."

"Taste like chicken," said Peleki.

"You said the pig was dog," said Gordon.

"Dis poodle dog," Inoke said, pointing to the mince-meat, "dis collie dog," he said, pointing to the pork. "You have dog, *palangi*? We come over to your house and eat him." Inoke nudged Gordon, causing his elbow to slip off the table.

"I'm not a dog lover," said Gordon. "I never owned one."

"*Gets es gut*," said Old Mama, showing brown stumps that were once teeth. If it were true that girls eventually turned into their mothers at a certain age, Miki-launi's prospects weren't pretty. Old Mama had fleshy love handles between her breasts and upper arms, which oozed from the armholes of her muumuu. Her gray, tangled hair flowed to her waist. Her cheeks, round as plums, squeezed her eyes nearly shut. She spoke with her hand held to her mouth, in an attempt to conceal her rotten teeth.

"Get it, *palangi*?" asked Inoke, his chin shining with pork grease. "Yeah, Mama. Cats are good. Horse, too. Yum, yum. I eat it all, even long pig."

"What is long pig?" asked Gordon.

"Stop!" said Mikilauni.

"*Pekkle*," said Old Mama.

"Get it?" asked Inoke, whacking Gordon with his elbow again. "People. I've even eaten a human bean."

"Tastes like chicken," interjected the sullen sister, Salote, her first words. She was the little sister, barely out of high school, although she was the largest of the three sisters in stature, built like a turnip, if you counted her hairdo. She was named after Salote, queen of Tonga.

Obviously the Kukula family was putting Gordon through a peculiar hazing, which brothers often did to the new boyfriends of their sisters, and Gordon tried to be good-natured about it, but then Inoke stepped over the line. "Sometimes when I look at Moopuna, I get so hungry, I think what is dis leetle black boy gut for? I eat him."

Moopuna's eyes grew big and he slipped halfway down his chair to get out of the reach of his uncle.

"I will put heem in the *umu* and cook heem right now," said Inoke, lunging across the table surprisingly quick for his size, and Moopuna screamed and disappeared under the table. Gordon felt him crawling on his shoes.

"Moopuna! Get back here and eat your dinner," called Mikilauni, but his food was left untouched.

Gordon didn't feel much like eating, either. The pork was pink and tough; despite all the hours sunk underground, it did not seem sufficiently cooked.

After countless helpings, Inoke looked over at the mound of pork remaining on Gordon's plate. "You going to eat dat?" he asked. Without waiting for an answer, he reached over and grabbed the meat off Gordon's plate with fingers thick as cigars.

After dinner, Gordon wandered into an empty room, a sort of den. Out the window he could see the gaping hole from which the pig had been exhumed, now smoking like a miniature volcano. On the back porch steps sat Moopuna, serving his time-out for leaving the table without permission. The back door swung open, and he looked up expectantly. Old Mama, clutching trash bags in both fists, tottered by him as if he weren't there.

Gordon turned away from the window and began to peruse the shelves, cluttered with knickknacks. One icon had ponderous breasts, beefy shoulders and calves, a blank stare, and an elongated, angry mouth. Was this a god of fertility or a god of destruction?

"Ah, here's the new uncle."

He felt his neck redden, having been caught staring at enormous breasts in a room he had entered uninvited. He looked toward the door to see who had addressed him. She was a thinner, shorter version of Mikilauni, in a black Spandex mini dress. She wore an armful of bangles and her hair was stacked a mile high.

"Excuse me?" he said.

"When we were growing up, Mama would call the men she had over 'uncles.' We have always referred to our lovers as uncles — a family joke."

"You're Kali?"

"Yes, the big sister."

"I thought your parents were together until your father died."

"They were. Sort of. Papa would go away for months, years at a time."

"To work?"

"Yeah. To work, to live with another woman for a while, whatever." Her lips curved into an ironic smirk. "Are you shocked, Uncle?"

"I thought you were raised Catholic."

"Oh, we are. And as islanders. That's why we're all so screwed up, trying to live the duplicity."

"Just because a culture doesn't share the same values as white western Europeans doesn't mean that it's screwed up."

"Don't you say all the right things now, *palangi?*"

"Your brother keeps calling me that. What does it mean?"

"White guy. Didn't you notice? You're the only one here." She sauntered toward him, one lean leg directly before the other, like a cat. "Did you have some multicultural lessons at the college?"

"Some," he admitted.

"Did they clue you in on what the smart white men didn't realize? Not the ones that came over to slaughter us poor, ignorant savages and blow up our islands, but the ones who came to save our souls — the missionaries. What they didn't realize is that you can put a coat of Christianity over the top of pagans, but they're still pagans at the core."

"I think the early Christians did realize it. That's why they let all sorts of pagan rituals seep into Christian celebrations, the adoration of the egg at Easter, the cutting of a tree at Christmas, both symbols of fertility, if I recall correctly." He could tell from her eyes that he had thrown her off guard by taking their conversation seriously.

"I wasn't talking about every fucking pagan in history."

"Sorry."

Her smile became a little more friendly then. "Mikilauni was brave to expose you to the whole clan so soon. That's a big mistake she makes with all her uncles. She can't wait to show one off. Wants to show Mama she snagged a man before he runs away."

"I don't see that Mikilauni would have any trouble keeping boyfriends."

"She works like a man."

"And what do you do?"

She clapped her hands once, accompanied by the ringing of her bracelets. "I take care of Mama."

Mama seemed perfectly capable of taking care of herself, but he didn't feel like sparring with Kali further. He turned to look out the window in hopes of discouraging any further conversation, watching Moopuna hugging himself against the November gusts.

"Ugly little kid, isn't he?" Kali's breath was warm on his cheek.

He sidestepped away from her, knowing that made him look defensive. "On the contrary. I think he's gorgeous."

Kali sniffed. "With that flat, nigger nose? His father was a black man, you know."

"So?"

"You might not care, but it's shameful to Mikilauni. She tried the coat hanger routine on herself, but she didn't know the right place to poke. Are you shocked by your good little Catholic girl?"

"This is all so very interesting, Kali, but I think we should get back to the party." He took a retreating step.

She smirked. "You don't have to run from me, Uncle. I won't bite. How do you like that fancy tattoo Mikilauni has on her ass? I've got one just like it. Want to see?"

"No."

"Ah, it's all right. Mikilauni and me have shared our uncles before. You know there is no word in our language for cousin?" She turned her backside toward him and leaned over the end table, causing her dress to inch upwards. The short skirt didn't have far to go, and she wasn't wearing stockings.

Actually, he did want to see. He wanted to pull the now-visible thong aside, unzip his pants, and shove in, and he hoped that she would struggle, because that would make it better. Strange how a man could desire a woman who disgusted him as much as one who attracted him.

Kali was a piece of work, having succeeded in bringing out the rapist in him, an aspect of himself he hadn't yet discovered. He looked away from her brown, trim ass, but not before glimpsing *them,* the nickel-shaped scars on her right haunch. He hustled to the door.

"Maybe some other time, *palangi.* You know where to find me."

At the door he paused, but didn't dare glance back at her. "How'd they get there?"

"Papa's way of extinguishing his cigar."

"I'm sorry," he muttered, and advanced down the hall in three long strides. Instead of turning left to join the party in the living room, he turned right toward the front door. He went outside, around the house, and found a gate leading to the backyard. He let himself in. Spotting him, Moopuna's smile began in the depths of his black eyes, then ricocheted into all the crevices of his face. Gordon took his hand, and wordlessly they dashed toward the gate. Kali was framed in the window of the den, laughing at him, but he didn't care. He routed Moopuna across the front lawn and loaded him into the new car seat he had bought for the back of his car.

"Isn't Mama coming with us?" he asked.

"We're not going home. You and I just need a break from all the fun we're having at Old Mama's."

"I wasn't having fun. Where are we going?"

"Where do you want to go?"

"For ice cream."

Of course, on Thanksgiving Day in Goldhurst, the ice cream shop and the drugstore soda fountain were closed. Main Street was like a ghost town, and there wasn't a single car in the K-Mart strip mall out on the highway. He drove around and around looking for something better than the 7-Eleven. He headed out to the freeway onramp and found the McDonald's opened.

Inside the restaurant, three workers stood idly talking behind the counter. Their only customer returned Gordon's gaze, but then nonchalantly looked away as if she didn't recognize him. Fine, if she wanted to play that game. Who else would wear red velvet gloves while wolfing down a sloppy Big Mac? Cecilia, he knew, would be at the Good News Center most of the day, serving turkey dinners to the needy. It was the perfect opportunity for Tiffany, the big phony, to sneak out of the apartment for a burger. Subsisting on a single communion wafer per day, indeed!

At the counter, he asked Moopuna, "So what will it be? Hot fudge sundae, no nuts? Anything to drink?"

Moopuna dropped his head and peered shyly through his dangling ringlets. "Can I have a number six?"

Gordon laughed. Moopuna didn't like half-cooked pork any more than he did. And no dinky Happy Meal for this boy; he didn't give a damn about the toy, but loved the nuggets and fries. Gordon's mouth watered at the thought of hot, crispy fries. He'd sworn off them for some time, but now he could use a splurge. "Two number sixes," he ordered. This was turning out to be a damn fine Thanksgiving after all.

He decided to avoid further eye contact with Tiffany by choosing a table at the opposite side of the vacant restaurant, but while he was filling drinks at the beverage bar, she approached him.

Moopuna aimed his forefinger at her and announced, "That lady has a flower growing out of her head."

"It may look like that, but it's not really. See, it's artificial." The woman bent down to allow Moopuna to inspect her hat. It looked like the same Victorian-style hat Gordon had seen Tiffany wear in church, except that it was trimmed differently, with a bright red flower shooting out of the brim like an antennae.

"Don't point at people, Moopuna. Sorry, Tiffany."

"Now, isn't that funny? When you came in you looked at me like you thought you recognized me. I thought, he must think I'm Tiffany. I'm Sandy, her twin sister, out here on a visit from St. Louis."

He scrutinized the woman. As much as she looked liked Tiffany, he could see the differences. Her face was fuller, sweeter, the muscles relaxed, the eyes, not set in dark hollows, but clear and bright. Her physique seemed heavier than Tiffany's but her woolen winter coat made it hard to tell.

"Good to meet you. I'm Gordon Clay."

"Gordon? Not Cecilia's friend, Gordon?" She bent her head toward him, whispering, "You *know*."

"Yes."

"Tiffany called me with the news on Saturday. Of course, I hopped the first plane out here. Cecilia told me all about you, how helpful you were. Isn't it miraculous? I'm still in awe that God sent roses to my own sister, of all women."

"Aren't you a little worried about her?"

"Worried? Why would I be worried? I'm thrilled."

"She's starving herself."

"She finds nourishment in the body of Christ. What I'm concerned about is the *pain*. If only she could find a way to escape the pain."

"Maybe a doctor should examine her."

"She prayed for union with Christ through the partaking of His passion. Her prayers were answered." She smiled serenely. "What does that have to do with a doctor?"

Moopuna clutched a handful of Gordon's pant leg and was tugging him toward their table. He went in the direction of his pants, stepping backward. "Well, uh, enjoy your stay in California." What else could he say? What exactly do you say to a stigmatic's proud sister?

Chapter Twenty-two

Mikilauni didn't say a word to him on the ride home from Old Mama's. As soon as the three of them walked into her house she ordered, "Go put your pajamas on, Moopuna." After he left the room, she turned on Gordon. "You deserted me! You're always deserting me!"

He would like nothing better than to retreat to his own house alone in peace, after all the commotion of the day, but he thought better of acting on his own selfish needs. "We did not desert you. We merely went for a little treat."

"To that ex-nun's place?"

"No, and please call her Cecilia. You know her name."

"What exactly happened the night you went over there?"

"Mikilauni, we've been over this. Her roommate has mental problems. You never told me where you went, leaving Moopuna all alone in my house."

"You said you were coming right back. You did come right back, didn't you? I didn't see any reason to take my poor baby out into the freezing cold in the dead of the night just because you deserted us both for that ex-nun. Where did you two go this afternoon?"

"I took Moopuna for a sundae. It's as simple as that. Your brother was terrorizing him."

"Shh! Listen." She looked toward the hall. He could hear it, too—the repeated squeak of bed springs. "He's jumping on the bed again, no matter how many times I tell him not to. Since you said no more spankings he knows he can do whatever he wants and get away with it."

Gordon pitched his voice down the hall. "Moopuna! Cut it out, man. Go brush your teeth."

She crossed her arms. "Like he's really going to do what he's told just because you asked him."

"Well, it's not worth beating him. You were hurt as a child. I've seen the scars, and now I know how you got them."

She flipped her long hair over her shoulder. "How could you? It was an accident. I sat on a hot radiator when I was a little girl."

"That's not what Kali told me."

"Kali! Don't believe anything she says! She hates me and she always tries to steal my boyfriends."

"She told me your dad used to . . ."

"A pack of lies! She wants to turn you against me." Her beautiful face crumpled; her full upper lip quivered. "Go to her if you believe her and not me! Kali always wins!"

Mikilauni gripped his shoulders and shoved him toward the door. He resisted, but she nearly overpowered him. Her fierceness alarmed him. He turned to her, tried to embrace her. She flailed her arms to keep him away.

"Honey, stop. Kali is just jealous of you."

She stopped swinging her windmill arms. "She told you that?"

"She didn't have to, it's obvious. Now tell me the truth about the scars. It wasn't the radiator, was it?"

She dropped her head against her wrist. "I can't! It's too shameful."

"Shameful for the one who did it, not for you, the victim."

"How come it doesn't feel that way? How come it feels like I deserved what I got?"

He encircled her in his arms and pulled her close. He kissed her hair, her fingertips. "No child deserves what you got."

From Moopuna's room came a loud thud that shook the house and then a howl. Gordon dashed down the hall, Mikilauni behind him. The throw rug was humped against the wall. Moopuna was face down on the hardwood floor. Gordon lifted him and set him on his outstretched knee. On the floor was a mini-pond of blood and spit, a tiny white object swimming. Moopuna sobbed, blood, tears, and spit running down his chin. He clenched his teeth and wiggled the tip of his tongue through the tiny hole where his right, upper-front tooth had been. Above his left eye was a triangular indention, matching in size and angle the corner of his bed. It began to bleed.

"Mama!" he shrieked, elbowing Gordon away and lunging for Mikilauni. He fell forward, squatted on his heels, and clutched her legs. She bent down, placed her hand on his head, and pushed it back to inspect the damage. "Oh, poor baby. See what happens when you don't mind Mama? God has punished you."

Gordon cringed. His mother had used the same expression on him, and he hated it. He had spent his whole childhood being afraid of God. He went to the kitchen to make an ice pack. When he returned, Mikilauni was seated on the floor, Moopuna huddled in her lap, trying to burrow his head into her breasts.

When Gordon pressed the ice against his forehead, Moopuna kicked and screamed. "It looks bad. We better get him to the emergency room."

"Oh, no, it's nothing. He'll be fine." She hovered over Moopuna, despite her breezy comments.

"He's not fine, Mikilauni. He may need stitches."

"Go into my top bureau drawer, would you? Right in front there are bandages."

In her bedroom, he opened the drawer. He ran his hand over the powders, old makeup, and lotions. He reached to the far back of the drawer, felt a box, and pulled it out. Condoms, a package of a dozen, two gone, but not used by him. He stood motionless, thinking back to their first night together. These had been here. She had sent him out into the cold for no reason. He replaced the condoms, withdrew the box of bandages next to it, then returned to Moopuna's room.

"Thank God it's only a baby tooth," he said. "Let's patch him up as best as we can, then take him to emergency."

"On a holiday night? The place will be packed! Hours of waiting."

He pictured all of Mikilauni's family lined up for liver transplants having eaten uncooked pork. "Still, we better have him checked out."

"No!" Her strident voice alarmed him. "He'll be fine."

"Then I'll take him."

"You can't. You're not his legal guardian. They won't treat him without my consent. You're overreacting, Gordon. Let's put him to bed."

Moopuna had stopped crying and was now staring blankly. His eyelashes fluttered, his eyes rolled back, and his body went limp.

"Oh, God. Now we're definitely going. He could have a concussion, internal bleeding." He scooped up Moopuna and tried to rise.

She caught his forearm, her eyes welling up. "Gordon, if we take him, I might be arrested."

"Jesus! How many times has he been to the ER?"

"Three. One wasn't even my fault, like this one. They'll never believe this was another accident."

"That's ridiculous. We'll just tell them what happened. Neither of us was even in the room."

She shook her head, hot tears spilling down her cheeks. "The county social worker there — she knows me, my family. Child Protective Services could take Moopuna away from me."

He looked at the small, motionless body. "Okay, I think I know what we can do."

He made the phone call to Henry Musgrave, and again, much sooner than he ever expected, he was bearing instead of turning, straining his eyes for movable landmarks such as ABORTION KILLS signs on flatbed trailers and resetting his odometer at steel bridges.

Mikilauni set a hand on his thigh and squeezed lightly. "Gordon, say something."

"I have nothing to say." His mind was swirling like a fierce red and yellow carnival ride, the kind that always made him vomit. His thoughts were going too fast, blurring like objects glimpsed at top speed, and he couldn't latch onto a single one to make sense of the situation. His wrecked beauty, her injured son. Their lives were too messy; he'd never be able to set things in order. He would have to accept them as they were or walk away.

"You're thinking, though," she said. "You're thinking what a horrible mother I am, that I am cruel and evil."

"I'm not. This isn't your fault."

"Tell me what you're thinking then."

"I'm a little overwhelmed right now. Just let me be."

"Just say something, Gordon. Anything."

Reaching out to still a single, swirling car on the carnival ride, he said, "I found your stash of condoms."

"Oh my God." She dropped her face into her hands.

"Why did you tell me that first night that you didn't have any?"

"You can figure that one out, can't you? I didn't want you to get the idea I had men over all the time."

"I wouldn't get that idea. And what if I did? If that's what you do, then that's what you do, that's who you are. I wish to hell you'd stop *presenting* yourself to me in a way you think might be more appealing. Just be you, that's all I ask."

She sniffled. She had been crying so quietly he didn't realize she had started up again. In a very small voice, she said, "What if you don't like me?"

"I do like you. I'm crazy for you." He avoided a near collision with the *L* word, the one he wasn't ready to proclaim to her, but she didn't seem to notice. He put his arm around her and she slumped against his chest. He stroked her long hair, until his hand came to pet one lovely, pendulous breast.

They fell silent. Finally Gordon said, "Promise me you'll never lay a hand on him again."

"I have already promised this. I've stuck to it. You don't understand how utterly alone I was, before you, how awful it was for Moopuna and me living at Mama's, how mean Kali and my brothers can be."

"I think I got a taste of that today. We're not leaving him at your mother's ever again. We go out, we hire a babysitter."

"If we ever do go out without him." She was staring out the windshield, her voice low and flat.

It was true that he preferred the three of them to be together. After Moopuna's bedtime was soon enough for lovemaking. He understood now that he hadn't been fair to her. She needed romantic dinners in dimly lit restaurants and getaway weekends at bed-and-breakfasts. He vowed he would give her more of that, if only he could find reliable care for Moopuna.

When at last they arrived at the Musgrave Llama Ranch, they found the driveway filled with cars. Of course all of Henry's kids and grand kids would be home, and Allegra would be hosting a big dinner for them.

"Damn, I forgot all about the holiday," said Gordon. "Let's go around back to the kitchen door."

He took Moopuna out of his car seat, and carried him against his shoulder. Henry, who had been expecting them, greeted them on the back porch.

"Sorry to barge in on you like this, Henry."

"It's all right. I know what ERs are like on holidays. Glad to help out."

Gordon and Mikilauni followed Henry into the house, and Allegra met them in the kitchen. She looked festive in a green brocade dress, the bodice embroidered with orange and gold leaves. From the great room came a flood of light, laughter, and squeals of "Movie! Sounds like eye. Die! Cry! *The Crying Game.* Yes!"

Allegra brushed the ringlets off Moopuna's forehead. "Oh, poor lamb! That is a nasty bump!"

"He was jumping on his bed and fell off," Mikilauni explained anxiously.

"Let's have a good look, now, shall we?" Henry led them through the kitchen, into his home office, and Gordon laid Moopuna on the examining table. Henry asked questions about the fall as he looked into his mouth, then shone a light under his eyelids. "Well, you folks could have saved yourselves the trip out here."

"No concussion?" asked Gordon.

"No, sir."

"You should have seen the way his eyes rolled back in their sockets." Gordon flung back his head to demonstrate. "It scared the hell out of me."

"Just exhaustion," said Henry. "Probably too big a day for a little guy."

"What about his tooth?" asked Mikilauni.

"You could double-check with his dentist, but I imagine the permanent tooth will grow in normally."

"He looks like a six-year-old at four," said Gordon.

Allegra came to the doorway, followed by the old spaniel Hunding, which began to bark. Moopuna awoke, blinking and rubbing his eyes, smiling shyly at Hunding. Soon he was laughing and using an old sock to play a game of tug-of-war with the dog.

In the kitchen, Allegra asked, "Would you like anything? Coffee? Pie? I've got pumpkin and grasshopper."

"No, thanks. We couldn't eat another bite," said Mikilauni. "My brothers roasted a whole pig."

Moopuna pointed at the counter. "I want that."

Allegra held her spatula over the pumpkin pie. "This one?"

"No, that." He was pointing at the aerosol can of whipped cream.

"Open wide." Allegra squirted it directly into his mouth. Moopuna swallowed and grinned, revealing the tiny space where his tooth had been.

"Pie actually sounds great," said Gordon.

"That's the holiday spirit. Stuff it down." Allegra got out a plate. "Which kind?"

"Some of each. And lots of whipped cream."

It had been that kind of day.

Chapter Twenty-three

It all came back to him. Walking on the pathway in Sutter Park, the duck pond to his right, the playground to his left, he felt a pain surge through his body, quick but acute, like tinfoil on a filling. He was reliving his profound unhappiness. The wearing of the Holter harness, the kid cop asking him to leave, merely one year earlier, what seemed like a lifetime ago. He no longer had dizzy spells, he had stopped monitoring his blood pressure, and he had to buy smaller pants just to keep them up. Life was good, and it was all because of Mikilauni and Moopuna.

He cupped his hand over his eyes, scanning the climbing structure for the little guy. The plan was to pick him up, meet Mikilauni here, and then the three of them were going downtown for Moopuna's first Susuki violin lesson. Gordon spotted the potato-shaped caregiver across the playground, talking to a short blonde woman in a navy blue suit. He was going to find Moopuna, and then he was going to swing him, in front of Potato Body and her partner, in front of God and everybody. Now he lay claim. Now he was Moopuna's . . . well, he was Moopuna's mother's boyfriend. Certainly that was *some* claim; he wished it were more. He wished Potato Body would come over and say, "Get moving, buddy," and he could reply, "Excuse me, I am the boy's *father.*"

Now the caregiver was pointing at him, saying something to the short blonde woman. Turning toward the parking lot in expectation of Mikilauni driving up, he saw a tall, muscular guy with a shaved head being pulled toward the playground by a dog on a leash. The dog had a German shepherd head and dachshund legs. It looked so ridiculous that Gordon admired the man's self-confidence at being seen with it. The dog started running in circles around a tree, wrapping the leash around the trunk like a ribbon wrapping a maypole. The man started running around the tree, too, but it was a lost cause. The dog was about three laps ahead of him and was a faster runner. The man was laughing at his predicament.

An open palm of money was presented to Gordon.

"Twenty-four dollars, right?" The short blonde woman was pretty close up, but thought her looks would be improved by drawing black circles around her eyes. Deep set lines around her little mouth harbored bitterness, perhaps toward him, maybe toward men in general. "Go ahead, take it. Even though you explained over the phone why you paid for my son's day care last spring, I don't quite understand it. I don't feel like owing you anything, so here." She moved her fingers closer to his chest, so he took the money, reached for his wallet in his back pocket, and put away the bills. She curved her hand over the side of her mouth and shouted toward the top of the climbing structure, "Gordie! Get down!"

Should he try again to explain himself to Carrie Clay? Thank God he had Mikilauni and Moopuna now. Thank God he wasn't the desperate, dizzy loser he'd been. "I just had to know your son was safe."

"So you actually bribed Annette to get information about Gordie? Too bizarre." She was looking in the distance at her son, a big lug of a kid with a shaved head, appearing much older than six. He was hanging by his arms from the top of the climbing structure, his fleshy potbelly peeking out from beneath his T-shirt, his baggy pants revealing three inches of boxer shorts at the waist.

"Gordie, get down from there. I'm not going to ask you again."

"Dad's taking me."

"Yeah, right," she muttered under her breath, then addressed Gordon. "It's a real coincidence you having a child in this day care."

"Oh, my girlfriend does. That day I came here looking for Gordie, I met Moopuna."

Her wide blue eyes were ringed with white, which was ringed with black eye liner like matching bull's-eyes. "This is too bizarre. You met your girlfriend here? My Gordie brought you two together?"

"Moopuna is her son. First I met him, then her."

"This is too bizarre." She was pretty when she laughed, despite the raccoon eyes. Mikilauni, who was approaching them, thought so, too. She looked from Carrie to him and then back at Carrie.

"Oh, hi, Mikilauni." He thought a kiss hello might smooth things over, but he wasn't used to greeting her like that in public. It seemed too effusive, and then the moment passed. "This is Carrie. She has a son here, too. We just met."

"Well, not exactly, just met," said Carrie, giving him a knowing look. "We've *talked* before." She must have seen the look of alarm on Mikilauni's face, because she added, "He's been telling me how you two guys met here."

Mikilauni gave Gordon a perplexed look.

"God damn it, Carrie, I told you I was coming." The shaved-headed, muscular guy with the stupid-looking dog walked toward them.

"Shit, Gordon, you never confirmed whether you were coming today or tomorrow."

"You know I take hot yoga on Fridays. I could never commit to a Friday." He had a burly Manchu mustache, his T-shirt was grimy, and a snake tattoo coiled his left bicep like the dog leash wound around the tree. He was nearly seven feet; Carrie came about up to his elbow. Gordon wondered as he always did when he saw a couple with such diverse heights: how could they comfortably have sex? But then, with this couple, that was a moot point.

Carrie glanced over at Gordon and Mikilauni as if she had forgotten they were there. "Gordon," she said to her ex, "this is Gordon Clay."

"That should be easy to remember," he said slowly. "What's your name?" he asked Mikilauni's right breast. "Are you Marquesan?"

"Close, but . . ."

Gordie charged his dad's gut with a beefy shoulder, causing the dog to bark and snap. Moopuna ran up and burrowed his face into Mikilauni's hip. There the six of them stood, lined-up facing each other as if they were about to dance a Virginia reel. An awkward moment passed and then Gordie kicked his foot toward Moopuna and announced, "Dirty skin."

The other Gordon apologized and made his son apologize. While Gordon, Mikilauni, and Moopuna walked away, she turned to have one last, lingering look at Muscle Man.

"Quite a hunk," said Gordon.

"Now who's jealous?" she said smugly. "He knew something about the south seas anyway. He was only about five hundred miles off."

"You told him close."

She shrugged. "There's a lot of open water in Oceania."

"He liked your breasts, especially the right one. Seems like a dickhead, except he's nice to his dog. What the hell is hot yoga, anyway?"

She laughed. "I've never heard you say dickhead."

"He travels a lot. Deserts his kid."

"Sounds like you had quite a chat. Nothing wrong with her, though, right? Why did you tell her we met at the park?"

"I didn't. She got it confused somehow."

"Why revise our history? Are you ashamed we met at church?"

"No, no. I just meant that . . . never mind." He stopped short of telling her the whole story, how he had met Moopuna at this park while looking for Gordie. If Moopuna hadn't been at home the evening he came to pick her up for the symphony, he might not have been nearly so interested in hanging around. It was best not to say anything.

The Susuki violin school was above an antique store on Third and Main. Moopuna had difficulty negotiating the stairs and holding onto the quarter-sized violin Gordon had rented, with an option to buy, at Bob's House of Music. Moopuna's knee bumped against the case and threw him off balance nearly every step, but he would not relinquish the violin, nor hold Gordon's or Mikilauni's hand. Stairs were enough of a novelty to him that he also saw them as a recreational challenge. A traffic jam of students, all shapes and ages, was building up behind them, shouts and laughter reverberating in the narrow stairwell. Gordon nudged Moopuna closer to the left wall to allow others to pass. Someone's hip knocked the violin out of his grip and it slid all the way down the staircase. Retrieving it, Gordon wondered how violins possibly survived children.

Upstairs, the vast room doubled as a dance studio, with barres and mirrors along one wall. The hardwood floors made the room acoustically live, too live for violins. The ages of the students spanned from preschool to high school, and most had a parent or two with them. The teacher, a fiftyish woman in retro bell-bottoms and embroidered gauze Mexican shirt scurried from student to student to help tune. One little girl approached the teacher and held up a violin with three strings trailing behind and asked, "Can you fix this?"

"Certainly. Just a moment, please, Jasmine."

The idea of so many needy kids, the noise, the confusion, and the amount of work needed to merely begin the session, caused Gordon's nerves to jangle. He removed his and Moopuna's violins from their cases and tuned them. A woman nearby him drew a bow across her son's E string and crinkled her nose at Gordon. "Do you know if this is right?"

It wasn't. Gordon turned the boy's violin, and then it occurred to him he could be of further assistance. He continued tuning, feeling purposeful, getting used to the commotion as he worked. Halfway around the room, he met the teacher.

"You're new here. Gordon Clay, is it, from the college?"

"Yes."

She took his hand and squeezed. "I'm Marilyn Gaubert. We spoke on the phone. You've brought your son? That's lovely. Thank you for the help with the tuning."

With bows laid before their feet, students began with arm rolls, small circles, then big circles. "Parents do it, too," called out Marilyn. "Now over your head. Palms together, push, push, push. Stand straight as poles. Now grow two inches."

Gordon glanced around at Moopuna and Mikilauni and all the poles. Next came holding the violin with chin alone, the arm placed diagonally across the chest. Gordon positioned Moopuna's violin properly, but stood nearby, ready to catch it if he released the pressure of his chin. Mikilauni followed the directions intently, angling her neck to hold her air violin as Marilyn circulated around the room making adjustments.

"May we get our bows?" asked a small girl.

"Yes, now bows," said Marilyn. "Everyone on the *E* string. Silent string crossings. No sound. Eek! No sound. Watch thumbs. Better thumbs! Now thumb, thumb, thumb, elbow, elbow, elbow. Oh, you guys almost did it!"

So much technique. He had had nothing like this starting out as a teenager in high school orchestra.

"Bows to the ceiling! Now ticktocks! Now fast, fast, slow. Fast, fast slow." Moopuna was starting to squirm, placing one foot on top of the other and sticking out his butt. Mikilauni worked through the bow exercises, her arm fluid, wrist bent, a perfect thumb. Gordon placed his bow in her hand.

"Not me," she exclaimed. "I'm just here to watch. You're the Susuki parent."

"You be one, too." He fitted his violin beneath her chin.

Her eyes and grin were white with wonder. "But I don't know how!"

"Then you've come to the right place."

He raised his arms to adjust the position of the violin beneath her chin, but there was no need. She had got it right the first time.

"Now 'Twinkle,'" said Marilyn. "*E* string only for newcomers. Eyes closed. Blind, but floating."

Gordon kneeled to help Moopuna keep his violin steady, but he could not stop watching Mikilauni, who wore the same look of sublime concentration that she conjured just before orgasm.

"Take a bow," said Marilyn. " 'Twinkle, Variation One.' Sit down if you don't know this."

The students continued through their repertoire with the instructions of "Take a bow. Sit down if you don't know this," after each selection. Twenty minutes later only two of the high school students were standing. By then, Moopuna had joined a group of preschoolers who were climbing onto the window seat, running its length, and leaping off, Moopuna's smile revealing the tiny black hole in his mouth. Gordon was disappointed that he wasn't interested in watching the older students play like some of the other four-year-olds, but maybe he would later, when he knew more about it. Mikilauni sat cross-legged on the floor, clapping enthusiastically each time Marilyn announced, "Take a bow."

At the end of the class, Gordon led Moopuna back to his spot to take a final bow. Mikilauni bent low, her head down, her expression solemn, looking like a concert artist who had had years of bowing experience.

She clutched his arm. "Do you think Moopuna did okay? It seemed like he was goofing off at the end."

"I think he did better than okay."

"You think so? Really?"

"Yep." He kissed the tip of her nose, beaded with tiny, glistening droplets of perspiration. "But you did even better."

"Oh, Gordon, do you really believe I can learn to play the violin? I've always wanted to play an instrument, but I never thought I could."

"I think you're especially capable of playing the violin. Dance talent and musical talent must be closely linked in the brain. Look, here's where you loosen the hair on the bow. Go ahead, twist. This is your instrument now."

Chapter Twenty-four

It was too early for him. He hoped he could stay awake at the wheel, charging along Highway 99 in the predawn dark. He had thought marathons were in the spring, maybe the fall, but not in December. They were on their way to Cecilia's target marathon, the event she had been training for all these months, not the Sacramento Marathon, she had once corrected him, but the California International Marathon — CIM.

She breathed in and out, slowly, deeply, and took another sip from her water bottle — hydrating, she called it.

"Are you nervous?" he asked.

"I've got a few little butterflies, but mainly I feel good. Well prepared." She was wearing a pair of pink sweatpants and an old gray sweatshirt, stretched out and holey at the neckline, over her usual ketchup shorts and mustard running bra ensemble. "I really appreciate you doing this for me."

The original plan had been for Tiffany to drive her to her race, but her fasting and stigmata had left her in such a weakened condition it wasn't possible. Gordon was looking forward to their conversation. Although he still conducted tutorials with Cecilia and saw her in class, lately they hadn't had much time to talk.

"I hope this didn't get you in trouble with Mikilauni."

He had confided that Mikilauni didn't like his spending time with her. "Oh, no. She actually made plans before I did, shopping the outlets with her girlfriends from the office, so I told her I had some out-of-town Christmas shopping to do, too."

"You didn't say you were taking me to my marathon?"

"I figured, why rock the boat?"

"If you expect to have a healthy relationship, you have to be completely honest with each other."

He laughed at her. "Spare me your sermons, Sister. What would you know about it?"

"I know you have to tell the truth."

"I did tell the truth. I am going Christmas shopping. Besides, she's got to get over being so possessive."

"Maybe she's afraid I'll say something negative about her."

"You know anything about a time she injured Moopuna?"

"Not for sure. I wouldn't want to spread malicious gossip."

"You — malicious? I need to know what went on." He told her about Thanksgiving night, how Mikilauni had begged him not to take Moopuna to the emergency room, and that Henry Musgrave had treated him instead.

Cecilia sipped her water thoughtfully. "I know Michael — Moopuna — came to preschool with a broken clavicle. She said he was reaching for something in a closet and a suitcase fell on him. It could be true, but that's a common injury in abused toddlers. A hand comes down too hard on a shoulder and the clavicle snaps. Another time he had bruises across his back and butt. Sister

Margie got into the habit of checking him for marks. Twice, she reported his injuries to Child Protective Services. I guess the second time, Mikilauni caught on, and she withdrew Michael from preschool."

"She had a terribly abusive childhood herself. Her family seems to think it's normal."

"You're really good for them both."

Inside the car it was dark and quiet, except for the sound of the heater blasting away. He wondered if CPS would allow him a consultation if he expressed his concern, but probably all their case files were locked up tight.

Cecilia sighed. "I hope Tiffany will be all right today. Jack offered to drop by, but you know how busy he is Saturdays, with confessions and all."

"Did the wounds open up last night?"

She nodded. "Last night, around ten. It's getting pretty predictable, every Friday. This is the fourth week now."

"It's a hard way to live."

"Oh, I don't know. Despite the suffering, I imagine it would be rather reassuring, knowing that Jesus had already chosen you, that he was saving a place for you next to him in heaven. Still I'm worried about leaving her today."

"Can't your neighbor Faye Marie check on her?"

"That blabbermouth? We're not letting her in on this."

"Ow, Sister! Name-calling!"

"You should have heard what she called me. It was simply slanderous and I'm still angry about it." She shifted in her seat, rubbed her arms, turned away from him to look out the window.

"Did it have something to do with my visiting you?"

"How'd you guess?"

"Who'd she tell?"

"Jack, and it was plain nasty."

He laughed. "The night I came over to help you with Tiffany, as I was going down the stairs, the old lady hissed some accusation at me. You've got to admit the sound of Tiffany's ecstasies is very incriminating."

"Oh! Oh!" She pressed her palms to her cheeks. "I never thought of that!"

"I'm sure plenty of people wonder about our friendship. Did you happen to figure out that Art Bunch set us up for Allegra's Halloween party?"

"Not true! You came with Mikilauni."

"He didn't know about Mikilauni at the time. I'd just started dating her. You should have seen the look on Allegra's face when she opened the door for us."

She slapped her thigh. "I wondered why I was the only student invited to a faculty party." She slid down her seat and laughed until she hiccupped.

"That's not good. Not before a marathon."

"You don't care what — *hic* — people say about us?"

"Hell, no."

"Thanks for being my friend, Gordon." She raised her palm between them like a stop sign. "I know, I know, it sounds trite, but I've been having a tough year, and I just want to tell you I appreciate you."

"Well, me too."

"I've always envied St. Clare for having St. Francis, and how St. Paula and St. Jerome had each other out in the desert. You know, the first ascetics founding religious communities were men and women living chastely together. Chastity canceled out gender differences. Men and women were equal in cooperative living. Their spirits were liberated." She threw her arms apart as if freeing a dozen winged birds.

"What happened to that idea?"

"People started talking smut. The sexes had to split up into monasteries and convents. I loved living in a community of sisters, but sisters and brothers would be even better." She drank deeply.

"Hadn't you better quit drinking? You're going to have to look for a restroom every mile."

"Ah, no. I'll sweat it out." She straightened, leaned forward, stared through the windshield.

"Oh dear, I just remembered Faye Marie and Miki-launi's mom are Bingo buddies. I've seen them there in the parish hall, Wednesday nights, yukking it up."

"Who cares what Faye Marie says? Hey, I knew there was something else I wanted to tell you. I ran into Tiffany's sister from St. Louis at McDonald's on Thanksgiving. I suppose she stayed with you guys for a couple of days."

Cecilia hiccupped again, then smiled.

"You think she's funny? Well, she did seem a little eccentric. I thought at first she was Tiffany, then I noticed the difference."

"Actually — I should tell you — you got it right the first time."

"What?" Gordon thought about the red gloves, what might be under them. "No! But she really did look like a different person, the fuller face, the bright eyes, mannerisms, everything."

"Multiple personalities are pretty common in stigmatics. I've been reading up on it. To escape the pain and the hunger, Tiffany becomes Sandy who doesn't feel the pain and can eat. At least now I don't have to worry about her starving herself."

"How strange. And Tiffany doesn't remember being Sandy when she's Tiffany and vice versa?"

She nodded. "It seems that way. I guess she sort of hypnotizes herself."

"You're going to have her committed, right? Because if she got into any of those convents she's applied to, it wouldn't be fair to them." Gordon tapped his temple. "It's all in her mind."

"I notice you're saying *mind* not *brain*. Perhaps the mind is the spirit, the soul, the presence of God within us. Extreme spirituality is a form of genius."

"I'm saying she's Looney Tunes."

"Aren't highly intelligent people frequently eccentric? Einstein, for example, and Beethoven? And some elite athletes—they go through bizarre training rituals which they believe makes them the best. Holiness is just another kind of single-mindedness. Take St. Simon Stylites, for instance."

"The pillar guy?"

"Uh-huh. Lived on top of a stone pillar for thirty-six years. People recognized his holiness and came to seek his guidance. This distracted his prayers so he kept building his pillar higher and higher."

Gordon imagined the saint pissing off the side of his tower, his admirers below greeting the droplets with upturned faces as if they were being doused in holy water.

She went on. "Saints possess a great talent for faith, like Mother Teresa. She's a saint now. I can feel her presence in my daily life. I know she's the right person to pray to for my musical ear."

"You *are* making progress." He tried to sound

encouraging. She had improved, but very little. With all his tutoring, she still couldn't pass first-year ear-training.

Gordon merged onto Highway 50 in Sacramento and drove onto Folsom. He got into a long line of cars dropping off marathoners on the dam. Parking of any kind was forbidden at the start, and the finish was 26.2 miles away on the State Capitol Mall. In the dark, he could make out thousands of runners jogging around and a long row of Port-a-Johns, with lines of runners in front of each one. Runners, it seemed, were forever stuffing their bodies or emptying them. Most of them were still in warm-up suits, but a few were ready to go in skimpy shorts, numbered racing bibs, caps, and gloves. Some runners wore plastic garbage bags, with holes cut for the head and arms. It looked weird, but the plastic kept the runners warm pre-race, and could be flung off at any time.

"What are you going to do with your sweats?" he asked.

"Oh, they give us a bag with our race number on it, and then they truck them to the finish." She was staring out the windshield. "Well, I guess this is it."

Abruptly, he was struck with the enormity of the task before her. Twenty-six point two miles seemed a long way to go, even though she had gone over twenty in her training runs. But that had been leisurely jogs; this was a race. He became afraid for her. "Hey, have you ever done this before?"

She smiled weakly. "No." She opened the car door. "See you at the finish."

"Good luck."

"Thanks," she replied, then hiccupped. The next moment she was gone, vanished into the mash of legs and elbows.

He had hoped to watch the start but, as his car was being waved off the dam, that didn't seem possible. He drove to the venue point closest to the beginning of the course. There he stood in the crowd, waiting for the runners to pass. The dawn broke, gray and cool, with gold veins streaking through purple clouds that threatened nothing but harmless sprinkles. The terrain of gravel and barren trees was still, except for the hushed voices of the spectators muttering various concerns for their sons, husbands, friends, mothers in the race: "If his legs don't cramp up . . . He forgot his Chapstick. He wouldn't eat a thing this morning. I hope she won't be disappointed. She'll do okay." and then finally, shouts of "Here they come! Here they come!"

The pack descended the dam, a lumbering, fat, five-hundred-yard, confetti-colored centipede, stretched across the width of the highway. Already the race leaders were surging ahead of the crush and jostle; the one out in front was the favored Kenyan, whose long, lean stride was like the leap of a gazelle, his upper body as still as a statue, a look of effortless calm on his solemn, narrow face. The pack followed, with yelps of excitement, reflections of euphoria on their fresh, determined faces, red, blue, purple, white, black, orange sweatshirts flying like kites in the air. Down the road they went, all styles of running bodies and running: short-legged and pounding, muscular and lean, animal grace and halting pummeling. It seemed impossible to spot Cecilia among the flashing flesh, but then there she was near the side of the road, pasty skin in red shorts and yellow top, jumping with each step, up over the sea of bobbing heads, one arm raised, two fingers splayed in victory as she shouted, "Gordon! Gordon!" And then they were gone, leaving in their wake enough discarded clothing to start a secondhand store, plastic water bottles and crushed waxed cups, puddles of spilled liquid, and a few lone runners squatting in bushes or watering trees.

Now he had lots of time on his hands. He went out to breakfast, then drove to the mall containing the Toys R Us, and snoozed in his car until it opened. Walking into the huge, high-ceilinged, garishly lit store, he thought, *heart, be still.* There was so much brightly colored, exciting junk, and he wanted to buy it all for Moopuna. He steered clear of the video game aisle, although video games was the one thing Moopuna had been asking for. Gordon was suspicious of them. What did they do for a kid, except maybe develop fast reflexes? Instead, he chose the deluxe set of Tinkertoys, a Twister game, a fire engine and accessories, puzzles, books, CDs, educational software, bike helmet, and a shiny blue and silver two-wheeler with training wheels and multicolored streamers. He had never owned a brand-new bike himself, always hand-me-downs. He paid for his purchases. An attendant who helped him out to his car remarked, "Gosh, you must have a lot of kids."

As he drove toward downtown Sacramento, it occurred to him that he didn't know when Cecilia expected to finish. When he'd asked her how she thought she'd do, she merely replied, "Oh, I'll come in somewhere in the middle." But what was the middle in terms of time? He parked his car on L Street and strolled down the Capitol Mall. The Kenyan had already come in at 2:16. The official time over the finishing gate now read 2:22. He thought it was safe to assume that Cecilia would be at least another thirty or forty minutes. He took a walk over to the K Street Mall for some more shopping. A massive red-lettered GOING OUT OF BUSINESS sign stood in front of a jewelry store. He peered into the showcase window and spotted a pair of jade earrings, quite reasonable with the markdown price, which he was sure Mikilauni would like. He stepped into the shop. Apparently the place had been in the process of going out of business for some time; the red velvet-lined glass cases were nearly empty. A squat, nervous-looking man with a toothpick-thin, gray mustache, and an unbuttoned, tiger-striped rayon shirt exposing several skeins of gold chains, raised his chin hopefully.

"Ah, and what can I do for you, sir?"

Gordon pointed at the jade earrings and took out his credit card. While the salesman was writing out the receipt, Gordon eyed a wedding set, two thin gold bands and a massive solitaire diamond, at least a carat. It was ostentatious, exactly what Mikilauni would love.

"Very reasonable, fifty percent mark down," said the salesman, who had caught Gordon admiring the ring. "You have a special girl?"

"Yes, but not that special, not quite yet."

"Buy it now — cheap. Then you'll be ready when the time comes."

Gordon nodded, considering the logic in this. He was in no hurry to pop the question. Then again, he hated to shop. It would be nice to have the ring if he ever needed it. "How much?" When the salesman replied, Gordon whistled. "No, thanks."

"Wait." He turned to look toward the back of the store, flipping a curtain aside, then returned his attention to Gordon. "Come closer. I'm the owner. I can give you an offer you can't refuse, but I don't want my wife to hear. She accuses me of giving away the whole store. What would you pay?"

Gordon looked toward the curtain. He was quite certain there was nobody behind it. Just for fun, he named a price, which was one-fourth of the slashed price.

"Sold!"

Gordon's hand wavered when he held out his credit card a second time. Noticing, the jeweler said, "It's nothing to worry about. I see that all the time."

Gordon had a warm, pleasant reverie of watching Mikilauni open the little green velvet box, her eyes popping.

With all his wheeling and dealing, he was later getting back to the marathon than he meant to be. He jogged down the K Street Mall, certain that he had missed Cecilia's finish and feeling bad about it. A steady stream of runners was trickling in, striding through the finishing gate. Each one was wrapped in what looked like a long sheet of tinfoil, a kind of lightweight blanket. Gordon searched the finishers. He checked the ones standing around the food and water stations and those collecting their belongings from the trucks. The digital clock above the finishing gate read 3:45. He was beginning to get worried. What if she was in trouble out on the course? Well, a volunteer would give her a ride to the finish. What if she was in trouble, but wouldn't admit it to anyone? This would be typical of Cecilia; he knew how badly she wanted to complete this marathon. He got into his car and drove in the opposite direction of the course on a parallel street, occasionally stopping to look for her. He parked and began walking on the course in the opposite direction of the runners. A light rain began to fall. He'd search for ten minutes more, then drive back to the finish and hope for the best. A patch of yellow caught his eye. She wasn't running; she was sitting on the curb, lacing her shoe.

"Oh, Cecilia, there you are."

She looked up at him, her orange freckles standing out against her pink, windburned cheeks. "Oh, hi! Where did you come from?"

"I drove out a little way to see how you were doing. Are you okay?"

"Oh, yeah, fine," she said, calmly. She didn't look fine. Her hair was frazzled, and her forehead was encrusted with salt. "I'm having a good race. Pretty much staying on my pace. Well, actually that was before I hit the wall a few miles back. My big toenail has been giving me pain the last ten miles." She stood, raised her heels and bounced on the balls of her feet. She winced. "Oh! Oh! There it goes! Something popped!" The front of her shoe bloomed red. "That feels so much better."

"Are you sure? It doesn't look better."

"Oh! There he is again." She was looking at a black man carrying a white wooden cross about three feet long, not Christlike, with the weight in back, but in front, like a miner carrying a pickax. "It's the cross guy! First I pass him, then he passes me. If there's one thing I have to do, it's beat him."

There must be some religious significance to this, but he couldn't figure it out. "Why?"

"Are you kidding? That thing must weigh at least ten pounds. If I can't beat someone carrying that much deadweight, I must be a real loser."

She shot off, head in front, elbows akimbo. Her determination reminded him of the day she had helped him with his car trouble. Loaded down with book satchel, clarinet, and guitar, she had resembled a little pack mule. That's how she went about everything — with dogged determination — her music, her religious life, her running. Nothing much came of her efforts; he wondered why she didn't just give up. From the distance, he could hear the P.A. system on the Capitol Mall, announcing bib numbers of finishers. It wasn't so very far away. She was almost there.

Chapter Twenty-five

He was hurrying to finish trimming the tree even though it seemed like a lost cause. The cats were stalking the ornaments on the lower boughs and batting them off. Target held the head of a miniature teddy bear in her mouth and was kicking it with her hind legs. Both Target and Bother were as excited as he was. They had never seen a tree in the house; he hadn't gone to the trouble in years. It was four days until Christmas and finals week at the college. He had all of Moopuna's gifts to wrap and the bike to assemble. He needed to find his mother's sugar cookie recipe and cookie cutters, stashed away someplace.

When he and Ruthie had cleared out the old family house after their mother's death, he had insisted on keeping the cookie cutters. His fondest memory of his childhood Christmases was not opening gifts on Christmas morning, which was usually anticlimactic and disappointing, but the rolling out of cookie dough with his brothers and sisters, the cutting of trees, stars, and gingerbread men, and the decorating of them with raisins, nuts, Christmas carols playing on the stereo. Eating the cookies, which were so sweet they made his teeth ache, had never been quite as fun as making them. Now he was eager to pass his favorite tradition onto Moopuna, if only he could find the cutters, buy the ingredients, and figure out how to make the dough.

Bother swatted a silver glass ball, shattering it to pieces. Gordon stamped his foot, and both cats darted down the hall, seeking hiding places. He was kneeling to pick up the jagged pieces when the phone rang.

"Hi honey, I'm afraid I've got some bad news," said Mikilauni. "There has been a death in the family." Her tone was even, matter-of-fact: surely it wasn't anyone in her immediate family.

"Oh, I'm sorry! Who?"

"My grandmother, my dad's mom. I haven't seen her since I was real little, but I should go to the funeral. Kali and Salote want to go, but of course they don't have the money, and Peleki doesn't want to go because he's got a lot of work lined up, and Inoke would have issues fitting in a plane seat, so Old Mama's sending me. Someone should be there to represent our side of the family. I have some vacation time from work . . ."

"Hold it. Where did you say the funeral was?"

"I didn't. Honolulu."

"You're going to Hawaii? When?"

"Tomorrow."

"When will you be back?"

"My boss said I can have the whole week."

"A week!" It was a blow. He felt like Mikilauni was deliberately depriving him of her and Moopuna's company on Christmas. This was irrational, of course. She couldn't help it if her grandmother died. Still, she could help leaving him stranded at Christmas. He hadn't much liked Christmas as an adult. Damn it, this year was supposed to be different. "Can't you go for the funeral and be back home in time for Christmas?"

"Oh, all that way for a couple of days? Moopuna hasn't met any of his relatives. I haven't seen some of them in ages. I want to travel around, see as much as I can."

"If only it weren't finals week. I could come with you."

"Oh, no, Gordon, no!" Her voice was strained and tense. It softened when she added, "I don't expect you to. Don't even think of it."

"What about Christmas?"

"Ah, that's a disappointment, I know. We can all have a Christmas when we get home. Moopuna can have a Hawaiian Christmas, then Christmas with you, and then his usual Christmas at Mama's. He doesn't know the exact day, it's all the same to him. He'll have all kinds of Christmases."

This was no consolation to him. Trying to control the resentment in his voice, he said, "I'll see you, won't I, before you take off?"

"Sure. We'll be over in an hour or so."

When he opened the door to Mikilauni only, she said, "You put your tree up. It looks good from the street."

He peered behind her, into the chilly darkness. "Where's the little guy?"

She stepped inside, shut the door quickly with a lunge of her round hips. She put her arms around him and kissed him. She must have spent the hour getting ready to come see him. She had on the knit red dress he liked with the plunging neckline, her hair twisted up with a few curling tendrils at her nape, and artfully done eye makeup. It was her special-occasion look rather than her just-stopping-by look. "I thought you might like a romantic evening for two."

"I thought you would want to spend the night. Then we could have romance and I'd get to see Moopuna."

"I can't spend the night, Gordon, I've got too much to do, but I can give you your going-away present if you're a good boy."

He resented her referring to sex as a present, and being called a good boy. He was perturbed at her for coming alone. "Where's Moopuna?"

She let her arms slide off his shoulders and fall limply at her sides. "At my house. With a babysitter."

"Not your mom, right? Because I told you I don't like him to be with her." His voice was deeper, more reproachful than he meant it to be, but he couldn't help it, recalling Moopuna sitting forlornly on Old Mama's back stoop Thanksgiving Day, hugging his little frame against the November blasts.

"It's Jenny, the teenager who lives next door. Don't worry, he'll be fine." She dropped her eyes to the carpet, her cheek twitching.

He could almost bet that she had left him at her mother's, but this was no time for accusations. He forced his tone to soften. "Will I get to say good-bye to him tomorrow, before you leave? I'd like to say good-bye."

She seemed perturbed with him, too, as if showing up alone in the tight, sexy dress hadn't produced the effect on him she was hoping for. "I can bring him by your office, early tomorrow, if we won't be interrupting anything. We don't have to leave for L.A. until ten a.m."

"Any time before then would be fine. I wish I could drive you to the airport, but I have to give a final." He rubbed her upper arms. "Do you really have to go?"

She nodded, her almond eyes tender.

He dropped his head to her cleavage, breathed in her

perfume, kissed her there. "Oh, Mikilauni, I'm going to
miss you."

In the morning, he found Art Bunch in the office, wearing a green T-shirt with a red Christmas stocking sewn
on it, reading, "Stuff it." Some students had, dropping
into it candy canes, Hershey kisses, and coins. One girl
had even given him a yo-yo, which he was working now.

"Mikilauni and Moopuna are dropping by. I want
you to behave."

Art's yo-yo floundered at the end of its string. He
stretched his neck indignantly. "I always behave."

"I mean polite, respectful. Look at Mikilauni's face
when you're speaking to her."

"Where would I be looking?"

"At her breasts." Allegra Musgrave appeared in the
doorway, her red Chanel suit and gold silk scarf a direct
contrast to Art's Stuff it T-shirt. "Are we speaking of your
delightful Mikilauni?"

Art wound the string on his yo-yo. "When have I ever
gawked at a woman's breasts while talking to her? Well,
maybe I sneak a peek, but not so anyone notices."

"Everyone notices," said Allegra.

"Including the woman," said Gordon. To Allegra, he
added, "Mikilauni and Moopuna are flying out to Hawaii
this afternoon. Her grandmother died."

"Oh, I'm sorry to hear that, Gordon."

Art began to croon in imitation of Elvis Presley, "I'll
have a blue Christmas without you . . ."

"Are you expecting her this very moment, or might I
have a private word with Arthur?" Since her Halloween
party, Allegra and Art frequently had a private word, no
doubt to arrange their trysts. Gordon was certain her

marriage was heading for destruction, but they acted like they couldn't help themselves.

"I'll step out a moment. I gave Mikilauni instructions on how to get here, but I don't think she's ever been on campus. I'll go keep an eye out for her." He walked down the hall and out the building. Then his cell phone rang.

"Hello, Gordon, hello! I can't believe it. We're here."

"You're where?"

"Honolulu. Oh, it's so warm! In the eighties. You wouldn't believe the difference."

"You said you were coming by this morning."

"A change of plans, honey. We were able to catch the red-eye on standby. It was way cheaper."

"You could have called me."

"In the middle of the night? Besides, there wasn't time. We're at the airport now, but I'm not quite sure where we're going to be when. We're going to be doing a little island hopping getting around to everybody, but I'll keep you posted. I'm so excited! It's so beautiful. I wish you were here. Here, I'll put Moopuna on. Moopuna, say hi to Gordon."

"Hi, Moopuna, how are you doing?" He forced a false cheerfulness into his voice, as adults do when they want to deceive children.

"Fine." He didn't sound fine. Sleepy, cranky, forced to do something he didn't want to do. Gordon couldn't get much more out of him before Moopuna hung up.

In a daze, Gordon walked back to his office and fell into his chair.

"What?" asked Art. Allegra had left.

"They're already in Hawaii, dammit. Something's just not right. I feel it."

"Well, um, did Mikilauni ever mention any old

Hawaiian boyfriends? Looks like you're being cuck-
olded."

"Oh, for Christ sakes, Bunch. Coming from you,
that's really rich."

"I know I'm a cuckolder myself, but — "

"There's no such word. The term I believe is *philan-
derer*."

"You've got to admit it's the major reason people
sneak around."

"It's the major reason *you* sneak around. Mikilauni
doesn't have an old Hawaiian boyfriend. She's never even
been to Hawaii."

"Okay then, think back. What is it, exactly, that's
bothering you? What reason did she give you for her
change in plans?"

"She said the red-eye was much cheaper."

"True enough. True enough." He was chomping gum,
nodding, and folding jazz band concert programs.
"You've got to trust her if you're going to have a decent
relationship."

Like Henry trusts Allegra was on Gordon's tongue,
but he said, "You've just hit on my trouble: Mikilauni has
given me reasons not to trust her."

"Like what?"

"She lies. For example, last night she said she was
bringing Moopuna over so I could say good-bye to him,
and then she didn't."

"Oh, well, no chance of good-bye sex with the little
tyke in tow. You can't fault her for that."

Gordon nodded, considering this. "Well then, the first
night we . . . uh . . . made love, she said she didn't have
any condoms. We were already to . . . were in bed and . . "

"Bummer."

"Yeah, right. I had to get up, get dressed, go out to the all-night market, and then, a month or so later, I found a pack of rubbers in her bureau. Why lie about that?"

"That would be so you wouldn't think she had guys over all the time."

Gordon rubbed the back of his head, gave his pony-tail a little yank of frustration. "I think I'm confiding in the wrong guy." Yet, it was true, by disclosing Mikilauni's faults to Art, they didn't seem so terrible.

Art snapped his fingers. "I know what. Call the mom. Say, for some reason, you can't reach Mikilauni by cell. Ask her for the phone numbers of the relatives she is stay-ing with, then you can call them up, and make sure she's where she says she is."

Gordon shook his head. "Sounds too underhanded. Besides, Old Mama doesn't speak English, and I don't want to involve the sisters. "

Art's eyes popped. "Sisters? She has sisters? You never told me she had sisters."

"Down, boy. The sister I talked to I wouldn't wish even on you."

"What happened — she get hit with the ugly stick?"

Gordon didn't mention Kali was just as beautiful as Mikilauni. "Ugly is right, man." He tapped his heart with his fingertips. "Ugly in here."

Chapter Twenty-six

He had promised to take Cecilia to Midnight Mass Christmas Eve, and she invited him to a late supper of meatless chili. Her chili was truly meatless, lacking his favorite ingredient, hamburger, but it was spicy hot and robust with onions and green peppers. He was setting the table for two and she was taking the corn bread out of the oven, when a female voice behind him said, "My, that smells fabulous! Oh, hi, Gordon."

He turned, then paused. Was it Tiffany? The face looked like Tiffany *and* Sandy, but was somehow different from both personalities. He'd never seen her without her head covered, for one thing. Her dark brown hair was cut close to the scalp in layers, pixie fashion. If the jeans she wore once fit her, they didn't now. They were a good three sizes too big, and her upper torso was lost in a man's plaid flannel shirt. Even if she did sneak away for a Big Mac on occasion as Sandy, she couldn't have done it often. She was bony thin, her bright eyes too big for her face. Could this cheery waif be a third personality?

"Tiffany," she prompted. "Remember?"

"Of course, I remember," said Gordon. "Hello."

She went to the silverware drawer, then laid a place at the table for herself. He glanced furtively at her hands. The skin was creamy and smooth. It was Saturday, her most difficult day of the week, second to Friday. He stole another glimpse of her hands. Cecilia had confided to him that on close examination, she'd discovered that Tiffany's hands had been pierced clean through. Now it appeared as if the wounds had never existed.

"More wine?" Tiffany asked him. She topped off his glass, then poured some for herself. "Did you hear it was supposed to snow tonight?"

"I did indeed."

"Oh, I wish it would! I was raised in Colorado. One Christmas morning when I was about ten, we woke up, and it had snowed so much during the night that I could leap into the snow out of my second-story window. I grabbed my sled and took the plunge. "

"The snow doesn't stay around here long," said Gordon. "It usually melts as soon as it touches the ground."

"Oh, I hope not this time. I prayed for a huge snowstorm."

Cecilia ladled out bowls of steaming chili. "What do you hear from Mikilauni?" She explained to Tiffany, "Gordon's girlfriend and her little boy are in Hawaii right now."

"She calls every day," he said. "Each time from a different place. She's moving around fast, trying to see all her relatives."

"Wouldn't most of them be at the funeral?" asked Cecilia.

"I don't know. It's a huge, extended family. She's always telling me about them, but I can't keep them all straight."

"How does Moopuna like Hawaii?" She passed him the cornbread.

"He seems a bit overwhelmed. All I can get out of him are hi and fine."

"Hawaii is something else," said Tiffany. "I got to take a summer course there, once."

Gordon couldn't get over what a changed person she was. She was cheerful and animated as they chatted about their favorite places around the world. Toward the end of the meal, she jumped up. "I have something special for dessert." She went into the kitchen and stooped to reach inside a corner cupboard.

Gordon leaned toward Cecilia and tapped the back of his hand.

Cecilia shook her head and rubbed her own hand with her fingertips, whispering, "It just disappeared."

Tiffany returned to the table with a Christmas tin. "I made these myself." She opened the container and offered its contents to Gordon.

"They're awesome." He selected a star-shaped sugar cookie, iced in yellow and trimmed with a silver ball on each point. "I loved to make these as a kid."

"Oh, me, too." Tiffany offered the tin to Cecilia. "It's been years since I've done it. Today, I just suddenly got the urge."

He bit into his cookie. "Hmm!" These were better than his mother's, not as sugary. "I want to make cookies with Moopuna. I know I've got my mother's recipe somewhere, but I can't find it. May I have yours?"

Tiffany laughed. "Sure." She went to the refrigerator and opened it.

"We better get a move on," said Cecilia. "If we don't get to the church soon, we won't get a seat."

A log thumped on the table, causing the plates to

jump. From the blue and white cylinder, Pillsbury's Doughboy grinned up at him. "There you go," said Tiffany. "My recipe. Making the dough is just a chore, right? Cutting out and decorating is the fun part."

"Right," he said, laughing.

"Go ahead, take it. I'll put it in a bag for you. Merry Christmas."

"Hey, thanks." He took another cookie, this time a reindeer. There he was, bonding with the stigmatic over Christmas cookies.

Cecilia was hurrying to clear the table.

"Oh, leave it. I'll do it," said Tiffany.

"Aren't you coming with us?" asked Gordon.

"I prefer to go to mass on Christmas morning. I like to see the kids out all over town, riding their new bikes, using their new roller blades. I hope some of them get sleds. They might need them tomorrow."

Descending the outside back stairs, Gordon muttered to Cecilia, "It just gets weirder and weirder."

"No, this is normal! You've never seen Tiffany as she naturally is. This is what she's been like most of the three years I've known her."

"Do you think the stigmata is gone for good?"

She shrugged. "The Lord only knows. It's nice to see her happy at Christmas. It cheers me right up."

By 11:30 p.m. the church was packed. He had to drive across the street to the college to get a parking space. They walked down the sidewalk toward the church just as a light dusting of snow drifted to their shoulders. The convent door opened and a line of nuns filed out, shrouded in black capes, their heads bowed.

Wearing her own matching, convent-issued cape,

Cecilia stopped to watch their progress through the side door of the church. "Oh, this is my first Christmas not being a nun. I miss my sisters!"

"Really?"

"I know what you're thinking — the nuns of your youth, cracking kids with rulers."

"Boys. Never the girls."

"Right. Men haters. The sisters that educated you did what they thought was right. They thought that's how you disciplined children. But sisters aren't like that anymore. We're a community living within the grace of God, working and praying together. It's a comforting way to live." She seemed to have forgotten that taking orders from Mother St. Paul hadn't been all that comforting.

They crossed the street and passed through the main entrance. The church was bright with red and gold bows attached to the ends of each pew and smelled of the pine wreaths mounted on the pillars and pine trees arranged around the altar. Overhead came the strains of "O Little Town of Bethlehem," sung by the high, sweet voices of a boys' soprano choir, the loft actually being used for its original purpose. Even the old pipe organ had been dusted off, its sonorous, reedy blast the epitome of church music.

Gordon and Cecilia walked up the center aisle and squeezed into two vacant spaces. She knelt, made the sign of the cross, and bowed her head in prayer. He looked around the church. Several pews ahead of him sat Old Mama, with Kali and Salote on either side of her. Salote, squat and heavyset, happened to turn and spot him. He nodded and lifted the corners of his mouth in a social smile. She did not acknowledge him, but whispered to her mother. Old Mama turned and leered at him. He nodded

and smiled again. She whispered to Kali, who twisted
around, pulled one side of her neckline down and up to
flash a bare shoulder at him.

Cecilia whispered, "Excuse me. I'm going to wish my
sisters Merry Christmas." She walked up the aisle to the
nuns in the front side pew. Kali watched her go, then
nudged her mother, sidestepped out of the pew, and approached him.

"Merry Christmas, *palangi*."

"Merry Christmas, Kali."

"I thought you'd be by to see me, Mikilauni being
gone *to Hawaii* and all, but I see you're with your other
girlfriend. I'll be talking to her when I get home. I'll tell
her I saw you. Shall I send her your *love*?"

"That would be great. Thanks."

Cecilia stood beside Kali, waiting to get by. Kali made
a show of genuflecting and bowing toward the altar, before returning to her seat, swishing her backside as she
went.

Cecilia stepped in front of him, whispering, "Is that
Mikilauni's sister?"

"Yep."

"Did I get you in trouble?"

"Nope." He'd already told Mikilauni during one of
their rushed phone conversations that he would be ac-
companying Cecilia to Midnight Mass, and she'd taken it
quite well.

While the Gospel was read, small children, wearing
costumes of angels, shepherds, lambs, birds, and one don-
key, pantomimed the first Christmas. He wished Moopuna was at his side to enjoy it. Better yet, he imagined
him peering out of one of the wooly lamb outfits, down
on all fours, baaing on cue. A wide-eyed infant was pre-

sented as the Christ Child, dressed in swaddling clothes and a disposable diaper, and resting his head against the flat chest of a three-foot-tall Mary.

He glanced over at Cecilia to find her ignoring the children's tableau, deeply engrossed in private meditation, which was quite unlike her. Her eyes were focused on her hands, the fingertips pressed in prayer, the palms slightly cupped. He had to lean forward to see what she held. It was a photograph of Mother Teresa, not with a rosary wrapped around her hands in solemn prayer, not holding a starving baby with the weight of the world on her brow; instead, her chin was tilted upward and she was laughing, as if there were no pain or strife in all the world.

Cecilia nodded, as if understanding some silent advice Mother Teresa was offering her. No, she was nodding to the beat of "Silent Night," which the children's choir was now singing. Her sense of rhythm had definitely improved. She reached in the deep pocket of her cape and withdrew a stubby pencil. She flipped her missalette on its side and wrote in the margin, then handed it to him, her gray eyes wide with expectation.

He studied what she had written, smiled, and nodded. She had correctly notated the rhythm of "Silent Night." It was an accomplishment, though a small one. Rhythmic dictation was much easier with a familiar tune, since the difficulty lay in remembering a new tune long enough to get it down on paper. He recalled reading about Mozart's ability to notate an entire mass after hearing it once.

Next, the choir sang "What Child Is This?" Cecilia flipped to the music section of the missalette, found a piece that contained many open bars of rests, and began using it like blank manuscript paper, notating the pitches of the melody in neat slashes on the staff, as fast as the choir sang them, then going back and filling in the stems and beams of the correct rhythms. He raised his eyebrows. This was another familiar tune, but her ability to get both the melody and rhythm down so quickly and correctly was impressive.

During the Offertory, Cecilia left the pew, as if she had a role in the ritual of presenting the gifts of wine, bread, and money. Moments later, she returned to her place, holding the objective of her errand, a blank sheet of manuscript paper which she must have begged from the choir director's binder. As the choir sang "Panis Angelicus," Cecilia set down the soprano and bass lines, then filled in the harmony in figured bass. She handed him her work, and, as he studied it, she pressed his arm, whispering, "I can do it." All their hard work was finally paying off!

Finally, during the recessional, "Joy to the World," the side doors were flung wide. Laughter and exclamations of amazement arose from the congregation. The night was streaked with white. Almost a foot of snow lay on the ground.

As Gordon and Cecilia crossed the street to the college parking lot, she accepted the arm he offered her, babbling happily and loudly. "It's all so obvious now! Always before, I could hear a part of the rhythm, two quarter notes, two eighths, say, but I never knew where to put them. Now, I get it. The downbeats keep my place! They're always one, so everything else has to fit somewhere in between."

"That's what I've been telling you."

"I know, but tonight I *heard* the downbeats. I *felt* them. They were coming right at me, hitting me over the head like baseball bats. And the melody. I heard the intervals as if you were shouting out the answers to me: up a fourth, up a third, down a second, down a second. It was so easy. And as for the harmony, well, it's so predictable, just a few chords. Did you check my work? I was right, wasn't I? Oh, you don't have to tell me. I was right! I know I was right!"

He laughed. Even if they were familiar tunes, this was a major breakthrough. Perhaps in the church, with all the good feelings of Christmas, she had been relaxed enough to leave her insecurity behind and truly *listen.* "I'm glad something finally clicked," he said.

"Clicked? Something didn't just click." She released his elbow, and dashed away, not to the parking lot, but toward the vacant lot beside it, running into the snow drifts, staggering as her foot sank, pulling it out, stumbling again, waving her arms over her head, shouting at the top of her voice, "It's a miracle! It's a miracle!"

He followed her, moving slower, sliding in his hard-soled shoes.

"Oh, isn't it marvelous? Isn't the snow magnificent? What a glorious night!" She spun around, holding out her arms, palms up, catching snowflakes as they fell.

"Yeah, great, Cecilia. It's cold. It's late. Let's get going."

"The greatest night of my life and this is how you act?"

"I can't help it. My feet are wet."

She bent her head as if to lick a snowflake off her palm, then stopped and stared at it. "Oh, my God! Oh, my dear God!"

"What now?" He caught up to her.

"Amazing. It's on every single snowflake!"

"What is?" he asked impatiently.

"*The Last Supper.* It's imprinted on every single one of these snowflakes!"

A chill snaked down his back. He imagined Leonardo da Vinci's entire painting in all its sprawling detail. "The *whole Last Supper?*"

"See for yourself." She scooped up a handful of snow and offered it to him.

"I don't see anything."

"It's there, all right. On every snowflake. Get closer, look carefully."

He crouched down and leaned toward her hands. Too late he realized what she was up to. The face full of snow stung, but it was refreshing, too. Relief enhanced his joy: not another miracle after all.

She sprang up and started to run from him.

"Not so fast, Sister. This means war."

He molded a snowball and fired it at her. It exploded against her nape. She yelped, tried to shake the freezing snow from her hood. She tossed a snowball at him. He ducked and hurled another chilly missile, striking her on the butt. Across the street the row of nuns were stalled on the sidewalk observing them, the tallest one, Mother St. Paul, shaking her head.

Cecilia didn't notice. In the center of the snow-lit field, she sank to her knees, her face lifted to the heavens. She blew the sky a kiss and shouted, "Thank you, Mother Teresa, thank you for this most amazing Christmas gift! A musical ear! Thank you for sending me a miracle!"

Chapter Twenty-seven

Mikilauni was pushing against his back. He wished she would stop. He rolled over, trying to sink back into sleep. It couldn't be Mikilauni, he remembered; she was in Hawaii. It was Christmas morning, and he was alone. He peered through mere slits and found Target pressed against him and Bother lying on his feet. His nose was so cold it tingled. The room was freezing, lit by an abnormal blue-gray cast. It was quiet, too quiet, not a single car on the street. He sat up with a start. Outside was completely white; the snow was up to the windowsill. He checked his digital clock; the display was dark. No electricity.

It didn't have to be this way! He didn't have to be alone in this cold house! He shot out of bed, feeling like Ebenezer Scrooge coming to his senses. He could take the next available flight to Hawaii and be with Mikilauni and Moopuna this very day. He put a sweatshirt over his nightshirt and stepped into his slippers. He wasn't quite sure where in Hawaii Mikilauni and Moopuna were, but he would find them. In the kitchen, he thumbed through the phonebook. First, he would call Old Mama's house asking for the addresses of various Kukula relatives, and then he would make airline reservations. He picked up the phone. No dial tone. He tried his cell phone to reach Mikilauni — no answer. What did he expect? It was the middle of the night in Hawaii. He'd have to drive over to Old Mama's house. Then he realized the snowplow had to come by before he could get his car on the road.

He was in a hurry, and yet he was stuck. He made coffee on his gas range, using a saucepan and a strainer. He took his coffee, which wasn't as bad as he expected, and sank into his recliner to think. Target came up to him and whipped him with her tail. He reached down and scratched around her ears. She shook her head vigorously, as if to rid herself of the human touch, her ears making a loud flapping noise. He loved that amazing sound, produced merely by the rapid whirl of soft, thin membrane. He loved his cats, but they were no longer enough.

He stared at the dark Christmas tree. He had stacked Mikilauni's and Moopuna's gifts under it the previous evening to be ready in case they returned home sooner than expected. Cecilia believed in miracles; the least he could do was hope. He went into a little reverie then, imaging the tree brightly lit and Mikilauni in her homey purple bathrobe sitting on his lap. He would shout out, "Wake up, Moopuna. Santa came!" Moopuna would dash into the living room and make a nosedive for the presents. Mikilauni had said it wouldn't matter what day it was, but Gordon knew better. There was no day like Christmas Day.

He realized that he hadn't bought much for Mikilauni: a Strings Is My Thing book bag, some classical CDs, the jade earrings from Sacramento. His main gift to her was a pricey top-of-the line Hoover because she had complained her vacuum cleaner wouldn't pick up anything. A vacuum cleaner — how romantic was that? What a fool he was; he acted like he knew nothing about women. He should have hired a substitute to give his final; any cock-

roach would have jumped for a few extra bucks around
Christmas. He never should have let Mikilauni and
Moopuna go to Hawaii without him. If she didn't already
have a Hawaiian boyfriend, she could certainly get one,
with all her relatives of relatives of relatives.

He pulled himself up, went to the bookcase, and removed the score of Wagner's *The Ring Cycle* from its
shelf. He stood on his toes, reached back, and withdrew
the small, green velvet jewelry case. He opened it. The
diamond sparkled back at him, reflecting the blue light
of the snow. He thought of a time several years ago when
he had watched, in broad daylight, the college's band
room being robbed of sound equipment and instruments.
He gave the thief a friendly nod, memorized his van's
license plate, and dialed 911. A few days later, when he
was asked to pick the guy out of a lineup, he was surprised to see that the culprit appeared the least like a crim-
inal. Gordon imagined if all the women in his life were
lined up, Mikilauni would be the least likely to be his
wife. Yet he loved her; he loved Moopuna. He didn't want
to be without them ever again, especially on Christmas
morning. With shaking fingers he wrapped the little box
in reindeer gift wrap and set it under the tree.

He showered and dressed for travel. He retrieved his
suitcase from the back of his closet and began packing. A
suit, shorts, a bathing suit, hard to believe in all this snow.
He was pulling boxers and socks out of his bureau when
Bother jumped on the top and paraded back and forth in
front of the mirror. Funny how cats couldn't recognize
themselves in a mirror whereas dolphins could, while cats,
it seemed, were at least as smart as dolphins. Bother understood what a suitcase meant, and she began to yowl in
protest at the sight of it. It was unfortunate that she had

sauntered into the bedroom at that moment. He had hoped to keep his leaving from her until the last minute.

Every few minutes he picked up the phone to listen for a dial tone, then looked down the street for the snowplow. He found an old transistor radio in the back of a top kitchen cupboard and batteries in a drawer. He tuned into a local station. As he expected, this was a record-breaking snowfall in Goldhurst. The highway had been plowed, however, and he could drive to the airport in Fresno as soon as the local streets were cleared. He went next door and asked his neighbor to take in his mail and feed the cats. There was nothing left to do but wait.

He realized he was hungry. In the refrigerator he found Tiffany's gift of cookie dough. He rummaged through several cupboards before discovering his mother's cookie cutters. He went to work rolling out the dough and cutting it. He was seated at the kitchen table with a second cup of boiled coffee, munching cookies warm from the oven when the lights flickered on. The snowplow came through midmorning. It was now possible to drive over to the Kukulas before heading out of town.

He secured the house, petted each cat good-bye. Slowly he drove through town, taking care not to skid on the icy roads. Kids were making snowmen and building snow forts, many of them young enough to have never seen snow in Goldhurst before.

A half dozen cars were parked outside Old Mama's place. When he rang the bell, he heard a child's footsteps on the hardwood floor. Could it be Moopuna? How was that possible? He tried the knob. The door was unlocked, so he stepped in. Moopuna stopped, one foot ahead of the other, frozen in a running position, staring up at him, his mouth slightly open, the gap of the missing tooth visible. Both his eyes were so severely bruised that it was hard to tell where one black eye ended and the other began. Old Mama was stopped behind him, also motionless, her hand in the form of a claw on his shoulder. Laughter and chatter wafted from the kitchen. There came the clicking of high heels.

"Who is it, Mama?" Mikilauni rounded the corner, dressed in her crimson, clingy dress and big gold jewelry. Her eyes widened at the sight of him. She paused. For an instant, the three of them appeared as a tableau. Mikilauni was quick to recover. "Gordon, honey, Merry Christmas! We got in late last night. We were just coming over to surprise you." She approached him, her arms extended for an embrace. He held up his palm, took a step back.

Mikilauni leaned toward Moopuna, the cords of her throat tensed. "Go on with Old Mama, baby."

Old Mama pulled Moopuna backward by the shoulder she clutched.

"Hold it!" Gordon dropped down on one knee and peered into Moopuna's face. The band of bruises was about three inches wide and extended across his eyes from temple to temple. There was little swelling, though. The injury was a few days old, probably four to be exact. Had her alleged phone calls from Hawaii been that easy to fake? "Moopuna, you poor little guy, what happened to you?"

Moopuna's lower lip pushed out, his chin bunched, misery zigzagged into the crevices of his face. Gordon realized he was reflecting his own expression. Moopuna rolled his melting chocolate eyes to Mikilauni.

"Tell him what happened," she coaxed.

"I climbed to the cookies and fell down," he recited.

"Oh! It was just awful," she said. "Mama had some Christmas cookies cooling on the counter, and Moopuna slid a chair over and stacked some blocks on top of that, and he went crashing to the floor, face down."

He hadn't taken his eyes off Moopuna. "Who hit you?" Gordon demanded. Moopuna gazed up at Mikilauni again, then ducked his head into his right clavicle. Was that the side that had been snapped in two by a swift blow to the shoulder? Was that the reason she had asked on which side a violin was held? An indignant rage seethed in his bowels, and yet his exterior was so cold and deliberate that, in his ears, his own interrogating voice sounded like another person's. "Was it Mama or Old Mama?"

Old Mama turned to Mikilauni, said something in pidgin, then snickered, covering her gaping toothlessness with her hand. Mikilauni laughed with her.

Gordon asked, "What did she say?"

"She said maybe you did it."

Gordon lunged for Moopuna, swept him into his arms, and stalked out the door. Mikilauni followed him down the porch steps, pounding his back, screaming, "Bastard! Let go of my son!" Her high heels skidded on the icy sidewalk and she clutched fistfuls of his overcoat to keep from falling, throwing him off balance. He recovered and kept walking to his car. "You can't take my son! " she screamed. "I'll call the cops on you. I'll get you for child abduction."

He muttered between clenched teeth, "You don't really want to call the cops, Mikilauni, now do you?" He reached his car and swooped Moopuna into his car seat.

Mikilauni pulled at Gordon's arms, trying to impede

his buckling the straps. "You've no right to him. You're nobody to him."

"That may be, but anybody can see this child needs protection."

"Where are you taking him?"

"To my place."

She stopped struggling against him. He finished securing Moopuna and straightened. He found her staring at his suitcase, stowed in the back seat.

"I was going to catch a flight to Hawaii."

Her eyes narrowed, the muscles in one cheek twitching. "You wouldn't do that for us. Up and leave on Christmas Day."

"Who else do I have?"

"Oh, Gordon honey, I knew you would overreact like this. Why do you think I made up that horrible lie? I'm coming with you. We'll talk it over."

"Stay here. I can't see you now."

She jutted her chin. "Then Moopuna stays, too."

"All of you, your whole family. There are five adults in that house right now, and not a single one willing to report this."

"Of course, not. If you had a family, you'd understand. Families stick together, they look out for their own."

"Yeah? Who's looking out for this child?"

"He isn't hurt bad. I know you don't believe it. You always want to think the worst of me."

He would not be baited. He locked and slammed the back car door. He got behind the wheel. She clutched his wrist with both hands. "Promise me you won't go to CPS."

"I won't promise anything, but for now, I'm taking him to my house. Christ, give me some time to think."

She did not reply. Just stood shivering in the street, watching him drive off. Kali and Salote came out on the porch, but they didn't try to stop him. Kali pointed at him, slapped her thigh. Some joke. He looked in the rearview mirror at Moopuna, staring out the window at Mikilauni. She stooped and waved. He remained motionless, not even a blink.

Pulling onto the icy street, Gordon tried to make light of the situation. "Did Santa come to your house last night?"

"I wasn't at my house."

"Well, then, did he come to Old Mama's?"

"No. There's no such thing as Santa."

Gordon's eyes darted from the road to the little sullen face in the mirror. How bad were his injuries? Did he need to see a doctor? He couldn't go to Henry Musgrave, not again. "No Santa? You've got to be kidding. Who told you there was no Santa?"

"I know it. It's your family doing it. All the presents were under Old Mama's tree many days before Christmas."

"Of course your family gives you things, but Santa gives you things, too."

"Not-uh."

"Yeah-uh." Gordon's enthusiasm sounded hollow in his own ears. Why did adults feel compelled to tell this lie to children, to insist they believe it? He himself had been a naive and sheltered child, believing in the whole rigamarole of Santa, Easter Bunny, tooth fairy, and leprechauns until after age ten, feeling utterly betrayed and foolish when he finally reasoned such beings were physically impossible. "Santa actually thinks you live at my house. He brought a whole load of stuff for you over there."

"Not-uh."

"Yeah-uh. Why do you think it snowed so hard last night? So Santa could land his sleigh." He could tell the bit about the snow and the sleigh was working. Moopuna's eyes widened; the beginning of a smile flickered on his lips. Gordon remembered now why this was important. Santa was magical. Santa was a miracle. All little children deserved the wonder of make-believe in their lives, especially one who was used as a punching bag.

Gordon pulled into his driveway. "Come see for yourself." He helped Moopuna out of the car and led him into the back door. Bother bumped against his legs and meowed furiously, scolding Gordon for leaving with a suitcase. Did they realize he'd been gone less than an hour, rather than days? He turned on the tree lights and sat on the floor before the tree. He set Moopuna on his crossed legs. "Come on, let's see what we can find for you."

Moopuna stared at the mountain of gifts, while Target whipped his leg with her tail. He held his palm out, and Target glided under it, raising her rear end to press against his hand. Moopuna petted the black W imprinted at the top of her head, and traced the black lines that flowed like tributaries into two black stripes running down her back. Purring, Target settled next to Moopuna, the graded spots on her sides connecting into swirling lines when she rested on her haunches. The cat seemed to soothe him.

"Aren't you going to open any of your presents?"

Moopuna's face clouded. "Mama said don't touch."

"Of course you can touch! They're yours."

"Don't touch. Mama learned me a lesson."

"Is that why she hit you? For getting into the presents too early?"

His chin bunched and trembled. "Mama say don't tell Gordon. She say I tell you, you won't like us no more. You won't like me for being a bad boy. You won't want to marry us and be our papa."

He didn't know how to reassure him about that one. His cell phone rang. He answered, expecting Mikilauni.

"Hey, Merry Christmas," said Cecilia. "I'm going for a run, and I want to drop something by."

"Sure, but I'm not alone. Moopuna's here with me. Turns out they never went to Hawaii. It's complicated. I'll explain when you get here."

Gordon picked up Moopuna and settled in the recliner to read *The Night Before Christmas*, but Moopuna didn't seem to be paying much attention. He locked his arms around Gordon's neck and stared vacantly. When he fell asleep, Gordon reclined back in the chair, the weight of the child on him, trying to think things through. A rap on the door roused him. He answered the door, Moopuna cradled in his arms.

The sudden brightness of the snow made him wince. There stood Cecilia in a rainbow-colored stocking cap, purple nylon jacket, black running tights, and orange mittens. She looked into Moopuna's face and sucked in air. "Oh, dear, what happened to him?"

"His mother smacked him. Anyway, that's what I think. Come in." Gordon carried Moopuna into his room, tucked him into his bed, and returned to the kitchen. "I've got cider. How about some of it heated up?"

"That would be great."

He prepared drinks, put cookies on a plate, and

brought the refreshments into the living room. "I'm so angry right now I don't want to see her. She's been at her mom's place this whole time, hiding his bruises."

"What used to make Sister Margie suspicious was that his injuries never matched up to the way Mikilauni said he got them." Cecilia reached for a cookie. "You made these?" She took a bite. "Hmm . . . good. Have you contacted CPS?"

Gordon selected a cookie, realized he couldn't eat, then tossed it back on the plate, causing it to break. "I'm not sure I'm going to."

"Oh, but you must. You're not doing her any favors. You're only enabling."

"Supposing she had to serve time. Even if she didn't, they would probably take custody. Moopuna would be placed in a foster home. Where does that leave me?"

"Maybe you could be the foster home."

"A single guy? No previous experience with kids? It's not likely. They'd give him to Mikilauni's mother or one of the sisters or brothers. They always place kids back in their family if possible."

"You've got to find a way to hold on to him. Suppose she didn't go to jail. Could you forgive her?"

"I'm beginning to fear we're not suited for each other."

"There is that saying: opposites attract."

"Yeah, right. She's a fun-loving, young woman and I'm a middle-aged stick-in-the-mud. I'm selfish, unwilling to commit. It's no accident I got this old without a family. I suppose I'm incapable of loving anyone."

"Oh, Gordon, that's not true. I feel your love every day." She said this without flinching, without embarrassment.

"Friendship I can do. I'm talking about commitment, the for-better-or-for-worse kind. I haven't been able to make that commitment to Mikilauni or any other woman. Somehow a little boy is easier."

"Oh, Gordon, hold on to him. I'll pray for you."

"I thought you might."

"Don't be cynical now." She sipped her drink, then looked up, with a start. "Oh, here! I almost forgot." From her jacket pocket she withdrew a small package wrapped in gold paper and red curling ribbon and handed it to him. "Go ahead. Open it."

Removing the wrappings, Gordon discovered a kind of pen, five points held together with a wooden brace. He turned it over in his hands. "Very clever, Sister. You could have used this in church last night."

"Let's try it out." Taking the device, she drew a musical staff on a newspaper.

"I feel bad. I didn't get you anything."

"Yes, you have, all the extra help in my music. And then *Saint* Mother Teresa gave me a miracle."

"Ah, yes. Your musical ear." He smiled, recalling her frolic in the snow. "Let's try a little dictation, right now."

She straightened, bristled. "That won't be necessary. I do not need to test my faith."

"Oh, really? What if your *gift* was just a one-time thing?"

"*Saint* Mother Teresa would not take back what she gives. It's a miracle. Have some faith, Gordon. It won't hurt a bit."

There was the sound of a car pulling up in front of the house. Gordon parted the blinds. "Oh, shit, she's here. What do I do now?"

Mikilauni's heels clanked on the porch, her keys jangled. When she let herself in, her eyes widened at the sight of Cecilia and Gordon seated together on the sofa. "This is cozy."

Cecilia stood. "Hello, Mikilauni. I was just leaving. Merry Christmas." She jogged the length of the living room in a few strides and was out the door.

Mikilauni watched her go, staring at Cecilia's trim, muscular backside in the black Spandex tights. "That's an outfit." She shut the door and pulled off her gloves, seeming to keep busy only so she wouldn't have to look at Gordon. She'd been crying; her makeup was smeared and pouches swelled beneath her eyes. "Did you sleep with her last night?" she asked casually. "Kali said you were pretty tight at Mass."

"You told me yourself: Kali is nothing but lies."

"I know you took her to Sacramento. Why didn't you tell me that?"

"I was trying to avoid a scene like this. Would you like some coffee or cider?"

"What do you have that's stronger?"

"I'll make us some hot buttered rum." He went into the kitchen and fixed the drinks. When he returned, she was staring down at the gifts under the tree. She tapped a huge box with her patent leather pointed toe. "Look at all this loot. I wonder who it's for."

He handed her a mug, but she set it on the coffee table, and sank to her knees on the carpet. She lifted a package and read the tag. "To Moopuna from Santa. Now isn't that cute?" She lifted package after package, "Moopuna, Moopuna, Moopuna. It's obvious who Santa thinks about in this house."

"Christmas is for kids. I wanted this Christmas to be extra special for him."

"But not for me? Our first Christmas together? I wonder if there's anything here with my name on it."

The ring. He'd forgotten all about it. He needed to distract her from the gifts so he could whisk it away undetected. "Don't you want to check on Moopuna?"

"I'm sure you're taking good care of him." She examined some more packages, tossed them aside. "You're a good uncle, aren't you?"

"Please don't call me that."

"Why not? I'm finding out the men in my life are the same as the men in Mama's life. They come, they go. How are you any different? Growing up, I had a dozen uncles. They gave me presents like you're doing here for Moopuna so I would like them, maybe let them put their hands in my panties." Her upper lip quivered, a tear bubbled at the rim of one almond eye. It was unclear if she was crying because of her own abuse or Moopuna's. His wrecked beauty.

He sipped his drink. "I guess I'm not in the mood to open presents."

"There must be some little thing . . ." She reached deep under the tree and retrieved the little box wrapped in reindeer paper. "Oh! What have we here?" She turned the gift around and around in her hands. "No tag."

In his haste he had forgotten to attach one. Here was his chance. He could snatch it away, saying it was for Ruthie, a niece, Allegra, even Cecilia if he had to. "It's for you."

"From *Santa*?"

"From me."

She blotted her moistened eyelashes with the back of her hand, leaving the imprint of a black butterfly. "Maybe you don't want me to have this after all. Maybe I've been a *bad* girl and I don't deserve nothing but coal in my stocking."

"No, I want you to have it." He hoped she didn't detect the flatness in his tone.

She held the gift in her palm and stared at it as if she had X-ray vision. The color in her face changed, her hand trembled slightly. This was his last chance to steal it away from her. *A mistake. It's just some earrings I'm sure you won't like. Come to the jewelry store with me. I'll let you pick out a pair.* One crimson nail slid slowly under the tape. She bared the box and stared at it. She placed it against her ear and shook it.

His heart began to pound. His ears filled with pressure. *Christ's sake, grab it.*

She snapped the case open. "Ah! Gordon, darling! It's so big! I had no idea. When did you decide to do this?"

When you were in Hawaii he thought to say, but he didn't want to spoil the moment. Gingerly, she removed the ring from its slot and put it on her finger. The huge gem slipped to her palm and she burst into tears. "It's not right for me; it's not meant for me."

"Mikilauni, honey, no! We'll get it sized."

"I never meant to hurt him! I never did! I just went like this . . ." She swept her arm out. "Like this . . . I went like this to get him away from the tree and he came out black and blue from ear to ear. I knew you would leave me if . . ."

He stooped and kissed her tears. "Okay, honey, okay. Of course you never, ever meant to hurt your own sweet boy."

She was staring at the diamond, holding it in place by squeezing her fingers together. "Oh, I never dreamed I'd get a real engagement ring. And this size! Kali will up and die green when she sees this!" She searched his face with wild, black eyes. "Are you sure you didn't spend too much, because if you did, we can go back and exchange it for a . . . I didn't expect . . ." She paused, composed herself, started again with resolve. "I won't be married any place but in the Catholic Church."

"Really? I was banking on the Chapel of Love in Vegas."

She slapped his arm with the gift wrap still in her hand. She was smiling again. They had passed through something dark and terrible. "Let's see . . . if we start announcing the banns this Sunday . . . sign up for the prenuptial class . . . then there's the invitations . . . my God, Gordon, already we're looking at June."

"June is fine," he said. June was an eternity away.

"A church wedding! Do you think people would laugh at me if I wore white?"

She actually looked best in red. He pictured her going down the aisle in a red satin, low-cut gown, a blooming bustle to accentuate her backside. He was letting her off too easy. He, the enabler. "What people? Wear whatever color you like. The hell with people."

"But an unwed mother in virginal white? Do you think it would be hypocritical? Wait a minute. Is this to get me to live with you? I won't live with you, Gordon, not 'til we're married. Wendy at the office has been living with Gary eight years now, and he refuses to tie the knot. I can't risk giving up my house and, then . . ."

"Keep your house. Except Moopuna stays here with me."

"Even when I don't? How will that look?"

"He stays here with me."

She lowered her lids, inspected her manicure. "Go ahead then. Haul him to day care, pick him up. Change the sheets when he pees the bed, stay up all night with him when he has a nightmare. You'll see how it is. You'll be begging me to take him back in a week."

She was scaring him, but he tried not to show it. He'd found a way to hold on.

Chapter Twenty-eight

Mikilauni sighed, the third time within ten minutes. He looked up from the stack of part-writing exercises he was grading to see her in profile, her chin resting on her knuckles as she gazed out the kitchen window, gone to her sun-drenched island once again. It was a Sunday afternoon, the day after Valentine's Day. From the center of the table, the dozen red roses he had presented to her were deploying fumes of decay. She had left them to wilt on the counter, and he had only doused them in a vase of water that morning, too late to offer them much hope.

All through January she had spent nearly every night at his place. He picked Moopuna up from day care and cooked dinner. He took pleasure in greeting her at the door with a chilled glass of wine when she came in from a hard day at Wiggins & Forrest. His kitchen counter, the coffee table, his bureau top and nightstand were strewn with *Bride* magazines, how-to books on wedding planning, and catering brochures, but so far the only decisive move she'd made was reserving Our Lady of the Apparition of Lourdes Catholic Church and parish hall for the second Saturday in June. Her effusive chatter about white Jordan almonds bound in squares of netting and honeymoon plans in the Caribbean were interrupted by bouts of sulking. Perhaps it was the weather. Torrential downpours had washed the snow away, leaving Goldhurst in mud and misery.

Gordon walked up behind her and massaged the tense cords of her neck. She did not respond to his touch, but continued to stare at the backyard, overgrown with weeds that bowed and dripped. The moisture seemed to encourage growth and rot at the same time.

"Remember you said we could take the train to San Francisco to the symphony?" she asked.

"We can do that. The train ride, I mean. I think Moopuna is too young to sit through a whole symphony, though."

She shrugged his hand away and wheeled around. "I mean the two of us. We can leave him with one of your students at the college. "

He nodded as if he agreed, while cringing inside. Somehow the thought of leaving Moopuna for a whole weekend was unbearable. It was irrational, he knew, but he had a nagging fear that harm would come to the child if he dared to relax his guard.

"I never wanted him."

Gordon glanced toward the back of the house. He could hear the muffled sound of a movie playing behind Moopuna's closed door.

"He ruined my body. I had a flat stomach before."

Gordon doubted it. Soft, low-slung bellies seemed to run in the genes of her family, judging by her sisters, aunts, and cousins. "Aw, honey, you have a sexy tummy."

"I'll never be free of him. When he's eighteen and out the door, I'll be in my forties, too old for any fun at all."

He tried to make light of it. "Ouch! I'm in my forties. Are you saying I'm over the hill?"

She cocked her hip against the counter and crossed

her arms, confronting him. "He's not going to match our other children. It'll be obvious you're not his real father."

"We don't need any more children."

"I want a girl. Girls are more fun than boys. She'd be ours. Someone we can love together."

He couldn't possibly love a child any more than Moopuna. "You're just stir-crazy. Why don't you get out? Go to the mall. Buy something pretty to wear." He withdrew a couple of twenties from his wallet.

She looked down at the money, up at his face, then out the window. "People at the mall are fat and ugly."

He laughed. He grabbed her shoulders and nuzzled her neck, tickling her so that she had to smile.

"We never do anything fun, never even go out for an evening alone."

For Valentine's Day, he had cooked a lobster dinner for her after Moopuna's bedtime, served it with champagne by candlelight, but it wasn't enough. "Okay, then, dinner out and a movie next weekend. It's a date."

"That's boring. Let's go dancing."

He thought of the local bars, loud with second-rate rock bands. Even as a teen he'd felt self-conscious gyrating before a dance partner, flailing his arms and legs for no apparent purpose. He had no idea how people danced these days; he would look even more ridiculous now. "Sorry, I never was much for dancing."

"Shit, you don't want to do anything! You don't even care much about doing *it* anymore. It's been two weeks."

"It has? Why didn't you say something? We can if you want."

"If I want? Why don't *you* want?"

"I do!" He tried to kiss her.

She squirmed away. "Forget it. If you don't want to go out with me, you ought to let me go out with the girls at work."

He shrugged. "Go if you like."

"What if a guy asks me to dance?"

"Then dance with him. You do mean just *dancing*, don't you? That would be enough for you?"

She didn't answer. After a moment, she held out her hand. "I guess I will go to the mall. Anything to get away from damn drip-drip-drip."

He laid the money in her hand and kissed her cheek. "Don't forget to shut your eyes."

"What?"

"So you won't have to see the fat uglies."

He stood at the picture window in the living room, watching her drive off. He wished he could feel something other than relief. He actually liked rainy Sundays, working quietly inside while drops tapped on the roof. He'd hurry up with the papers and then go for a walk with Moopuna. He had bought him a red raincoat and matching galoshes, which the boy called his fireman costume. He loved to put it on and go stamping through puddles. Gordon recalled his mother scolding him for deliberately stepping into water; now he gleefully joined Moopuna in the fun. Later they'd cuddle before the fire and read e.e. cummings from his book of children's poems:

> when the world is mud-luscious . . .
> when the world is puddle-wonderful.

After class one Tuesday in March, Cecilia approached his podium, bearing her ear-training test like a breastplate.

"B-plus. Not bad."

"Not bad? It's great!"

He laughed. "You are getting very good at rhythm. Let's work on harmonic dictation at your tutorial this afternoon."

"I'm pretty good at harmony, too." She cocked her shoulder to her ear and let it drop. "In fact, I really don't need to take up your time anymore. I know how busy you are."

"Not so busy." Sometimes he was in a rush to leave campus, eager to pick up Moopuna from day care around 3 p.m. so that they could have some time together before he had to start dinner.

"And I'm sorta busy, too. I'm planning to do more hours at the rehab center. They're paying me now."

He would miss their weekly tutorials. The track was muddy like every place else in town, and there had been no dinner invitations since Christmas Eve. Her demeanor had changed, too. She stood farther apart from him, her tone was softer, her arms no longer animated in flailing gestures, but held relaxed at her sides. He could think she was purposely being cool toward him, but he observed her treating others in the same, detached manner. She was drawing herself inward, setting herself apart from humankind. Oddly, it pained him. They were friends. And yet, he was a man; she was a woman. He was engaged to be married; she was a nun, not technically, but committed to her heavenly spouse. "How's Tiffany?" he asked.

"The same, about." After a two-week respite at Christmas, she was back to her usual routine of manifesting open wounds on Fridays, which gradually closed over during the week. "How's Mikilauni?"

"Busy with wedding plans."

"Oh, good. Well, there's something I've been meaning to ask you. Would you write me a letter of recommendation?"

"Sure."

She laughed. "Wait, you didn't even ask what it's for. I'm applying to several universities that have a music therapy major. I hope I'll get accepted at Arizona State. They have a good program."

"Music therapy. When did you decide all this?"

"Working in the cardio rehab, I see so many of the patients find joy and hope through music. For them, music is a kind of medicine."

He had always imagined her staying in Goldhurst after finishing school, like nearly all his students, going about her routine of caring for the aging nuns at Our Lady's convent and helping out at the hospital. "When will you leave?"

"In May, as soon as the semester ends, if I'm accepted. I've connected with a parish down there, St. Anthony's. They need some help in the church office and, when I told them my background, they offered me room and board in the convent. It's practically empty, I guess."

"Is it an order you'd like to join?"

"I'm not ready to commit to any order yet. I still need to focus on the work St. Mother Teresa has chosen for me." She grinned ruefully. "This will be my third order; I better get it right this time."

"Of course I'll write the letter. Be sure you get one from your supervisor at the hospital."

"I've already asked."

"I'll miss you," he blurted.

He saw it, he was certain, a pinkish hue backlighting the sienna constellations across her nose. "Oh, I'll be around a while longer."

"After you go, I mean." He didn't care if he flustered her. Maybe that's what he was going for.

"Me, too." Quickly she turned from him, flapped her palm behind her, and was gone.

Chapter Twenty-Nine

That first Friday in April was so sunny Gordon had to squint to watch Moopuna swinging. He didn't need pushing now, pointing his sturdy, brown legs to the sky, then cocking them back for his arcing descent. He had grown up these past five months; next fall he'd be starting kindergarten. Gordon lunged in front of him with outstretched arms and wiggled his fingers, pretending to tickle him. Moopuna's laugh was quick, the movement of his legs loose and fluid as he kicked the air.

"Come on, my little man," said Gordon. "Time to go." Without hesitation, Moopuna leaped off the swing at the apex of the arc — "Hey, watch out! That's too high!" — and landed gracefully on sure feet.

They walked together to the Sutter Park parking lot. Moopuna stopped abruptly and stared down a side street. "Can we visit Mama?"

Gordon was surprised that he remembered the route they had walked several times last fall, between Mikilauni's house and Sutter Park. "Mama's not home. Remember, she has to work late during tax time."

"Can we just walk to her house? I want to see it."

"Sure, why not?" Gordon took Moopuna's hand to cross the street.

"Do we got a 'vorce?" asked Moopuna.

"Now you know we don't," said Gordon. "We'd have to live out in the country for that."

"No, not a *horse*, a *'vorce*. Bisrat's family got one. Now she has to live sometimes at her mama's and sometimes at her dad's."

"Oh! A *divorce*." Gordon laughed and swung Moopuna up to ride on his shoulders. "I doubt if we'll ever get that far." Mikilauni had stalled on the wedding plans. As far as he knew, nothing had been done in a month.

When they arrived at her house, they found her car parked in the driveway. Gordon pressed the doorbell button, Moopuna still astride his shoulders.

She answered the door wearing her yoga gear, blue batik Capris, and a stretch top with spaghetti straps. Her eyes popped when she saw them. "What a surprise! There's my big boy!" She reached for Moopuna and he fell into her embrace, hugging her with his knees as well as his arms. Behind her was her rainbow-colored yoga mat laid out on the floor and, wafting from the CD player, a tinkling sort of music of chimes and finger cymbals. Gordon wasn't sure why she had this sudden interest in yoga. He'd watched her one evening, moving from one contorted pose to another. She seemed to lack the patience, breaking off in the middle of an *om* to hiss, *shit*, through clenched jaws. He thought she should spend her time practicing the thing she was good at, the violin. Moopuna seemed to go along with the lessons merely because it was what Gordon wanted him to do. It was actually Mikilauni who was making great progress. Each lesson when Marilyn Gaubert said, "Sit down if you don't know this," she stood longer.

When she set Moopuna on his feet, he stood hesitantly, staring down the hall. "Mama, can I see my old room?"

"Old room? It's your regular room, baby. Same as always. Go on." Moopuna ran down the hall as she shut off her music. "I just stole away from the office for an hour to unwind." She rotated her head and rubbed her neck. "I've got to go back tonight."

"You told me. And Saturday and Sunday."

"April fifteenth is not far off."

"I know. Well, we're glad we caught you. We can have a bite together."

"Sorry, I made plans with the girls."

"Cancel out on the girls." Gordon looked above her phone, where she posted take-out food numbers. "I'll order pizza."

"All right, then. Make it a veggie."

"Since when did you turn vegetarian?"

"It's better for you, body, mind, and spirit. I've been reading up on eastern religions. What do you think about reincarnation?"

"Not much. It seems like a made-up dream. Wishful thinking. No more plausible than heaven."

She looked down at her hands, found a hangnail, and began to scrape it. "This guy . . . this guy at work . . . he believes it. Wouldn't it be wonderful to get to live over and over?"

"People who believe in reincarnation want their lives over with. They dread going through all that pain and suffering again. They want to go to Nirvana — heaven. Stick with Christianity. You'll get there a lot quicker."

She glanced up, searching his expression to see if he was teasing her. "I wouldn't want to get my lives over with. I want second and third chances. I would like to get it right just once." She managed to rip the hangnail off. He saw a pale strip of raw flesh. She winced, sucking in air.

He reached out, pressed his thumb against her finger to stop the flow of blood. "Is this life so bad?"

The phone rang beneath his hand.

"Oh, I'll get that!" she said, a bit too intensely.

He ignored her and took the call himself. A man's voice with a thick accent came on the line. At first he couldn't understand him. He listened a while longer, then addressed Mikilauni. "It's Anatole's. They want to know if they should keep the deposit on the catering."

"Tell them to send it back. We're not using them."

Gordon delivered the message, then hung up. "Who are we using?"

"I don't know. I haven't had time to make any decisions on the wedding."

"Decisions don't take a lot of time." He removed two catering brochures from the counter, holding up first one, then the other. "Here, what will it be? Stuffed grape leaves or taquitos?"

She ran her fingers through her hair and shook her head. "I don't know."

"Stuffed grapes leaves or . . ."

"All right, taquitos."

"There! Wasn't that easy? Now, Jordan almonds or M&Ms with our names on them? I'll decide this one — M&Ms. Jordan almonds are hard as rocks. Now, about the honeymoon . . ."

"Gordon, why are you doing this?"

He held up two other brochures, his voice becoming increasingly strident. "The Caribbean or Hawaii? Better choose the Caribbean, you and Moopuna just got back from Hawaii. Oh, I forgot. You didn't really make it there, did you?"

"You bastard!" She slapped his arm. He grabbed her wrist and she attempted to twist out of his grasp.

"I have a right to know, Mikilauni. Is the wedding on or off?"

"I think . . . I just think we're rushing into it."

"There. That's all I wanted to know. Now, postponed or canceled?" She continued to struggle against his hold. He moved his hand to her fingers, grasping the big, glittering diamond between his thumb and forefinger so that if she pulled away, the ring would come off.

She went limp, bowed her lovely head, smelling of Midori.

He quelled his voice to nearly a whisper. "Postponed or canceled?"

She searched his eyes. "I just need more time. How's . . . how's October sound to you?"

"October is fine. We can decorate with jack-o'-lanterns. You can rent the mermaid costume again . . . I'll wear my Groucho Marx glasses."

He got the reaction he was going for. She laughed and hugged him tightly. Their kiss was long and deep. It felt to him as if she almost meant it.

After the tax deadline, Mikilauni began taking turns with Gordon, picking Moopuna up from day care. Late on a rainy Monday afternoon in the middle of May, he arrived home to find the kitchen yellow with light and her smearing pink icing on a cake. The top layer was lopsided and bald patches of chocolate cake surfaced through the goo. Moopuna was perched on the counter with his own knife, doing more gouging than smoothing.

Gordon bent to kiss them both. "Hi, what's the occasion?"

"It's not my birthday," Moopuna said solemnly.

"You're right, baby. It's nobody's birthday." She smiled up at Gordon. "We've already been through this."

"Can we have candles?" asked Moopuna.

"Yes, we can have one candle," said Mikilauni.

"Can I blow it out?"

"Yes, you can blow it out." In answering Moopuna's questions, her voice rose in pitch and enthusiasm. Her look was hungry, as if she were feasting on his countenance. It wasn't like her, so cheerfully accommodating and maternal. Had she been apart from her son so much during the past two months that she actually missed him?

Moopuna's forehead wrinkled either in concentration of the movement of his knife or in consideration of his next question. Finally he asked, "Will there be presents?"

Mikilauni and Gordon laughed. He was relieved that Moopuna still liked presents; he had never wanted to open any at Christmas. Gordon had stored them all away, planning to remove the Christmas paper and replace it with birthday wrap when the time came in July.

In the wake of Moopuna's knife was a trail of brown cake crumbs. "Jesus," he exclaimed, "there's dirt on the cake."

"It's not dirt," said Mikilauni, "it's chocolate and don't swear like that."

"It's dirty! I'm glad this isn't my birthday cake. I don't want no dirt cake." He dropped his knife and clambered off the counter.

"Wait. Let's get those paws." Smiling faintly, she rubbed each sticky finger with the dishcloth and dried them on her apron while Moopuna squirmed. "Hold it, now. Let me see that mug." She squatted before him, looked full in his face, folded him in her arms and squeezed. "There. Now go." She waited for him to dash out of the room before remarking to Gordon, "I want to be sure he's raised Catholic. Did you hear him swearing?"

He got a beer out of the refrigerator and sat at the kitchen table, watching her try to repair the cake. She looked almost happy, like there was no other place she wanted to be, nothing she'd rather be doing. But her shoulders were raised, her body tensed, as if there were a boiling frustration raging within her demure domestic-goddess exterior.

"Stop looking at me," she said.

"Why can't I look at you? You're a lovely sight."

"You're boring into me." She turned to take the dinner out of the oven. He called Moopuna, and then they all sat down to pot roast, potatoes, carrots, and chocolate cake. Afterward Gordon and Mikilauni cleared the table together. As she scraped the dishes over the garbage, he ran hot, sudsy water in the sink. She came alongside him and nudged him aside with her hip. "I'll wash."

"No, you cooked."

She put pressure on his hip and handed him the dish towel. "I'll wash, you dry." She removed her ring and set it on the windowsill over the sink.

When they finished, she put on her coat and announced, "I'm meeting the girls for drinks."

He didn't believe her, of course. "Don't be late."

"Oh, but I will be. I'm sleeping at my own house tonight. I wouldn't want to disturb you coming in late on a school night."

"Thoughtful," he said, watching her face.

She dropped her heavy lids over her dark, sad eyes and kissed him. "Well . . . good-bye."

He listened to the decisive click of the back door.

Much later he awoke, alone in the dark. Thinking things over, he pictured her ring sitting on the windowsill. Had she left it behind? He couldn't remember witnessing her replace it on her finger. He'd check for it in the morning. Dozing, he visualized Bother leaping up on the sill, knocking the ring into the drain. He sat up with a start, his heart thumping. It was a ridiculous concern; even if the ring were bumped into the sink, the drain stopper would catch it. Still the image was worrisome enough to haul him out of bed. In the kitchen, he flicked the switch, squinting in the sudden light.

The ring was where she had left it.

Tuesday he heard nothing from her. It was not too unusual for a day to pass without seeing her, but at least she answered the messages he left on her cell. He was certain he would meet her Wednesday, at her violin class. Even when Moopuna didn't make it, once because he had a miserable cold, another time to attend a birthday party, Mikilauni was in attendance and dutifully taught him the lesson afterward. When Marilyn Gaubert asked, "Where's Mikilauni?" Gordon felt embarrassed to admit he didn't know.

After the lesson, he took Moopuna for a treat at McDonald's. While the boy played on the playground, he called Wiggins & Forrest. One of her drinking buddies, Wendy Hatch, told him that Mikilauni had quit. When he pressed her for more details, she primly told him company policy did not allow her to divulge information about previous employees. She knew something, but she wasn't about to share it with him.

Now he was angry. It was obvious that Mikilauni leaving her ring bore supreme significance. Still he could not believe their relationship was completely over. She had left behind something far more precious than a diamond. He and Moopuna drove by her house; it was deserted, the carport vacant. He cruised the parking lots of the few nightspots in Goldhurst, searching for her car. Moopuna complained from the back seat; he was tired and wanted to go home. Gordon swung the car around: he had one more idea. There in front of the Kukula residence, amid her brothers' trucks, he found her car parked on the lawn. So she was holed up at Old Mama's, not exactly a place where he wanted to confront her, but at least a place where he could find her.

The next day when Gordon walked up the path at Sutter Park, Moopuna ran to greet him. "Where's Mama?"

"She's at Old Mama's. Want to go visit her?"

Moopuna shook his head. "Uncle Inoke will try to eat me. You call her. Tell her to come over to our house."

"I'll try." As he reached for his cell, Carrie Clay sauntered up to him and said, "You seem like a nice man, certainly nicer than the Gordon Clay I've shared my life with."

"Gee, thanks."

She looked like she was having a bad day. Her pale skin was splotched, her raccoon eyeliner smeared down to her cheekbones. Her set mouth seemed to have sunk deeper into the bitter parentheses enclosing it. "I don't know if I should tell you this," she said. "I mean, some people like to know. But then some people resent the person who tells them. You seem like the kind who would like to know."

"What? Just tell me."

She looked down at Moopuna. "Why don't you go swing some more, sweetie? The adults need to talk." When he dashed off, she said, "Your girlfriend — I mean, I assume she's still your girlfriend since you take care of her little boy — she's, uh, seeing my ex. You met him, the other Gordon Clay."

The towering skinhead loomed in his mind, along with his half-German shepherd, half-dachshund. "Are you sure?"

"She was over his place a lot, mornings, when I dropped Gordie off. She was very chatty, like we're friends or something."

He recalled that Mikilauni and this other Gordon had seemed attracted to each other the first day they met. Gordon had misjudged the guy, the power that lay in his muscles, his stature, his tattoos. He wasn't surprised Mikilauni had left him for someone else; he was just taken aback by her choice. What could they possibly have together, but sex? She was looking for stability, a father for Moopuna; this guy couldn't even be a father to his own son.

"Are you all right? Have I done the right thing?"

"Yes, yes. I'm only thinking."

"Have you seen her lately?"

"Who? Mikilauni?"

"Isn't that who we're talking about? Gordon skipped town, stole off in the night owing two months rent. I'm guessing he set sail again, and I have this morbid sense of curiosity. I want to know if your girl went with him. None of my business, really."

"I . . . I don't know. I think she's staying at her mom's. I've seen her car parked there."

One eye twitched. He wasn't certain if it was dust in the gusty wind or his gullibility that irritated her. The cadence of her speech slowed, the volume increased.

"Brace yourself. Gordie said there was some talk of her selling her car to her sister and pawning the engagement ring to raise some funds."

"That boat of his — he can actually sail that thing to the South Seas?"

"That's one thing he can do right — sail."

Gordon looked down at his shoes. The sun-streaked blades of grass appeared to shimmer. He took an involuntary step back to regain his balance. "Any ideas where they might be headed?"

"Somewhere in French Polynesia. Gordon is always harping about how clean it is down there, how cheap it is to live. I think he likes it because the women go topless. Hey wait, she's some kind of Polynesian, right? Where's she from exactly?"

"That's one of those things I could never pin her down on."

"And she abandoned her kid? That's cold, man. Well, you don't have to feel stuck with him. You know she's got family. Lucky for the kid he probably won't land in a foster home. Are you all right?"

"I just . . . I never expected it would end like this." He felt weary, as if more had gone on between Mikilauni and him — marriage, divorce, custody battles.

"Maybe it's not an end. Maybe she's just on a holiday, one last fling, you know?"

"What I was wondering — is Gordon religious?"

"Oh, please." She rubbed her blackened eye. "He's a

vegetarian, meditates, calls himself a Buddhist. It's all a good excuse to shirk responsibility. He's way behind in child-support payments. You don't have to answer this. but my curiosity is morbid as hell: did she get off with the diamond?"

Just then Moopuna charged him, legs and arms pumping, his grin revealing the gaping hole in the upper row of his flashing teeth. He reminded Gordon of Mikilauni: bright whites but with something missing. He leaned toward the boy and flung his arms wide.

That evening, he left Moopuna with a neighborhood teen while he drove to Mikilauni's house. When he pulled up in front, the sunset was a pink puddle in the western sky; the crickets made the dusky air vibrant with life. A middle-aged woman was swishing a broom across the porch.

"Excuse me, ma'am. I'm looking for a friend of mine, Mikilauni Kukula, the woman who lives here."

"I'm her landlady, name of Mrs. Pete Lambert. She's gone. Left the place a mess. Left all kinds of stuff behind, too. Clothes, toys, even furniture. Must be some kind of rich. Left something that belongs to the college, too."

"I can take care of that for you."

The woman went into the house and returned with the violin, Goldhurst College stamped on its case. He regretted that Mikilauni had left it behind. She had been getting pretty good.

Chapter Thirty

The phone rang. A woman's anguished voice came on the line. "Gordon? Gordon Clay? Michael is not in his bed. He's gone. Taken from you."

He awoke with a start. He sat up, listening to his heart pound. He eased his head to the pillow. It was just a nightmare, the recurring nightmare that never would allow him to completely relax. He would never get back to sleep now. Already the nagging urge was pushing him out of bed. He groaned, swinging his legs over the edge of the bed, feeling the stab of pain in his lower back, the tight muscles in his legs.

This had become his cross to bear, his road to Calvary, trudging down the hall in fear that someone had wrenched Michael from him. Although he had legally adopted the boy, he never felt he had any real claim to him. Every day he dreaded the clack of Mikilauni's stiletto heels on his porch announcing her return, or a letter with a Dallas postmark from Kali and her husband's lawyer, or a phone call from Inoke or Peleki in Tonga. Even Salote, whom he saw occasionally, now as big as Old Mama, draped in a blue smock behind a K-Mart checkout counter, could abruptly begin a custody battle against him. Old Mama had died, but there was an endless supply of Kukulas — aunts, uncles, cousins — all who had more legal right to Michael than he.

Gordon entered the boy's room and sat in a chair to watch him sleep. Michael could only fit in the bed lying diagonally, his feet hooked over the corner of the mattress. The light from the hall shone on his face, revealing dark facial hair above his lip and at his temples, causing him to appear older than his twelve years. "Moopuna," Gordon whispered, like forming a kiss — Moopuna, the musical, exotic name he had been forbidden to use since Michael was in the second grade with a Hmong student named Kau. The other kids taunted them both on the playground, jeering "Moo, Kau, Moo, Kau."

Although Gordon and Michael rarely attended mass, the boy was adamant about participating in his weekly religious instruction class, preparing for his confirmation. History was his favorite subject and, this year in seventh grade, he loved his study of the Middle Ages and the Catholic Church in all its glory.

Against the wall was Michael's saxophone, reminding Gordon that he had a lesson that day with Art Bunch. Sometimes Gordon felt a little jealous because Michael thought Uncle Art was way cooler than he. In his middle-school jazz band, Michael took most of the solos, mimicking Art's gyrations. Art was still in cahoots with Allegra, who was now a widow running the llama ranch on her own, and forever Art's "body mate."

Gordon had been disappointed when Michael had switched from violin to sax in the fifth grade, but he himself had found an active life in the Goldhurst musical community. Besides teaching at the college, he had several classes at the Susuki School, delighting in his young students' able fingers. He performed in the Goldhurst

Community Symphony, wincing when it drifted out of tune, but happily partaking in the music making nevertheless.

Gordon had a few dates with women over the years, but he'd never gone crazy for one again, not like his Carrie, not like Mikilauni. Ah, Mikilauni of the almond eye and flashing teeth, her round hip jutting in the hula, her lithe arm guiding a bow across a violin, his Polynesian princess. He liked to imagine her at the stern of Clay's sailboat, her long black hair whipping in the wind, her glaze fixed on the white sands of a distant island, like those she had escaped to in her mind. He hoped she was happy and that Clay was good to her. Was she in love with the other Gordon Clay? He didn't believe it. Mikilauni belonged to no one.

Bother entered the room, scolding him with her high-pitched morning mew. The calico was old and crotchety, her flabby white stomach swinging as she walked. Target had to be put down, but last Fourth of July, Michael had found a stray, fluffy white and gray kitten, its eyes runny and sealed shut, shaking with fear under a bush in their yard. Coltrane, asleep on the pillow next to Michael's head, was now a frisky, long-haired male, an endless bother to Bother.

It was nearly five a.m. Gordon turned to face the computer on Michael's desk. It was his habit to instant-message his best friend, his soul mate, nearly every day. The Internet created a kind of disembodiment, a convenient method of having an intimate relationship with a celibate. Cecilia was living in Springfield, Missouri, a Sister of Mercy. She was at work on her Ph.D. in Music Therapy, studying the benefits of music for autistic children at the Mercy Children's Hospital.

He found her online and instant messaged her.

"Can't sleep, huh?" she wrote back.

"Same old, same old. How's *your* work going?"

"Great. I've finally got Donovan beating a drum instead of his head against the wall!"

"That is progress."

"You see, Gordon, God had a plan for me all along. It was necessary for me to study the basics to understand how my autistic kids also struggle to learn. If I had been born with great musical talent, I may not have been able to reach them. How's Michael?"

"Great, except he has a sax lesson today. Art is going to pound him for not practicing."

"Say hi to Art for me. Did you happen to see the *National Inquirer* this week?"

He had bought it to send to her, just in case she'd missed it. The cover story was about Tiffany McClary, now Sister Veronica, who lived in a cloister near Medjugorje, Bosnia Herzegovina. The photograph depicted her, not as a sister, but as a priest, Father Damien. As Father Damien, Tiffany had grown black chin whiskers, lowered her voice several octaves, and taken on the power of faith healing. Pilgrims who visited the Apparitions of the Virgin Mary in Medjugorje and received Father Damien's blessing left behind their crutches and wheelchairs. The article did not mention if they had to buy new ones when they returned home. Many of the faithful believed in Tiffany's ability to bilocate, simultaneously remaining in the cloister as Sister Veronica and healing pilgrims on Apparition Hill as Father Damien.

Gordon typed back, "I hope you don't believe everything you read in the *National Inquirer*."

"I don't have to. I believe in miracles."

Gordon liked best to remember Tiffany, not as the hysterical, anorexic stigmatic, but as the wide-eyed pixie in oversized jeans, thumping down a roll of cookie dough as a Christmas gift to him. "Do you think she still takes Christmas off?"

"I don't know. Why don't you visit her Web site and ask her?"

"Maybe I will." That a faith-healing, bilocating stigmatic with multiple personalities even maintained a Web site was both ludicrous and hilarious. If St. Francis of Assisi only knew what he had started. "Hey, I'm signing off now."

"Keep the . . . whatever."

He chuckled at their old joke. He still couldn't swallow Catholic dogma, but he did know that a tone-deaf woman could have a successful career in music, that a person could bleed from wounds produced by mere thoughts, and that cats that needed a home would always find him. He had a son just by doing what Cecilia had suggested: he had just held on.

Call it love, call it faith, call it whatever. He believes.